KRISHNA

The Super Consciousness

The Highest Pleasure
Love and Serve

THIS BOOK IS BORN
THROUGH:

OM PRAKASH NEMANI

First published in 2018 by

Becomeshakespeare.com
Wordit Content Design & Editing Services Pvt. Ltd.
Unit - 26, Building A -1, NrWadala RTO,
Wadala (East), Mumbai 400037, India
T: +91 8080226699

Wordit Art Fund helps deserving authors publish their work by
providing monetary support. To apply for funding,
please visit us at
www.BecomeShakespeare.com

© ISBN - 978-93-88081-32-0

Contents

Foreword		*v*
About The Author		*vii*
Acknowledgment		*ix*
Introduction		*xi*
1.	Vedanta – Intensely Practical	1
2.	Know your potential	10
3.	Being in the world and yet above-Perfection of renunciation	17
4.	Laws of Thought	28
5.	Be Chaitanya – Delete Past Data	40
6.	Learning Humility	46
7.	Spirituality - The way of life	52
8.	Tree without roots life without love	61
9.	Realization of God	69

10. First step towards Gyana and Bhakti   75

11. Live in Present- Be Positive   83

12. Be different   95

13. Nature the enjoyer and Consciousness   102

14. Make life simple   110

15. Duty is divine consciousness   115

16. Material and Spiritual Reality   126

17. Dharma and Adharma Deva And Asuras   135

18. Fear –Ego and Maya   142

19. Mukti –Liberation   150

20. What We Believe In-Super Consciousness   158

21. The Great Ancient Epics Ramayana
     Mahabharat Gita   164

22. The Supreme Wisdom   171

23. Salvation through Karma Non Attachment   184

24. The way of Knowledge   197

25. Detachment   204

26. Humanity and Human Consciousness   213

27. Expansion of Consciounsess   218

Foreword

Sadguru Ramesh Ji
Poorna Ananda
Ashram Hyderabad

A New Meaningful life

Our universe has manifested from Super Consciousness, which is formless, omnipresent and omnipotent. It is the source of the creation. It sustains the creation and merges back the same creation into itself at the end of the life span of the creation.

Lord Krishna was the *Avatara Purusha*, the direct manifestation from this Super Consciousness hence he could himself be called as Krishna – the Super consciousness. He revealed such secrets in *Bhagwat Gita* that only the purest source could reveal.

Lord Krishna was not an ordinary or extra ordinary human being but was a complete divine being. The *Gyana* which he revealed through *Bhagwat Gita* is the testimony of his being the purest form of consciousness. At many places in Gita he revealed this secret of himself being the super consciousness but not many have been able to focus on this aspect and considered *Krishna* as another Demi God.

Nemaniji has taken up this task of not only clearing and clarifying this aspect in his book but even tried to bring out new meanings to important shlokas of Gita which are applicable to common man for daily use through which common man will be able to live a much happier and joyful life.

This task of bringing out new hidden meanings in *Gita* could be done only by a person who has practically lived such life and is spiritually evolved. To know the hidden meanings of what *Krishna* has prophesized, one need to achieve the state of *Krishna* himself and Nemaniji in his meditation and intense contemplation has definitely been quite close to understand what *Krishna* must have meant in some of the shlokas.

In this book Neamaniji amazingly, has written such a difficult and serious subject in such simple words. The whole book has come out beautifully with examples and stories in almost every chapter making it a very interesting reading. The examples are quite striking and impressive. I believe the reading of this book will leave impact on the minds of the readers and they will find that teachings of *Gita* and *Upanishads* are very much relevant and adoptable in the present times.

I would definitely like people to read and contemplate on this book and try to live life which has been brought out through this book and which is more suitable in the present time with present living style.

May Swamiji shower his choicest blessings on Nemaniji and on all the readers?

*Sadguru Rameshj*i
Poorna Ananda Ashram
Janwada Hyderabad India

About The Author

Om Prakash Nemani, born on 5th September 1936, in Kanpur is a graduate in commerce. He did his early schooling in Kanpur and graduated from Lucknow University. He was awarded Gold Medal and Chancellor's Medal by Shri V.V. Giri, former President of India.

He started his career as a Probationary officer in State Bank of India. Since, he belongs to a business family he left the job after five years of service and started his own manufacturing unit. He is widely travelled and has vast experience of various fields of business.

Since, last 3 years he has come in touch with Sadguru Rameshji and is moving ahead on his journey on the path of spirituality. Nemani considers him a common man just like you living with family, earning his livelihood and moving in a society with very strong belief systems of happiness through materialistic success. His first book was HAPPINESS 24/7. It was widely appreciated and liked by the readers. He has now written this book to explain how the philosophy and teachings of Gita and Upanishads can be adopted and practiced in the context of present life and one can achieve the highest pleasure of love of the life and service to the mankind.

He can be reached via his face book page or via email at ompnem@gmail.com. Book can be ordered on Amazon and other on line portals..

Acknowledgment

I completed my first book Happiness 24/7, blended with simple spirituality in Dec 2017. I am thankful to word it Art Fund for publishing my debut novel via @ Be Shakespeare and agreeing to publish this book as well. They helped me to make both the books available on Flipkart, Amazon, Infibeam.com, Google play, Snapdeal and Kindle.

I got very good response from my friends and dear ones. Sadguru Rameshji of Poorna Ananda Ashram, Hyderabad gave me all the encouragement. He further inspired me to continue to write. Once I was attending the study group of GITA SAR and suddenly I got the idea of writing something on consciousness. SRIMAD BHAGWAT GITA can be the guide and I started studying GITA. I consulted the following commentary of BHAGWAT GITA and other related books and articles. I took the help of the following to write this present book.

Srimad Bhagwat Gita	Jayadayal Goyandaka
Srimad Bhagawat Gita as it is	Swamy Prabhupad
Dis Illusions	Yogi Shri Rameshji
Don't make a problem of anything	J. Krishnamurti
Mahabharata	C Rajagopalachari
The Bhagavada Gita	S. Radhakrishnan

Adhyatama Marg	Dr Julian Johnson
My Gita and other books	Devdutt Pattanaik
Articles of Speaking Tree	Times of India.
Autobiography of a Yogi	Sri Sri Paramhansa Yogananda
The complete works 9 volumes	Swami Vivekananda
Set of books	Osho
Books and Pravachans	Sri Sri Ravishankar
Books of Sri M Living with the Himalayan Masters	Swamy Rama

I am glad that I could write present book bringing out hidden meanings in *Gita* in a most simple way to make them understandable and adoptable by common people like me to make their life happy and free from all worries and tensions.

I am thankful to my sons Arun Nemani, Ajay Nemani, my daughter in law Archana Nemani and entire family who extended their full support and encouraged me all the times. I am thankful to my friend, spiritually enlightened Shri Aditya Ajmera who gave me valuable advice on every step. The book cover has been kindly designed by Smt Kiran Agrawal. I acknowledge the cooperation extended to me by the entire team of our organization specially Mr. Venkateswarulu.G, Mr. LijoLona, Ms Sushma Rasaily, Mr. Manjunath HS and Mr. Ankit Singh and my friends Mr.Shashi Mohan Jha and others.

Introduction

I, with the blessings of my Guru Sadguru Rameshji, ventured to write a book titled "Happiness 24/7, blended with simple spirituality". It gave me the confidence to proceed on the journey; I got very good response of my first book "Happiness 24/7" from my loving gentle friends and readers.

I was encouraged to write a book on awareness. This is titled as **KRISHNA THE SUPER CONSICOUSNESS** – constantly self remembering wherever you are; remember yourself. It is also known as self consciousness. Normally we are loose bags. No crystallization, no centre, just a loose combination of many things without any centre. We become part of the crowd, constantly shifting and changing with no matter inside. Awareness makes us our own master- not a controller. We are present in every moment continuously doing or not doing but having constantly one thing in our mind our consciousness; "That I am." The constant remembering of the self creates a subtle energy and we become a crystallized being.

The very idea of writing on this subject encouraged me to study *Gita* intensely and with the object of revealing the hidden heart touching ideas of *Gita* I proceeded on this journey and found that ideas may become intelligible to others also. I also studied books on *Upanishads* and full range of books on Swami Vivekananda, Swami Rama, Sri Sri Ravishankar, Osho, Sri M and other eminent spiritual Gurus.

The meaning of *Srimad Bhagwad Gita* is very profound. By reading its teachings, introspection, meditation and contemplation; unique, strange and ever new ideas and emotions continue to arise, whereby the mind and intellect, being thrilled, become contended. While writing this book, meditating and contemplating on *Gita* and other spiritual books of eminent writers. I have been very much spiritually benefitted.

The dictionary meaning of consciousness is "To be aware of things happening outside" we infer that a person is conscious as long as some or all of his sense organs are active. In the spiritual domain, consciousness has a different connotation and meaning. *Upanishads* have clearly identified consciousness as a separate entity from our gross manifestation of body, mind and intellect including the sense organs. They proclaim that consciousness is the life force of our gross manifestation and we are declared dead when consciousness is withdrawn.

Upanishads have further explained that the mind is the eye of the eye. This is a clean and simple statement. Even if the eye is open and all the images that are in front of us and are falling on our retinal screen; but if our mind is not concentrated we don't see anything. We might be thinking of something else and therefore 'seeing' something else. Therefore 'The eye of this eye is the mind' – because it is the one that sees, it observes, it decides, it chooses.

The 'eye' sees everything but the eye does not see itself. You can see your eye in a mirror as an image, but the eye does not see itself, but because it sees everything, we do not doubt its existence. Somewhat similar is the case of *Atman*, the consciousness which is the eye of the mind.

That consciousness is absolute stillness without any movement at all. Therefore, the closer the mind goes to this state of stillness, the more it is able to comprehend. This is talked, in *Upanishads*; there is no difference in its quality at the basic source of all human beings. In deep sleep condition all three faculties of body mind and intellect remain inactive. We feel a temporary bliss during this period due to lack of any activity, physical or mental. There is also a possibility for us to remain in perpetual and pure state of blissfulness.

One who lives in and operates from the field of pure consciousness does not get entangled in worldly activities and their consequences. As a result such a person remains always happy, even in the midst of immense problems. This state is attainable through continuous practice.

Srimad Bhagwad Gita holds an incomparable and unique position in world literature. It recalls the divine voice of Lord *Krishna*, through which many of His mysteries and inner secrets are revealed. The *Bhagawad Gita*, full of Lord's extraordinary thoughts and views from the very heart was never excelled in the past, nor would ever be, in the future.

The teachings of *Gita* are *Yoga* and the teacher is *Yogeshwara*. In Indian philosophy *Guru* has a very important role in one's life. *Guru* gives us knowledge, teaches us *Yoga* which tells us how we can bring *Gyan* in our practice. By touching the feet of *Guru* we are overwhelmed by the spiritual power of the *Guru*. All unwanted *Sanskars* of the disciple are burnt and get purified. His all worldly desires get attracted towards divine and the curtain of *Maya* is taken off and he experiences, Bliss *(Param Ananda)*.

God has given man the power to imagine (intellect). This is a two edged sword. It can create and destroy as well. One can use it to get rid of his ignorance or to cut the head of some one. Spirituality teaches the intellect to move on right path.

Knowledge *(Gyan)* is not seen by eyes only but it has to be adopted and practiced. When we start believing truth not only by our mind but adopt it for our whole presence then only the darkness of ignorance will be replaced by light of knowledge. *Atma Gyan* does not just require bookish knowledge but it requires its adoption and firm belief.

God is Honey and social organization is Honeycomb. Both are important. As body is of no use without soul, one should try to help and grow these social organizations as worship of God. A house holder busy in looking after his wife and children is doing a great social service. A person who does not have family or has not engaged in marriage and having children should accept to help and take responsibility of a family.

A yogi, having family is very useful in the present context of the requirement of the world. A yogi should earn his own livelihood. He should not become a burden on already economically over burdened society. God can be seen or realized by one's own efforts not by having any religious belief system or because of mercy of some powerful person.

Everyone has *Chetna (Atma)*. It is fact because body remains same but the moment *Chetna* or *Atma* leaves this body, it becomes in active and is declared as dead i.e., of no use. This *Chetna* or *Atma* is pure, peaceful and joyful. The proof of this is that a child does not discriminate in his treatment or response. Every human being appreciates beauty. A famous writer JOHN O' DONHUE has said, "The human soul is hungry for beauty; we seek it everywhere-in landscape, music, art, clothes, furniture, gardening, companionship, love, religion and in ourselves. When we experience the beautiful, there is a sense of homecoming".

The teachings of *Bhagwat Gita* taken in the appropriate context could present solutions to current pressing problems. The soul in its original state is an embodiment of purity, peace, love and truth. When we live with the awareness of being soul these qualities are manifested in our thoughts, words and actions. There is no scope for vices to influence the mind. It is only with this awareness that the soul can connect with soul.

To gain spiritual bliss, I humbly urge all to study this book for their own forward progress in the world. While reading, this book please make your mind receptive, curtailing the feelings which say; 'I know that, I know what he is saying, I know everything'.

1. VEDANTA - INTENSELY PRACTICAL

What is there in the reading of Vedas?
The Shrutis, the Purans and doing sacrifices?
Freedom alone takes off the weight of the dreadful world,
And manifests Self-blessedness.
Here is the truth; the rest is all shop-keeping.

It is essential that basic principles of ethics should be such which can be carried into our everyday life, the city life, the country life, the national life and the home life of every nation. For, if a religion cannot help man wherever he may be, wherever he stands, it is of not much use; it will remain only a theory for the chosen few. Religion to help mankind must be ready and able to help him in whatever condition he is. It should be helpful everywhere equally to servitude or in freedom, in the depths of degradation or on the heights of purity.

Swami Vivekananda in his lecture delivered in London on 10th Nov 1896, has proved that the philosophy of *Vedanta* is very good and absolutely practicable in every part of our lives. It is not a mere intellectual gymnastics. *Vedanta* teaches oneness- one life throughout. The ideas of *Vedanta* covers the whole field of life, it enters into our thoughts and covers the whole fields of life.

In various *Upanishads* we find that this *Vedanta* philosophy is not the outcome of meditation in the forests only, but that the very best parts of it were thought out and expressed by brains which were busiest in the everyday affairs of life. We cannot conceive any man busier than an absolute monarchy, a man who is ruling over millions of people and yet, some of these rulers were deep thinkers.

Bhagwat Gita is the best commentary we have on the *Vedanta* philosophy, curiously enough the scene is laid on the battlefield, where *Krishna* teaches the philosophy to *Arjuna*; and the doctrine which stands out luminously in every page of the *Gita* is intense activity, but in the midst of it, external calmness. This is the secret of work, to attain which is goal of the *Vedanta*. Inactivity, as we understand it in the sense of passivity, certainly cannot be the goal.

If inactivity or passivity is the goal of life then the walls around us would be the most intelligent, they are absolutely inactive. Clods of earth, stumps of trees, would be greatest sages in the world; they are inactive.

Vedanta does not treat activity combined with passion as real activity. *Vedanta* aims at the real activity combined with eternal calmness; the calmness which cannot be ruffled, the balance of mind which is never disturbed, whatever happens? And we all know from our experience in life that is the best attitude of work.

Many times people ask how one can work, if they do not have passion for work. I also thought in that way years ago, but as I am growing older, getting more experience, I find it is not true. The less passion there is the better we work. The calmer we are the better we work. The calmer we are the better for us, and the more the amount of work we can do. When we let loose our feelings filled with passion we waste so much energy, shatter our nerves, disturb our minds and accomplish very little work. The energy which ought to have gone out as work is spent as mere feeling, which counts for nothing.

It is commonly known that the man who becomes angry never does a great amount of work and the man whom nothing can make angry accomplishes so much. The man who gives way to anger or hatred, or any other passion cannot work; he only breaks himself to pieces and does nothing practical. It is the calm, forgiving, equable, well balanced mind that does the greatest amount of work.

The *Vedanta* preaches the ideal; and the ideal as we know, is always far ahead of the real, of the practical, as we may call it. There are two tendencies in human nature; one to harmonies the ideal with the life, and the other to elevate the life to the ideal. It is a great thing to understand this, for the former tendency is the temptation of our lives.

Now if any one comes to preach to me a certain ideal; the first step towards which is to give up selfishness to give up self-enjoyment, I think that is impractical. But when a man brings an ideal which can be reconciled with my selfishness, I am glad at once and jump at it. That is the ideal for me what I think is practical, is to me the only practicality in the world.

If I am a shopkeeper, I think shop keeping the only practical pursuit in the world. If I am a thief, I think stealing is the best means of being practical; others are not practical. We all use this word practical for things we like and can do. We have to understand that *Vedanta*, though it is intensely practical, is always so in the sense of the ideal. It does not preach an impossible ideal, however high it is, and it is high enough for an ideal.

In one word *Vedanta* teaches us one word that you are divine. You are Master of your senses. *Vedanta* says, a man who does not believe in himself is an atheist. Not believing in the glory of our own soul is what the *Vedanta* calls atheism.

I am the master of my senses. I will not allow them to blackmail me. I will not allow my guilt to overpower me, if I have committed some sin sometime I will not allow my fear blackmail me if I have committed some wrong. I will not allow myself to drag in temptation, anger, hurt or the criticism of others. I will not get attracted to somebody out of my desire or lust for sex.

Most of the time we think that this is ideal but cannot be reached so easily; we can try slowly to progress on that path. *Vedanta* insists that it can be realized by everyone. There is neither man nor woman or child nor difference of race or sex nor anything that stands as a bar to the realization of the ideal, because *Vedanta* shows that it is realized already, it is already there. You are Divine, You have all the power. You are the master.

All the powers in the universe are already ours. It is we who have put our hand before our eyes and cry that it is dark know that there is no darkness around us. Take the hands away and there is light, which was from the beginning. Darkness never existed, weakness never existed. We who are fools cry that we are weak; we are impure. Thus *Vedanta* not only insists that the ideal is practical, but that it has been so all the time; and this ideal, this Reality, is our own nature. Everything else that we see is false and untrue.

The *Vedanta* recognizes no sin, it only recognizes error. And the greatest error, says the *Vedanta*, is to say that I am weak, that I am a sinner, a miserable creature, and that I have no power and I cannot do this and that. Every time you think in that way you, as it were, rivet one more link in the chain that binds you down, you add one more layer of hypnotism on to your own soul.

The *Vedanta* also says that not only can this be realized in the depths of forest or caves, but by men in all possible conditions of life. We have seen that the people who discovered these truths were neither living in caves nor forests, nor following the ordinary vocations of life, but men who we have every reason to believe, led the busiest of lives.

It is very practical for us, whose lives, compared with theirs, are lives of leisure. If we cannot realize them, it is a shame to us, seeing that we are comparatively free all the time, having very little to do. Our requirements are as nothing compared with those of ancient compared with the demands of *Arjuna* on the battlefield of *Kurukshetra*; commanding a huge army; and yet he could find time in the midst of din and turmoil of battle to talk the highest philosophy and to carry it into his life also. Most of us here have more time than we think we have, if we really want to use it for good.

Wherever there is a false idea of reconciling fleshly verities with the highest ideals or dragging down God to the level of man, there comes decay. Man should not be degraded to worldly slavery, but should be raised up to God. At the same, we must not look down with contempt on others. All of us are going towards the same goal. The difference between weakness and strength, difference between virtue and vice, difference between heaven and hell, difference between life and death are of degree only and not of kind because oneness is the secret of everything. We have no right to look down with contempt upon those who are not developed exactly in the same degree as we are; condemn none; if you can stretch out a helping hand, do so. If you cannot fold your hands, bless your brothers and let them go their own way. Dragging down and condemning is not the way to work. We spend our energies in condemning others. Criticism and condemnation is a vain way of spending our energies.

Every one knows his disease; it requires no one to tell us what our diseases are. Being reminded of weakness does not help much; give strength and strength does not come by thinking of weakness all the time. The remedy for weakness is not brooding over weakness, but thinking of strength. Teach men of the strength that is already within them. Instead of telling them they are sinners, take the opposite position say, 'You are pure and perfect and what you call sin does not belong to you'.

The principles of *Vedanta* or the idea of religion or whatever, you call it will be fulfilled by its capacity for performing this great function. The ideal of faith in ourselves is of the greatest help to us. Throughout the history of mankind if any motive power has been more potent than another in the lives of all great men and women, it is that of faith in them. Born with the consciousness that they were to be great, they become great. Faith in us will do everything. I have experienced it in my own life, and I am still doing so, and as I grow older that faith is becoming stronger and stronger. He is an atheist who does not believe in himself. People say that he is an atheist who does not believe in God. But it is not selfish faith, as per doctrine of oneness have faith in all because you are all. Love for yourselves means love for all love for animals, love for everything, for you are all one.

To be able to use what we call *Vivek* (Discrimination) to learn how in every moment of our lives, in every one of our actions, to discriminate between what is right and wrong, true or false, we shall have to know the test of truth, which is purity, oneness. Everything that makes for oneness is truth. Love is truth, and hatred is false, because hatred makes for multiplicity. It is hatred that separates man from man; therefore it is wrong and false. It is a disintegrating power; it separates and destroys. Therefore, in all our action we have to judge whether it is making for diversity or for oneness. If for diversity we have to give it up, but if it makes for oneness, we are sure it is good.

It is through the heart that the lord is seen, and not through the intellect. The intellect is only the street cleaner, cleansing the path for us, a secondary worker, the policeman; but the policeman is not a positive necessity for the working of society. He is only to stop wrong doing. Intellect is necessary for without it we fall into crude errors and make all sorts of mistakes. Intellect checks those; but beyond that do not try to build anything upon it. It is an inactive secondary help; the real help is feeling love. Do you feel for others? If you do, you are growing in oneness. If you do not feel for others, you may be the most intellectual giant ever born, but you will be nothing, you are but dry intellect, and you will remain so. And if you feel, even if you cannot read any book and do not know any language, you are in the right way The Lord is yours.

Vedanta says that you are all prophets and all must be prophets. The book is not the proof of your conduct, but you are the proof of the book. How do you know that a book teaches Truth, because you are the truth and feel it so? If we ask what is the proof of the Christ and Buddha of the world? That you and I feel like them. Our prophet soul is the proof of their prophet soul. Your God head is the proof of God himself. Every one of us will have to become a prophet and we are all that already.

I will like to narrate a very ancient story-

A young boy said to his mother, "*I am going to study the Vedas. Tell me the name of my father and my caste*". *The mother was not a married woman, and in India in those days the child of a woman who has not been married was considered an outcaste; he is not recognized by the society and is not entitled to study the Vedas. So the poor mother said, "My child I do not know your family name; I was in service and served in different places; I do not know who your father is, but my name is Ram Pyari and your name is Satya Prakash.*

The little child went to a sage and asked to be taken as a student. The sage asked him, "What is the name of your father and what your caste is?" They boy repeated to him what he had heard from his mother. The sage at once said, "None but a *Brahman* or pure heart could speak a damaging truth about himself. You are a pure soul and I will teach you".

He who shines through the eyes is *Brahman*. He is the beautiful one. He is the shining one. He shines in all these worlds. A certain peculiar light which comes of the pure man is what is meant by light in the eyes, and it is said that when a man is pure such a light will shine in his eyes and that light belongs really to the soul within, which is everywhere.

We may invent an image through which to worship God, but a better image already exists, the living man. We may build a temple in which to worship God, and that may be good, but a better one a much higher one already exists the human body.

The *Vedanta* says that infinity is our true nature; it will never vanish, it will abide forever. But we are limiting ourselves by *Karma*, which like a chain round our neck has dragged us into this limitation. Break that chain and be free. Freedom is our nature our birth right. Be free and then have any number of personalities you like. Then we will play like the actor who comes upon the stage and plays the part of a beggar. Contrast him with the actual beggar walking in the streets.

The scene is, perhaps, the same in both cases, the words are, perhaps, the same but yet what difference. The one enjoys his beggary while the other is suffering misery form it. And what makes this difference? The one is free and the other is bound. The actor knows his beggary is not true, but that he has assumed it for play, while the real beggar thinking that it is his too familiar state and that he has to bear it whether he likes it or not. We cry all over the world for help but help never comes to us; we cry to imaginary beings and yet it never comes. But still we hope help will come and as such life is passed and the same play goes on and on. So our lives spend, in hoping, hoping and hoping which never comes to an end.

Vedanta says, "Give up hope" why should you hope? You have everything. What are you hoping for? If a king goes mad and runs about trying to find the king of his country, he will never find him, because he is the king himself. So it is better that we know we are God and give up this fool's search for Him; and knowing that we are God, we become happy and contented. Give up all these mad pursuits and then play your part in the universe as an actor on the stage.

Bible says, "If you cannot love your brother whom you have seen, how can you love God whom you have not seen. If you cannot see him in human face, how can you see him in clouds or in images made of dull dead matter or in our brain only? You are a religious man start seeing God in men and women.

We cannot see impurity without having it inside ourselves. Our whole life is to carry this into practice. In this process one great point we gain is that we shall work with satisfaction and contentment instead of with discontent and dissatisfaction, for we know that Truth is within us, we have it as our birthright, and we have only to manifest it and make it tangible.

There is no good in thinking whole life that I have done evil. I have done many mistakes. Bring in the light and the evil goes in a moment. Build up your character and manifest your real nature the ever-pure and call it up in everyone that you see. I wish that every one of us had come to such a state that even in the vilest of human beings we could see the Real self within and instead of condemning them say, "Rise who is always pure, birth less and deathless, rise almighty, and manifest your true nature. This is the one prayer, to remember our true nature, the God who is always within us, thinking of it always as infinite, almighty, ever good, ever beneficent, selfless and limitless.

All truth is eternal. Truth is nobody's property; no race, no individual can lay any exclusive claim to it. Truth is the nature of all souls. Who can lay any special claim to it? But it has to be made practical to be made simple, so that it may penetrate every pore of human society and become the property of the highest intellects and the commonest minds of the man and woman and child at the same time. Let us try to make things simpler and bring about the golden days when every man will be a worshipper and the Reality in every man will be the object of worship.

2. KNOW YOUR POTENTIAL

There is nothing you cannot be
There is nothing you cannot do
There is nothing you cannot have
You are the most magnificent,
The most remarkable, the most
splendid
The God has ever created

One day my grandson asked "*Babaji* what is your philosophy of life" I was an eighty year old still writing and still functioning physically and mentally but quite helpless when it come to formulating 'a philosophy of life'.

I wondered how I dare reach this age of eighty year without a philosophy; without anything resembling a religious outlook; without arming myself with a battery of great thoughts with which to impress my young interlocutor, who is obviously in need of a little practical if not spiritual guidance to help him navigate the shocks of life.

This morning I was pondering on the absence of a philosophy or religious outlook in my makeup and feeling a little low because it was cloudy and dark outside and gloomy weather always seems to dampen my spirits.

Then one day clouds broke up and the sun came out, I felt an uplift of spirit. At the same time I realized that no philosophy would be of any use to a person so susceptible to changes in light and shade, sunshine and shadow. I was a pure and simple; a sensualist; sensitive to touch sounds of every description, a creature of instinct, of spontaneous attractions, given to illogical fancies and attachments. As a guide, philosopher and friend I am of no use to anyone, least of all to myself.

Each one of us is a mass of imperfections and to be able to recognize and live with our imperfections, our basic natures, defects of genes and birth hereditary flaws- makes for an easier transit on life's journey.

In our imperfect world there is far too much talk and not enough thought. The TV channels are awash with TV *Gurus* telling us how to live and they do so at great length. Too many know all! A philosophy for living? You won't find it on your TV sets. You will learn more from a cab driver or street vendor.

I asked myself what is my philosophy of life. I got the answer. Ask yourself, "What makes you happy. The answer is simple it is neither the sunshine nor the birdsong, nor the bedside book and all other little things that make life worth living. It is better that we find out for ourselves. Now I understand that my philosophy of life is to be happy all the time, in all situations under all circumstances and my mission of life is to get enlightened.

We are not rational creature who feels; we are emotional creatures who rationalize. We mistrust fellow humans and so yearn for something beyond humanity, someone who comforts us, indulges our hungers, our insecurities and our inadequacies, without judgment. It is the acknowledgement of emotions in our life.

It is well understood that it is not enough to simply instruct a seeker or a student. Unless, the heart feels secure, the head will never receive new ideas. Everybody needs an anchor, a support, someone to lean on; the comforting hand of God. In Hinduism *Bhagwan* or God is seen as part of his being. This is not appropriation or inclusion; this is evolution, a journey from the limited to limitless. It is also a journey from the physical to psychological; God is not 'out there'; God is also in us and in others.

In the pre *Gita* period, God was a concept. In the post *Gita* period, God became a character in human affairs. The old abstract words – *Purusha, Brahmana, Prajapati,* And *Atman* – were gradually overshadowed by two new words; *Ishwara* and *Bhagwan*. *Ishwara* referred to the seed of divinity and *Bhagwan* referred to the fully developed tree of divinity, laden with fruits and flowers. *Ishwara* is associated with *Shiva*, the hermit whose marriage to *Shakti* creates the world. *Bhagwan* is associated with *Vishnu*, the householder who's awakening results in creation and whose slumber results in dissolution.

Between awakening and sleeping, Vishnu takes many forms to walk the earth including that of *Krishna*. *Vishnu* presupposes the existence of Goddess, who is nature, the mother of humanity, as well as culture the daughter of humanity. The God of Hindu mythology is visualized sometimes male, sometimes female, sometimes both and sometime neither. The God *Brahma* is not worshipped as he is visualized as the unenlightened householder, who seeks to control the Goddess, chasing her relentlessly against her will, and so loses his head to *Shiva*. *Shiva* is worshipped as the enlightened hermit who is turned into an enlightened householder by the Goddess. *Vishnu* is worshipped as the enlightened householder who takes responsibility for the Goddess and adopts various forms to protect her while she provides for him; becoming *Ram* when she is *Sita* and *Krishna* when she is *Radha, Satyabhama* and *Draupadi*.

The Hindu idea of God, presented through language and the liberal use of metaphors is located inside humanity not outside. It is what makes humans yearn for and find meaning. It is what makes humans outgrow fear and expand the mind for others. It is what everyone can be. This rather psychological understanding of God is unique to Hinduism and distinguishes it from western mythologies.

God wants everybody to be *Bhagwan*; see his slice of reality, his insecurity and his vulnerability, and comfort him without making him feel small. Everyone has that potential. So do you, if not you, then surely there is somebody else.

As the mind expands, everyone will accept how helpless they really are. How limited our control over the world is. We will discover how every organism has little control over his or her own capabilities and capacities that are dependent on their natural material tendencies or *Gunas*, which in turn is shaped by *Karma*. It will dawn on us that we are not agents who can change the world we are merely instruments of the world that is constantly changing.

At times, we see our inability to control our mind. How is it that despite unwillingness, humans do bad things? History tells, the upright *Yudhishthra*, could not stop himself from gambling away his kingdom, his brothers, their wife and even himself. *Pandava's* grand uncle *Bhishma* and tutor *Drona* were fighting on the *Kauravas* side. This gives an acknowledgement of the role emotion plays in cognition. Unless the heart feels secure, the head will not accept the reality revealed by *Darshan*; the reality that humans are helpless before the force of nature; that *Karma* determines the circumstances of our life and *Guna* determines the personality of people around us. We can, at best, understand these, but we cannot control them. Attempts at control only contribute to inescapable and often dreadful consequences that haunt us lifetime after lifetime, generation after generation.

Darshan reveals that humans are propelled by desire, animals by fear, plants by hunger, but what eventually manifests depends on the *Guna* that constitutes each individual. *Guna* is the nature of one's nature, the root of its diversity and dynamism. The *Atma* within observes the dance of *Guna*.

The *Gunas* are three, *Tamas*, *Rajas* and *Sattva*. The tendency towards inertia comes from *Tamas Guna*, The tendency towards activity from *Rajas Guna* and the tendency towards balance from *Sattva Guna*. The three *Gunas* cannot exist without the other. They are like three phases of wave: *Tamas* being the movement downwards towards the nadir, *Rajas* being the movement upwards towards the crest and *Sattva* being the balance; the point at which there is a pause.

In the elements, *Tamas Guna* dominates which is why they have a tendency towards inertia, unless acted upon by an external force. In plants and animals, *Rajas Guna* dominates, which is why they grow and run to overcome hunger and fear to survive. In humans, the *Sattva Guna* dominates, which is why only humans are able to trust and care for strangers, empathize and exchange. But it does not mean that all humans are *Sattvik*. While humans have a strong *Sattvik* component compared to animals, plants and minerals but amongst humans there is a differential distribution of all three *Gunas*.

Different *Gunas* dominate at different times; *Tamas Guna* is dominant in a child who follows the adult parents. *Rajas Guna* is dominant in a doubting, fiercely independent, energetic youth who strives to make his own path. *Sattva Guna* is dominant in the mature, who understand when to be silent and when to speak, when to follow and when to lead.

Guna may determine our body and our personality. *Karma* may determine the circumstances of our life. But humans have power to create their own identity by creating and claiming property. Society values people more as proprietors, than as residents of the body, for property is visible and measurable. As a result mine becomes more important than me. The gaze shifts from the inside to the outside.

Economists value wealth, Educationists value literacy. Politicians value power. Feminists value gender. Employers value skill. Physicians and surgeons value body; society is not interested in person but what a person is; his hungers, his fears or his potential. Things matter more than thoughts. Property becomes a substitute for feelings. Hence the purpose of life has become all about acquiring more and more material things.

Animals and plants do not measure or compare. They fight for as much territory as they need to survive. But humans can measure the size of their property and hence compare. This ability to measure and delimit reality is called *Maya*. *Maya* establishes the structure, divisions and hierarchies of society, in which we locate our identity and the identities of those whom we compare ourselves with.

We can qualify these yardsticks as unwanted illusions or necessary delusions that imagination can easily overturn.

When value comes from what I have, then the more I have the more valuable I become. And so I want to ensure that I have more than you. All conflicts in the *Ramayana* or *Mahabharata* also speak of conflicts generated by comparisons. Humans very instinctively evaluate and compare. In *Gita Krishna* distinguishes between *Asuras* and *Devas*, we position *Devas* as better than *Asuras*. When *Krishna* speaks of the three *Gunas*, our minds position *Sattva* as better than Rajas and Rajas as better than *Tamas*.

In nature, there is pecking order. It is necessary for survival. Humans dominate to grant themselves value and feel good about themselves. Social structures are designed to grant humans identity. They are invariably based on comparison of the social body, what we have, wealth, knowledge, contacts and skills. People think that I am better than you because what I have is bigger or better or faster or richer or prettier or cheaper or nice or nastier than yours. But comparing our titles and estates we validate ourselves, make ourselves feel significant and relevant.

The *Gita* requires us, not to renounce work but to do them, offering them to the Supreme in which alone is immortality. When we renounce our attachment to the finite ego and its likes and dislikes and place our actions in the eternal, we acquire the true renunciation which is consistent with free activity in the world. Such a renounce acts not for his fleeting finite, but for the self which is in us all.

Ultimately, I learnt that to be alone is to be God. When the wrong people leave your life, the right things start happening. Wrong people come to one's life with all their negativity; get rid of them and come out of this. Individuals in our life have their positive and negative influences. Human mind unwillingly gets drawn to all undesirable things and thoughts. The cognitive faculty of human brain quickly latches on to the bad rather than good.

When people leave your life, you do get a new perspective. Now you are free to exercise your volition, unclouded by other's thought patterns. One has to develop his potential to aspire to spiritual enlightenment. It is an individualistic process, yet not selfish or self centered. People come and go when their time is up in their life. Develop love to be alone. Because it's different from being aloof; remember, to be alone is to be God and the highest objective of human existence is to get to the Godhood that's within the reach of all.

> This whole wide earth my bed,
> My beautiful pillows my own two arms,
> My wonderful canopy the blue sky,
> And the cool evening air to fan me
> The moon and the stars my lamps,
> And my beautiful wife, Renunciation, by my side,
> What king is there who can sleep like me in pleasure?

3. BEING IN THE WORLD AND YET ABOVE- PERFECTION OF RENUNCIATION

In enjoyment, is the fear of disease?
In high birth, the fear of losing caste;
In wealth, the fear of tyrants;
In honor, the fear of losing her;
In strength, the fear of enemies;
In beauty, the fear of old age;
In knowledge, the fear of defeat;
In virtue, the fear of scandal;
In the body, the fear of death;
In this life, all is fraught with fear;
Renunciation alone is fearless.

Mere renunciation brings unhappiness and frustration. Renunciation without being aware of the purpose of life creates problems for the renunciates and for the people of the world who look for examples from them. The people of the world think that renunciates are the best examples to be followed. But we find many householders who are superior to renunciates. The inner condition is more important than the external way of living.

Even after renouncing wealth, home, relatives, wife and children one cannot easily renounce the lust for name and fame, nor can one easily purify the ego and direct his emotion towards self realization. Cultivation of a new mind is a necessary step for enlightenment.

Decide that no matter what happens, you will do what you get out to do. If one is determined, possible distractions will still be there but one will continue on his path and remain undisturbed. *Sankalp* (determination) is very important. One cannot change his circumstances, the world or his society to suit him. But if one has strength and determination one can go through his process of life very successfully.

Attachment is one's mother and anger is father. If they both die, one has nothing to do. Once, one is able to give up attachment, anger and pride; meditation will become his very nature. Then he will not have to pose for meditation for whole of his life and his life will become a sort of meditation.

There is a famous story that once a *Guru* of a swami asked him to do a particular *Sadhana* for forty one days to achieve enlightenment no matter how much your mind attempts to dissuade you from completing the *Sadhana*; you should not leave that place. *Swami* followed the practices for thirty nine days and nothing happened.

Then some powerful thought came into his mind, "What a foolish thing you are doing wasting your time in a lonely place, cut off from the world". He thought he is wasting the best period of his youth. So on thirty ninth days his mind advanced reason after reason against this *Sadhana*, he started thinking, "What difference two more days possibly make". He has not experienced anything even after thirty nine days.

He started walking on the street, leaving the place of *Sadhana*. When he was walking on the main street he heard some musical instruments being played. There was a woman singing and dancing. The theme of the music was, "There is very little oil in vessel of life, and the night is vast". She was repeating the phrase again and again. The sound of the *tabla* drums seemed to call to me, "*Dhik, Dhik*! Fie on thee, fie on thee! What have you done? I felt dejected and went back and completed my practice for the remaining two days.

Then he walked back to the city once again and went to the house of the singer. She was a beautiful and famous dancing girl. She was considered to be a prostitute. When she saw a young swami coming towards her house, she called his servant, a large and powerful man to stop him and not to let him in. She commanded, "Stop Young *Swami* this is the wrong place for him".

Swami insisted to see her, saying "She is like my mother. She alerted me with her song. I would not have completed my practices. I would have failed and I would have condemned myself and felt guilty the rest of my life."When I got up to go she said, "I promise to live like your mother from now on. I will prove that I can be mother not only to you but of many others as well. Now I am inspired".

The next day she left for *Varanasi*, where she lived on a boat on *Ganges*. In the evening she would go ashore and chant on the sand. Thousands of people used to join her. She wrote on her houseboat, "Don't mistake me for SAINT. I was a prostitute. Please do not touch my feet". She never looked directly at anyone's face and never talked to anyone. If someone wanted to talk to her she would only say, "Sit down with me and chant God's name". She later took *Samadhi* in the *Ganges*.

When awakening comes we can completely transform our personalities, throwing off the past. Don't condemn yourself. No matter how bad or how small you think you have been, you have a chance to transform your whole personality. A true seeker can always realize the reality and attain freedom from all bondage and miseries. In just one second you can enlighten yourself.

There is a great difference between physically giving up and actually giving up. If one has given up all material possessions, yet is attached to what little one he has then he has not really given up. It is good to have a middle path with no extremes. Have what is necessary and have no craving for more. *Krishna* says in *Gita*, "This *Yoga* is not for one who eats too much or too little, or sleeps too much or too little. There is a beautiful sentence in the *Ishuvarya Upanishad* which says 'Let go and rejoice. When you let go you suffer.

Once when Swami Vivekananda was wandering around India, a young man came to him and said, '*Sir, I want to renounce everything and become a Sanyasi. Swamiji said 'great' you must be a mature man to be able to do that! What is your education? The young man said that he had not completed his high school, Swamiji asked, "What about your background?" The young man replied that his parents were dead. He had nothing, no home. Swamiji said, "Then what are you going to renounce? The young man said that he wanted to give up what little he had and become like the Buddha. Swami replied, "Buddha had a whole kingdom to renounce, but you have nothing to let go. Go and make some money first, even if you have to steal. And when you have a Lakh of rupees in your hand, you can come and say, Swamiji, have this much, I am going to give it up and become a Sanyasi and then I will accept your request.*

Frog, lone among all creature that we know of, passes through quite a metamorphosis that swims around in the water and discards its tail. Then it begins to live both on land and in water. It is a great transformation that takes place. It is also in some way a reference to a spiritually advanced being or a *rishi*, who in his complete spiritual understanding, has discarded his tail; like a frog that can live both in water and on the land, *rishi* is in two worlds at the same time – the material and the spiritual. When tail is discarded, one no longer remains a tadpole; he is fully grown and can live in two worlds-here and there at the same time.

Live in the world of the spirit, anchored in the world of this world. A beautiful example is that of the lotus, which grows in the water, taking all its substance from the mud underneath, yet not a drop of water will stick to its petals. So also, derive all your substance from the world and yet remain unaffected by it. Some people think that it is not possible. One has to try.

If one remains trapped by the attractions of this world, it means one is not trying hard enough, and if that be so it only means that one's priorities are not yet decided – that is all. People have this approach – we will work hard for anything- for instance, a promotion or a fat bank balance, but where spiritual development is concerned, a short cut would be nice.

No *Upanishad*, no religious teacher has said that we must renounce this world and live in isolation. It is so difficult for a person to go away, sit in a cave and meditate. It is impossible because we carry our mind with us; we are not free from the mind which comes with us wherever we go. Even if we do go away, how do we find out whether we have progressed spiritually, sitting alone then? Spirituality can be tested only in society, in the midst of people.

Of course, when one has performed all one's life work and discharged one's responsibilities, then one is free to go. But there is no point in running away prematurely, for trivial reasons. That is what is called the '*Vairagya*' of the monkey. I get upset with my wife; we have a big quarrel; so I renounce everything and go off to *Varanasi*. One has to be very mature to be free; then one can physically go away somewhere.

Possessing more than necessary only creates obstacles for oneself. It is waste of time and energy. Fulfilling wants and desires without understanding needs and necessities deviates one from the path of awareness. Desire is the mother of all miseries. When the desires for worldly attainments are directed towards attaining self awareness, then the same desire becomes a means. At this stage the desire, instead of becoming an obstacle, becomes a useful instrument for self realization.

This can be explained by a simple simile. A candle light is extinguished by the breeze very easily, but if that light is protected and allowed to catch the fire, it will grow into a forest fire. Then the breeze helps that fire instead of extinguishing it. Similarly, when an aspirant, with the help of discipline, protects the fame of desire burning within, it grows more and more.

The obstacles which are supposed to obstruct the path of self realization are not really obstacles. Attachment is one of the strongest obstacles created by us. With the help of non attachment we can overcome such obstructions.

There are four ways of removing these obstacles. First – If there is no object, the human mind cannot become attached to it. Renouncing the object is one way, but it seems to be quite difficult for ordinary people.

Second – While having all the objects of the world, if we learn the technique of using them as means, then the objects are not able to create obstacles for us. On this path, attitudes need to be transformed. One who has transformed his attitudes can change his bad circumstances into favorable ones.

The third way is the path of conquest, in which one learns to do his actions skillfully and selflessly, surrendering the fruits of his actions for the benefit of others. Such a person becomes detached and safely crosses the ocean of life.

Fourth – By self surrender one surrenders himself and all that he owns to the Lord and leads a life of freedom from all attachments. This path seems to be easy but is really rather difficult.

The impulses of attraction and repulsion residing in every object of the sense are the two robbers who constantly rob man of his spiritual wealth. Those impulses are known by the names of desire and anger and that of those two; again desire is the dominant force, for it is a grosser form of attraction because anger has its roots in desire.

Desire springs up from attraction and anger ensues from desire. Therefore, with the eradication of desire anger too gets automatically eradicated. Desire as insatiable by nature, it can never be satiated by enjoyment. It can be clarified that butter and fuel when added to fire, strengthen it, even so the more we indulge in sense enjoyments the stronger is our appetite for enjoyment.

Desire is the root of all evils. Man is forced to commit sin against his will neither by *Prarabdha* nor by GOD; it is desire alone which leads man to develop attachment for various objects of enjoyment and drags him to sinful acts. *Prarabdha* is merely concerned with the enjoyment of the fruits of action done in a previous life. It does not possess the capacity to lead anyone to sin. GOD being the very embodiment of compassion and greatest friend of all created beings can never lead anyone to sin. The only enemy therefore, that drive a man to sinful acts is 'desire'.

The mind, the intellect and the senses are not ordinarily under control of man; 'desire' holds its sway over them. This is what is said, that mind and intellect is the seat of desire. Therefore to pursue spirituality one has to drive out this enemy i.e. 'desire' from his mind, intellect and senses or to suppress or crush it in their very strong hold, failing which, like an enemy entrenched in one's own house, it will destroy his valuable possession in the shape of human existence.

This formidable enemy of man in the spiritual path, viz., 'desire' takes hold of the senses, mind and intellect by tempting them with ideas of false happiness to be derived from enjoyment of worldly objects, and covering the knowledge of the *Jivatma* through the instrumentality of the mind, intellect and senses throws it into the dark cell of transmigration. Nay, depriving him of real wealth in the form of GOD-realization this arch enemy of man robs him of inestimable blessings of a human birth.

The senses are said to be greater than body; but greater than senses is the mind. Greater than the mind is the intellect; and what is greater than the intellect is the self, the consciousness. The senses even of a wise man who is practicing self control forcibly carry away his mind and the senses moving among sense objects the one of which is mind is joined and takes away man's discrimination. It leads to the fact that senses are not only more powerful than the mind but conjoined with the mind they are even more powerful than the intellect.

So long the soul does not exercise the control over intellect, mind and sense and forgetting its inherent power submits to their control, the senses misleading the mind and intellect succeed in dragging them forcibly behind them along the wrong path. That is to say, the senses first of all win over the mind by tempting it with prospects of enjoyment; then the sense in conjunction with the mind win over the intellect; and they all combine to bring the soul under their thumb.

Nevertheless, in reality the mind is stronger than the senses, the intellect is stronger than mind and the soul is the strongest of all. The soul possesses the power to kill desire. Once man realizes the strength of soul, he can easily establish full control over the intellect, mind and senses and kill desire.

It is true; the soul possesses infinite strength, and can uproot and destroy the enemy of man, 'desire'. In fact, it is the strength derived from the soul that makes everything else powerful and active in the world. But the tragedy of it is that it remains forgetful of its strength. That is how desire, hidden in the intellect, mind and senses tempts the soul with prospects of enjoyment and keep it entangled in the world.

The total renunciation is wholly abstaining in thought, word and deed from vile deeds such as thieving, adultery, lying, duplicity, chicanery, coercion, violence, taking forbidden food, indulgence in frivolities etc.

We have also to follow renunciation of actions motivated by desires. We should cease to perform with a self motive, sacrifices, charity, penance, worship and other action motivated by desire, which are generally performed with a view to obtaining agreeable objects, such as wife progeny and wealth etc or with the object of securing freedom from some ailment or saving oneself of other calamities.

If by chance one is confronted with a duty, secular or sacred, which is outwardly motivated by desire but the omission of which is calculated to cause pain to anyone or interference with the time-honored institutions of Action and Worship, there is no objection to one's performing it disinterestedly and only for the good of the world. Such act will not be deemed to have been performed an act motivated by desire.

One should also renounce the thirst for enhancing one's honor, fame social prestige and whatever objects of a transient nature, regarding them as an obstacle to GOD realization.

One should also not ask for money or bodily service from another for one's own gratification. One should also not seek to attain one's selfish end through any one by any means whatsoever – all this is included in taking service from another with a selfish motive.

Story Explaining experiencing *Maya*

Narada went to Vishnu and asked him the meaning of Maya. In response Vishnu said, "I will explain after you quench my thirst. Go fetch me some water".

Narada went to river to fetch water. But as he was collecting the water, he saw a beautiful girl. He got attracted and married. Narada was involved in the family and felt content. Suddenly he lost his wife, his children. So he remembered of Vishnu who said, "where is my water, I am still thirsty".

Narada asked, "From where does this pain and suffering come from? Vishnu smiled and said, "I thought you had full knowledge of Maya before you set out to fetch water for me".

Narada bowed his head in realization. He knew Maya but had never experienced Maya. Knowledge of Maya is not experience of Maya. Unless one experiences Maya, one will not be able to empathize with those who are trapped in Maya.

Devotional Service into the supreme personality of GOD head is the ultimate goal of life of all **YOGIS**; one who always thinks of ME within himself is best. All acts should be performed in conjunction with the supreme Lord. The purpose of life is indicated to be renunciation and attainment of transcendental position above the material modes of nature.

Real renunciation means that one should always think himself part and parcel of the supreme Lord. Therefore, he has no right to enjoy the results of his work. Since, he is part and parcel of the supreme Lord; the results of his work should also be enjoyed by the Supreme Lord. This is actually *Krishna Consciousness*. The person acting in *Krishna* consciousness is really a *Sanyasi*, one in the renounced order of life. By such mentality, one is satisfied because he is actually acting for the supreme. Thus, he is not attached to anything material; he becomes accustomed to not taking pleasure in anything beyond the transcendental happiness derived from the service of the Lord. One who is satisfied in himself has no fear of any kind of reaction from his activity.

Sometimes we are confused about our duty and lose all composure because of weakness. By nature's own way the complete system of material activities is a source of perplexity for everyone. On every step there is perplexity. The world situation is such that perplexities of life automatically appear without wanting such confusion. No one wants fire yet it takes places and we become perplexed.

The wisdom therefore advises that in order to solve the perplexities of life and to understand the science of solution one must take the help of a spiritual *Guru*. We should understand how the man in material perplexities does not understand the problems of life? He is actually a miserly man who does not solve problems of life as a human and who thus quit the world like cats and dogs without understanding the science of self realization. This human form of life is most valuable asset for the living entity who can use it for solving the problems of life; therefore one who does not utilize this opportunity properly is a miser. On the other hand there is a *Brahmana* or who is intelligent enough to utilize this body to solve all the problems of life.

So it is with our God. He is waiting for us to give up all cheap things in our lives so that he can give us his beautiful treasure, that he has all the time for us. But we have to give up our desires first. Why are we holding onto things, which God wants us to let go of. Are we holding on to harmful or unnecessary possessions which we have become so attached to that it seems impossible to let go.

Sometimes it is so hard to see what God has in the other hand, but we must believe that God will never take away anything without giving us in return something precious in its place.

---

4. LAWS OF THOUGHT

MY THOUGHTS, MY KARMA, MY DESTINY.
The laws of thought are that, whatever,
We are interested becomes our world.

All great sages and spiritual people have identified thoughts as the most potent strength of a human being. Just as fire heats up environment so thoughts have the power to transform the personality of the person; who comes into contact with them. Thoughts transformed *Arjuna* to face life's challenges. Thoughts turned the robber *Ratnakar* into *Valmiki*.

Most of us feel that thoughts are random and automatic, but they are powerful too. They seem to come from a certain depth in our being and influence our feelings and action. We feel somewhat passive in relation to our thoughts as they quickly change our mood for better or worse alter the crucial decisions of our life and so have a strong impact on our current and future reality. However, once we start observing our thoughts and introspecting deeply, there comes the realization that they are not aligned at all.

Upanishad says," We always look outward and never look within, thus we destroy ourselves. Only the courageous person looks within".

When you face your madness with courage, then your intelligence will search for sanity beyond the maddening mind.

Krishna, Buddha and all other enlightened masters tell us that your interstate is Happiness. Some philosophers now a day say "In the absence of happiness sadness exits". But what *Krishna* says you have not to just believe but your experience will tell you that but for that you have to see yourself clearly. You will find that you are happy inside, only you have allowed sadness to overpower you. If you look into the mind, you will actually see that the mind is the cause of your unhappiness. The truth is to be happy is effortless, but to become sad, we feel something which is borrowed.

Thoughts mirror our deep-seated formations about which we are and what the world is. These are often misleading because they are based on the ignorance of our present and previous life times as well as the collective ignorance of humanity. Therefore, our personal evolution can proceed only when we start working with our thoughts in a conscious and active manner.

The science of psychology has found that whatever we mentally pay attention to whether in a conscious or unconscious manner we are that and we end in becoming more like that. That's why it is advocated that if we can create a mental attitude that is filled with hope, positivity and which anticipates good and favorable outcomes; we will make considerable progress. That's why there is wide spread belief that if you think positively all your problems will be magically sorted out.

But there is a growing dissent that power of positive is overrated because if the reality does not match one's positive expectations, people experience severe frustration, which may take them downhill. What is the way out, then?

Perhaps, the answer lies in thinking not just positive thoughts, but thinking transcendental. The *Yogi Vasistha* narrates, that the end of an epoch when the universe had dissolved, the creator God, *Brahma*, wished to make a new universe. However, he was puzzled to see that several universes, each having its own creator, had already been created. Through enquiry, *Brahma* became aware that 10 young men, who were sage *Kashyapa's* sons had created these universes.

The 10 young men wanted to aspire for that, which would never make them despondent. They realized that neither any positive thought, nor any possession whether on earth or anywhere in the universe will bestow permanent bliss on them. Then 10 young men concluded that only if they could become *Divine* and attain creatorship of the universe, they would attain eternal joy. Thus, they contemplated that they are *Brahma*, who is liberated and full of self knowledge and that creation exists within them.

At its pinnacle, the thought is omnipotent. When the sage's sons could become creators through intense aspiration, we can explore the unknown and untapped power of thought. Why should we limit ourselves to wishing for a good job, health, peaceful mind, confidence, harmonious relationships and meaningful life? Why not dream big, the best possible way? Why not contemplate that transcendent between oneself and Divinity?

If we live in such a reality eternally, there will be pure bliss. Just concentrate on creating this omnipotent thought form by constantly reminding yourself that everything, big or small, living or non living, past or present is *Brahma*, universal consciousness.

Scrutinize your life; see what you have booked in your thoughts. According to Law of thought, you keep noticing only what you have booked in your thoughts and the same appears in your life. If you have booked love, joy and peace, you will experience them. So don't wait anymore. Go ahead and create the formula for success, prosperity and happiness and get maximum satisfaction for your life through your thoughts.

There are people who can create bad thoughts howsoever, good the situation is, so we can create good thoughts, however, bad the situation may be. We have to be firm that situations and state of mind have no connection. We have to take care of our state of mind. Situations may come and go but our state of mind will make our behavior.

One should always focus on what you want, not on what you don't want. By force of habit, one often repeats negative statements like, "I don't want illness", "I do not want to meet with an accident", "I don't want to witness corruption". But now make it a point to tell the nature what you want in place of what you don't want. With this you will stop unknowingly attracting the negative things in your life.

Whenever, you think or say negative words like, "This should not happen" immediately become aware and tell nature, "What should happen". Tell nature what you want instead of conveying what you don't want. This is the right prayer. Repeat to yourself time and again, wherever possible.

We often tend to give in to the age old habit of thinking and speaking negatively, without even being aware of it. As a result, we unknowingly keep repeating negative words and thereby contradict our own prayers. For example, at one moment a student says, "I wish to pass the exams, but how can I study so much? The very next moment he says, "I hope I don't fail" This is a double prayer, one negates the other.

Many a times your prayer fetches the opposite result. But you fail to identify where exactly you are going wrong. Hence it is essential to repeat positive sentences multiple times. People who experience negative results in life lose their faith in GOD. Hence, it is necessary to understand the laws of thought and implement them in one's life.

In order to gain clarity on the laws of thought, let us go through an example which you may relate to. Suppose you have gone to a showroom for buying a new vehicle. You see a variety of models of vehicles with different colors. You place an order for the model and color you have liked. You know that you will receive the vehicle after a few days. Now, what happens during this waiting period? Wherever you go, you spot more and more vehicles of the same model and color that you have chosen.

You feel surprised, "Where have so many vehicles of the same model and color suddenly come from? But actually they were there, you have started noticing them now suddenly because they came into your thoughts and became a part of your world. You were travelling the same route before. Many of those vehicles had passed you by even earlier, but you hadn't noticed them. Now they suddenly seem to appear out of nowhere. Why did this happen?

The reason is that earlier you were not interested in them. As soon as you got interested, you booked one for yourself and you started noticing them. We learn from this example that the thoughts in which we are interested become our world. Therefore, see what you have booked in your thoughts.

People have very different conceptions of their final destiny. Some think in terms of annihilation and cessation of all our functions. Others believe that beyond death there is eternal life. Eternal life to me is that we keep walking. If we walk in the presence of GOD on this earth, we do it partially. In the afterlife I believe that we will walk in the presence of GOD fully.

On ageing, many a time's people start living sedentary life. The same thing was happening to me also. Fortunately, after meeting *Sadguru Rameshji* I understood that spiritual walking is like physical walking. It is moving towards productive goals like creating happiness, nurturing loving relationships, working hard, spreading peace, serenity and tranquility.

We may have stymied by a tepid attitude of life, lukewarm, no passion for life and become plain neutral in a pejorative sense. But when faced with death, we can no longer remain neutral. So always make a Mantra of life, walk, walk and walk. Doing so will help you resolve health issues and remain fit and alert. There is also a spiritual dimension to this, because as embodied beings, our body is an important part of our spiritual nature.

If we do not continue walking; the lack of motion depletes our energy. There are times when we need to be still but not motionless because motion is energy. When I watch trees grow, I notice how imperceptible their growth into full glory is. They look so tiny in the beginning but there is an inner growth that finally manifests in full outside growth.

Spiritual walking is like that. There are times when we may stumble and fall. There are moments when our energies are depleted by stress, dysfunction and regression. But there is an inner momentum and if we make the right choices, that will keep pushing us forward till we realize our destiny.

There is a thought how can we tie up the spiritual world with material world. The material world is important so long as we remain detached from the results of our walking. Will we always be successful? Perhaps not! Will we always attain our goals in this life? May be not! But by the very fact that we are walking and creating motion and energy in sync with creative forces in the universe, we are walking with the correct attitudes which influence our choices, inclinations and our intellectual and emotional life.

Spiritual walking is to walk in the present. Though, we integrate our background history and past consciousness by relating them to our walking in the present. Each step that we take today is taken in the present. If we have any regrets, the very forces that propel us forward are also the spiritual forces that bring renewal and rebirth, helping us to overcome those regrets.

We tend to get used to the rut and routine and begin to love that as the sole option available to us. A sort of mental complacency sets in and we don't want to alter that. The human mind does not like to break a set pattern. But until the set and fixed pattern is broken, how something new and even more exciting can be welcomed.

New beginnings are often disguised as painful endings. We resist and often resent the changes. But change is the key of life, because despite change being seemingly painful, it is ever necessary.

What's perceived as painful and undesirable often paves the ways for something better; at least different. In difference lies life's momentum and progress. Apparently, painful endings have a silver lining. They carry positivism in their wombs. They are the indicators of a better and greater tomorrow.

When Hiroshima and Nagasaki were nuked during the last days of Second World War in 1945 on August 06 and 09 respectively, Albert Einstein said, "Though it is terribly painful, new lives and purposes will emerge from the ashes of two great cities and they will become even greater.

The pain and trauma of near annihilation gave birth to stronger determination and resolve. Most importantly it removes the complacency that tends to set in when everything falls in a predictable routine. When life throws challenges at us howsoever, difficult and cruel they are the human spirit ought to triumph in the end. Hidden opportunities make us more determined and fill us with life preserving energy. Until we are out of our peaceful slumber no epochal event can be expected to happen.

Change for the better always comes after a seemingly hopeless situation. The significance of a drop of water is to get merged into the river; when pain becomes unbearable it turns into remedy. We often perceive painful things through tunnel vision. We don't let other options and opportunities emerge out of them. So broaden your vision by deepening your perceptions and take path in perspective. Mind you, it will open up a plethora of positive outcomes that will become clear in the long run. All we need is a pair of eyes unblinking by fear, apprehension and prejudice.

We all know Banks carry in their Balance sheet Non-performing Assets, the unrecoverable loans. Banks burdened with these Non-performing Assets are said to be stressed. Like

Banks people do have their non-performing assets which impose a crippling load on them. These Non-performing assets are Hate, Fear, possessiveness, ego, etc.

Hate is the most dangerous and deadly of all our NPAs. This causes the maximum damage not only to our emotional and physical well-being, but to the health and well being. Hate is the most negative and most oppressive of our NPAs and the quantum of hate seems to be growing all over the world, often fuelled by sectarian strife ignited by differences in religious or ideological beliefs.

The other most common NPA of which hate is a derivative is fear. All hate of any form, can be traced to fear. I hate my enemies because I am afraid of them. I hate your practices – religious or political or even dietary – because I fear that they will overcome and supplant my beliefs and practices.

If hate is linked to fear, fear can be linked to possessiveness. I fear and hate my neighbors across my national border because they might take away from me that which my national ego – which is often given the name of patriotism, covets and wants to possess at all costs, even at the ultimate cost of war and mutual destruction.

Possessiveness, fear and hate give rise to the NPA of anger and aggression, which sparks violent confrontation, physical or verbal between conflicting concepts of nationhood or of political, cultural or religious convictions.

How can one get rid of these baneful human NPAs which end up hurting us more than any eternal adversary can? It's easier said or written about that done. For all these hurtful NPAs spring from the fundamental NPA of a discrete, individual ego which is not just separate form but is at antagonistic variance with all other beings with whom it must ceaselessly and relentlessly compete in order to ensure its own survival.

The first step towards this distant goal is to consciously try to see things from not our own perspective, but from that of others. It's a trick of mental eyesight which is sometimes called empathy or compassion. And it's the first move we can make to avoid the danger of spiritual bankruptcy.

Our thoughts influence our physical health. The present reality can be that we are physically unwell, but if we create thoughts and talk about being unwell then that vibration slows down the healing.

While we are taking medicines for healing, we need to be aware of our role and the role of our reality in healing. Our thoughts and words radiate to the body. The thoughts and words of the family create a collective vibration in the house, which we absorb as it affects the body.

Unaware we create thoughts that we or our family member is unwell. To not create this thought, we should create a thought that our health is perfect and normal.

Daily practice of early morning affirmation for perfect health along with visualization of health will start replacing the thoughts of being ill. Early morning and before sleeping, at regular intervals during the day affirmation radiate healing energy to the body. Two belief systems reduce soul power. First is that our emotion is dependent on external situation or people. Second is the negative emotion is normal in the current scenario. When we label a negative emotion as normal we allow the mind to create that emotion.

When the soul is creating and experiencing any of its 7 qualities of purity, peace, happiness, love, power, knowledge and bliss, we will be comfortable. But if we label the negative emotions as normal and create them, we will not be comfortable.

When the body does not get its original elements, we get suffocated. Relationships experience suffocation because the two souls exchanging energy are suffocated. When the soul gets healthy our desires start reducing; relationships get smooth; addicting to substances and technology are no more; we do not need people's approval and appreciation.

We need to forgive those who did what was not right for us and forget all that happened. In spite of knowing it; sometime we are unable to do it. Forgive and forget is also a *Sanskar* which we need to create. Misunderstandings can run so deep that they get carried over from one generation to the next. Not only that tight knot of hatred and anger that can never be unraveled, gets formed. So think wisely. Thoughts make words meaningful; in fact all human actions are made meaningful.

To make it a *Sanskar* it needs to be done repeatedly. To do it often we must begin with ourselves. When we make a mistake we keep thinking about it and keep re -living the past, this becomes our habit. Not being able to forgive ourselves creates a *Sanskar* of not being able to forgive and then we find it difficult to do it for others also.

We understand our, other people understand their *Sanskar's*, have compassion for them, they are in emotional pain and we must support them. We need to do the same for ourselves. Treat yourself like another person and have compassion for self.

When we do not forgive ourselves or we believe we cannot forgive our self we radiate hurt, guilt and anger to ourselves. We stop loving ourselves and it becomes difficult to live without self. These emotions deplete us and chances of making a mistake increase.

When we create a positive affirmation like – I am a Divine being or I am a powerful being, it creates a positive pattern on the soul. Repeated thinking of a positive line increases soul power, our words and behavior are then based on the quality of that affirmation.

When we make a big mistake, we start cursing ourselves and create a negative affirmation – I am wrong, I can never forgive myself, I should be punished and so deplete soul power. Depleted soul power makes more mistakes and then again creates guilt.

To release the past and stop the repetitive pattern of self anger and guilt, we need to consciously create the right thought.

Daily create a thought - I am a pure soul. My every word and behavior is full of God's knowledge and purity. It was a past Karmic account. It's over; never to happen again. My every *Karma* is accurate.

We need to empower our self daily so that we are stable and face the consequences of any past Karmic account the right way.

We are accompanied in our journey by the GOD of the impossible. By walking we move to higher levels of consciousness. In this walk we carry people along with us. We influence the others and begin to relate more with significant others and less with those who are sometimes a drag on our energies.

So, as embodied spiritual beings, let us keep walking past the clouds of doubt and distress, despair and fear and hopefully we will still continue walking in the corridors of eternity.

Power of Positive thoughts.

Once an astrologer told to the parents of a boy that boy is going to die at the age of 28 years and boy over heard that. It gave thought to the boy that he has such a short span of life and he will die without accomplishing anything.

The boy went to his *Guru* and informed him of it weeping. *Guruji* told to the boy that prediction is wrong. Don't worry – but you will have to experience death face to face on that fateful day. During the intervening years the boy forgot about the prediction when he attained the age of 28 years his *Guru* asked him to go to a mountain peak some 1100 feet high and some sixty miles from *Rishikesh*. He asked him to perform nine days *Durga Puja* there. The person performed *Puja* with all mountains chanting and reciting the Hyms of the mother Goddess.

One day he climbed to a height of 20000 feet and saw a temple of Divine mother. There were pine trees all around. Suddenly he slipped on the pine needles and began to roll down the mountain and felt as if his life is finished but he plummeted downward after about 500 feet and was caught by small thorny bush. A sharp branch pierced him in the abdomen and that held him. There was a steep drop below - and the bush started swinging with his weight. First he would see the mountains and then the Ganges far below. He closed his eyes and then opened them again. He saw blood flowing where the branch pierced his abdomen but that was nothing compared to stark imminence of death. He paid no attention to the pain because of the larger concern, the anticipation of death.

5. BE CHAITANYA - DELETE PAST DATA

Creativity is the highest peak of your consciousness; hence it is painful and arduous. To be uncreative is comfortable; it is a downward journey. You need not to do anything, nothing is needed on your part; the gravitational pull is enough. When you are coming down from the hill; you can just turn your car engine off; the car will go on rolling down. If you are going uphill, effort is needed.

Many things have to be dropped when you are moving upward; unnecessary weights have to be dropped. Think! You are carrying so many luggages; it is all unnecessary, it is useless. But people go on collecting. We will collect any king of rubbish, hoping that some day it will be of some use. We are greedy and feel empty, so go on stuffing ourselves with every kind of thing.

We are so full of ego and ego is a great weight. One cannot move upward unless we put our ego aside, and that is the greatest pain.

Every experience that we have, consciously or unconsciously gets captured, mapped and tagged in our *Chitta* (Mind). In yogic tradition our *Chitta* mind is like a database. Thus, we retain memories of everything we have experienced not just in this life but also in our pervious lives.

No one likes to suffer; yet we undergo suffering. Einstein once said "I cannot believe that God plays dice with the cosmos". It is we only who create sufferings for ourselves. All life is imbued with suffering that is so pervasive that it engulfs the entire planet and across species. Einstein was not prepared to accept that nature was being governed by the laws of chance. The Doctrine of *Karma* has its roots in cause and efforts theory.

To begin with the Doctrine of *Karma* divides people into two categories, the active and the contemplative. The active ones are those who believe in external action as a means of unfolding of the self. Their sensibility is still colored by stains of duality. But if they perform their duty in an unselfish way their sensibility is purified.

Thus they achieve a higher platform of understanding. They also start looking at things as a kind of divine play. So is the case with the working of the cosmos. We find that nature is conservative with a few disturbances here and there. Our insistence on rational reasoning causes needless psychic suffering. Action is the outcome of want and desire.

A contemplative man of higher sensibility slowly becomes desire less and hence obtains from self centered action. Freedom from action leads to devotion to knowledge. Through unselfish action, the seeker gradually eliminated his trivial worldly desires and attains the level of purer sensibility. When one is aware of transitory nature of life suffering can be accepted as a primordial nature of change.

The main reason of our suffering is also that we retain our memories of everything. These twists and knots of our mind, which we retain because of our past memories and experiences distort our understanding of reality and make us, see the world in a particular way. As long as our *chitta* is twisted and knotted in this way, we will always remain unhappy.

The twisting of *chitta* often makes us feel that we are victims and so we often engage with the world as martyrs; at other times as heroes, striving to create a better world. A twisted *chitta* prevents us from appreciating the reality. We are not able to see the reality that, even as the most certified of all villains imagine themselves as a victim, martyr or hero.

It all comes down to memories, buried deep in our being, that shape our view of the world. With all the data about our existence being captured by digital technology, we all want the right to be forgotten.

The outer world floods our brain and senses with a continual stream of data input. Messages from the environment around us flow into our brain, which then processes it. There is nonstop competition from the outer world to grab our attention. What should we do, if the input we receive daily is predominantly information filled with things that put us into states of fear?

For destroying all these past memories, we need to worship Shiva, who has the power to destroy all the past memories. His ability to wipe out memories makes him *Yogaeshwar*, Lord of *Yoga*.

We are always in search of the methods to make ourselves happy. In this search, sometimes we find the easiest method of taking drugs, which we find chemically induces happiness and unsustainable. We resort to parties and shopping to distract our minds. We also resort to another method to distract our mind with repetitive meaningless activities that stop us from thinking and make us forget time, like video games and rituals. It all work for some time, but not for long. Even bollywood and TV shows are also not able to distract our minds. These are all temporary measures not to achieve happiness but to forget and distract our mind from miseries.

The good news is that we have a choice about where to focus. We can decide whether to focus on what is temporary and negative or what is positive. We have free will to determine with what we want to flood our being.

One solution is to fill ourselves with the peace existing already within us. We all have clam inside us all the time. It is free from the problems and conflicts of the outer world. It is like a sea of tranquility that lies in the stillness within us. We can dip into those healing water any time we want through meditation.

Meditation allows us time each day to turn our attention away from the problems of the outer world to swim in a sea of peace for a while. We then experience moment of bliss, joy and happiness.

Our *Vedas*, *Upanishads* and in *Gita* also Krishna the *Yogeshwara* has told us the easiest way to wipe out these past memories and experience as *Yoga* and meditation. It recommends eight fold paths of *Yoga*.

Yoga is defined as *Chitta Vriti Nirodha*, removing the twists and knots of our mind, using the eight fold path. This includes *Yama*, revisiting our relationship with others; *Niyama*, revisiting our own behaviors, Asana reorienting our postures; *Pranayama*, reorienting our breath; *Pratyahara*, introspection without external distraction *Darana*, awareness, *Dhyana*, attention and finally *Samadhi*, the cleaning up of all those memories that create divisions, gaps and hierarchies in our mind making us feel trapped alone isolated and abandoned.

This cleaning us makes us *Chaitanya*, one whose mind has been purified of all kinds of old data. We see the world afresh, with a rebooted mind free of prejudices, biases and perceptions.

We can balance our lives by being aware of what is happening in the world outside and even do our best to help make it a better place and we can also tap into the peace within us through meditation. We can then flood our being with bliss and joy. When we find our own inner tranquility, we then become a source of calm that radiates to others, to make the outer world more peaceful.

For trading the correct path and move on, we require a *Guru*, which is like GPS, *Guru* Processing system. For finding the right path in the unknown universe, we require a *Guru*, who can process for ourselves and guide. A real *Guru* is one who is born from time to time as a repository of spiritual force which he transmits to his disciples.

The current of this spirit force changes its course from time to time, just as a mighty stream of water opens up a new channel and leaves the old one for good. Thus it is seen that old sects of religion grow lifeless in the course of time, and new sects arise with the fire of life in them.

Men who are truly wise commit themselves to the mercy of that particular sect through which the current of life flows. Old forms of religion are like the skeletons of once mighty animals, preserved in museums. They should be regarded with the due honor. They cannot satisfy the true cravings of the soul for the highest, just as a dead mango tree cannot satisfy the cravings of a man for luscious mangoes.

The one thing necessary is to be stripped of our verities- the sense that we possess any spiritual wisdom and to surrender ourselves completely to the guidance of our *Guru*. The *Guru* only knows what will lead us towards perfection. We are quite blind to it. We do not know anything. This sort of humility will open the door of our heart for spiritual truths. Truth will never come into our minds so long as there will remain the faintest shadow of *Ahamkara* (Egotism). All of us should try to root out this devil from our heart. Complete self surrender is the only way to spiritual illuminations.

A real *Guru*, even after considering his disciple too week, to receive the lessons of spirituality will try more and more to teach and educate him. Every man is capable of receiving knowledge, if it is imparted to him in his own language. *Guru* speaks truth boldly, without any fear that it may puzzle the week. Real *Guru* is not selfish; he always wants his disciples to come up to the same level of his knowledge.

There is a set of people who say that there is sin and sorrow and death in the world, but at the same time there is another set of people who say there is God, there is no pain no misery, only happiness. It is our choice to follow. The highest imagination that can break all the bondage is that of the personal God – the super consciousness. When I think I am *Brahman*, I alone exist; so with others. Therefore, each one is the whole of that principle.

This universe comes forth from *Brahmn* and will return to *Brahmn*.

A person is what his deep desire is. It is our deepest desire in this life that shapes the life to come. So let us direct our deepest desire to realize the self.

The self, who can be realized by the pure in heart, who is life, light, truth, space, who gives rise to all works, all desires, all odors, all tastes, who is beyond words, who is joy abiding this is the self dwelling in my heart.

Smaller than a grain of rice, smaller than a grain of barely, smaller than a mustard seed, smaller than a grain of millet, smaller even than the Kernel of grain of millet is the self. This is self dwelling in my heart, greater than the earth, greater than the sky, greater than all the worlds.

This self who gives rise to all works, all desires, all odors, all tastes who pervades the universe, who is beyond words, who is joy abiding, who is ever present in my heart, is *Brahmn* indeed. To him I shall attain when my ego dies.

6. LEARNING HUMILITY

To cultivate the quality of Humility is one step towards enlightenment. By being humble we gain much and lose nothing. Prayer and contemplation strengthen our will power in cultivating this inner quality. There is a famous dialogue between *Rama* and *Hanuman* where *Hanuman* says to *Rama*, "Eternally we are one and the same but as a human being, I am still a *Sevak* and you are master". Modern man tries to have the position of a master without attaining anything.

A man went to see a master who was seated on a high platform teaching many people. The man held a distinguished position in society. So he resented at being treated like all the rest of the students, without getting special attention. His fellow persons asked the organizers to offer him a seat on platform by the side of the teacher. The organizers said that the teacher do not permit for this. They argued why he can't become a master? The teacher who was seeing all this said to that man, "You don't become master right now, because you will be hurting yourself and others as well. You have to understand from the very beginning that the spiritual path can tolerate everything but ego".

Ego places a veil between the aspirant and the process of learning. When one becomes ego centric he isolates himself and thus, is not able to communicate with his teacher and conscience; and does not follow the instructions of the teacher. Such an ego needs immense austerities and modification without which all knowledge drains away.

On the path of spirituality if one keeps on looking at the sky and continue walking, he will stumble and fall down. One has to learn to bow down his head and then walk without stumbling. For going through this hazardous journey of life, one should learn to be humble. Ego and pride are two stumbling blocks on this journey. If one is not humble, he cannot learn; growth will be stunted.

When one begins to tread the path of spirituality it is essential to be humble. Ego creates barriers, and the faculty of discrimination is lost. If discrimination is not sharpened, reason does not function properly and there is no clarity of mind. A clouded mind is not a good instrument on the path of enlightenment.

There must be renunciation and there must be action; in reconciliation of the two, the crown of life resides. It is not action that ought to be renounced, but the fruit of action. Be sure that the ego has been annihilated in the ocean of consciousness. Be sure that it is not lurking somewhere in the inner dark chamber of your heart. Its ways are various and its forms are numerous. Action greased with love gives a glimpse of eternity and perpetual joy.

Once a person who was moving on the path of spirituality met a scholar of *Vedanta*, who was head of the department of philosophy in a renowned university, the aspirant put some questions to the professor.

The *Upanishads* appear to be full of contradictions. In one place they say that *Brahman* is one without a second, somewhere else they say that everything is *Brahman*. In a third place they say this world is false and *Brahman* alone is truth. And in a fourth place it is said that there is only one absolute reality beneath all these diversities. How can one make sense out of these conflicting statements?

This question of that aspirant was replied by a *Sadhu* in the Himalayas. He was always naked, having no clothes or any other possessions. When the aspirant asked the same question to him he said, "Bow down first. You can't ask about *Upanishads* with a swollen ego. Unless you bow down your ego how you can learn these sublet truths.

As long as one is not prepared in his mind and wants to examine the *Guru* he is not prepared to learn. *Guru* can resolve your all questions, provided you are prepared and have emptied your mind to receive.

Sadhu then explained to the aspirant that there are no contradictions in the teachings of *Upanishads*. When the student starts practicing, he realizes that the apparent world is changeable, while, truth never changes. Then he knows that the world of forms and names which is full of changes is false, and behind it there exists an absolute reality that is unchanging.

In the second step, when he knows the truth, he understands that there is only one truth and that truth is omnipresent, so there is really nothing like falsehood. In that stage he knows that reality which is one and the same in both the finite infinite worlds. But there is another, higher, state in which the aspirant realizes that there is only one absolute reality without second, and that; "that which is apparently false in reality a manifestation of the absolute one".

These are the levels of consciousness and there is no contradiction in them. The teachings of *Upanishads* are not understood by the ordinary minds or even by the intellectual mind. Intuitive knowledge alone leads to understanding them. In fact, whenever, anybody, knowingly pose such questions to others without being humble just to judge their knowledge, one can never get the answer. One should rise above argumentation and allow his intention to flow uninterruptedly to solve such subtle questions.

People have different views regarding touching the feet of a sage or *Guru*. People should know that it is said in *Upanishads* that one should touch the feet of a *Guru* because he gives the best part of his life, surrendering it at the lotus feet of the Lord. People ordinarily recognize you only by your face but face of the *Guru* is not here; it is with his Lord. People find only feet here, so they bow to the feet. One should have the humility when touching someone's feet.

All kicks and blows of life teach us something. No matter whence they come, they are blessings in disguise, provided we learn our lessons from them. Buddha said, "For a wise man, there is nothing to be called bad. Any adversity of life provides a step for his growth, provided he knows how to utilize it.

A human being knows enough, but that knowledge needs to be brought into daily life. If this is not done, the knowledge remains limited within the boundaries of knowing only. We all know what to do and what not to do, but it is very difficult to learn how to be. Real knowledge is found not in knowing but rather in being.

We read and hear lots of *Pravachans* and teachings from various *Gurus*. They are all full of *Gyan*, but we don't practice them. The achievement depends upon practice, not just on verbal knowledge of them. Knowing is not of much use unless practiced. Knowledge is mere information. Practice gives direct experience, which alone is valid knowledge. We don't allow *Gyan* to interfere in our day to day life. We need a *Guru* to tell us that this *Gyan* is not interference, but teaches us how to live.

Nine miles outside of *Badrinath* there is a side trail which leads to the valley of flowers. In summers the flowers in the valley are in full Bloom. For first few hours they are very soothing to the senses and stimulating to the mind. But slowly people start feeling that their memory is slipping away. People get so disoriented that they are not able to remember anything even their names. People remain aware of their existence only and have a hazy idea that they are there.

The fragrance of those flowers is so strong that one stops thinking rationally. Under the influence of that fragrance one forgets about his education or any other social strength; one has so much joy because of the influence of the fragrance. Actually it is not meditating; it is like the influence of *marijuana* or *hashish*; but people think they are in mediation. One goes to college and might have read many books. Then one lives on the opinion of others, who call them educated.

When we compare direct knowledge and the so called knowledge we find which is real and which imitation is. Those who live on the opinions of others do not ever have the ability to decide and express their own opinions. Informative knowledge is not the real knowledge. Unless one has control over mind there is no meaning of such knowledge. Without any discipline; control over the mind is not possible and without control of the mind direct experience is impossible.

For practical knowledge it is important to live under the guidance of a *Guru*, who has direct knowledge of the values of life with its currents and crosscurrents.

Most people do not know what it means for misery to strike in the form of life. But for certain people, when it really strikes, everything that they valued in their life is taken away, and a deep sadness settles. There are many ways to handle this sadness. Some people just sit in a corner and drive themselves mad, making everybody miserable. There are others; who, when they become sad, find a way of doing some useful work. Usually, it is people who have been hurt like this, who become great *Karma Yogis* in their lives.

One can make any emotion into a creative force in their life. It is not a negative force. There is no negativity in the existence. We may think something is negative and something else is positive, but a light burns because negative and positive wires together. Negative is as important as the positive.

When your sadness is reminding you that you are incomplete, it is good. Make use of your sadness to grow. When sadness sets in, if you become more compassionate, more caring, more humble and more loving you have some sense in you. When you get sad, if you get irritable and angry and thinking that the whole world is wrong, you are a fool. At that moment, if someone meddles with you, your sadness can very easily become anger.

So it is in your hand to make this sadness a source of anger or you can convert this sadness into love and compassion. It is very easy to become compassionate when you are sad. One has to learn to use all his emotions creatively. It is not just happiness which is important. If one has not known sadness, he will never mature. It is only sadness and pain which matures a man. One can never understand, without sadness and pain, what is happening with him and what is happening with anyone else around him.

When one grows older, has seen all ups and downs of life has faced utter sadness and has enjoyed great pleasures of life; becomes mellower. Things are not as black and white and one becomes more tolerant. One can see the good in things much more easily rather than getting enraged as he used to do when he was young.

---

7. SPIRITUALITY - THE WAY OF LIFE

Quote by Swami Rama

All the great religions of the world have come out of one truth. If we follow religion without practicing Truth, it is like blind leading the blind. Those who belong to God love all. Love is the religion of the universe. A compassionate one transcends the boundaries of religion and realizes the undivided, absolute reality.

God has given human beings an unparallel mechanism to live life in the universe. Science has developed lots of medicine, equipments and systems to assist body which is tiring and depreciating. But science is unable to assist the inner mechanism of the Being. There is no way to help Being inside.

Spirituality is the only way which teaches us what we are inside and what we require to increase our inner strength. Spirituality is not religious. It is not simply being good or to renounce this world. It also does not mean that we should not have desire or goals in life. It does not restrict us to have any sensual pleasures. It also does not ask us to be away from the pleasure of senses.

Desires and goals are necessary in life for the progress and growth of humanity. Just think if we do not have desire to combat the heat we will never require shade to save ourselves from this scorching heat. If we do not desire to wear good clothes, we would have not grown from the barbaric age when everyone used to live naked. These all scientific inventions and technological developments are there because we have the desire to make our life happy and to facilitate navigation in the life.

But just think? Even after having all these developments and facilities in life, we have no guarantee that we will be happy all the time. Even after having all sorts of comforts a small thorn can make our life miserable. Then jealous, hatred, anger, hurt, ego, sex desire and many such other emotions can make our lives burning from inside and we may not feel cool even in a iced cold environment.

Spirituality is the only thing which can give us strength to combat all these emotions. We many times console ourselves by taking them as natural instincts. If they are natural they should be same in every being. But we find that they differ amongst each individual. Two brothers and sisters will have different magnitude and impact of these emotions.

Spirituality is the only way to control them. When we start on this journey, we try to find out the short cuts and accept defeat very soon. We try to advance many arguments and reasons for our failure. We do not accept if anybody has advanced on this path. We start finding out some or the other faults with them and satisfy ourselves that they are in no way better than us and feel fully convinced that whatever we are doing is quite natural and we cannot improve upon that.

Sometimes when we hear some spiritual discourse or come across some spiritual person, we start thinking on moving on this path of controlling our emotion or treating them as our diseases.

But sooner when we are not able to proceed and forget the teachings, we just leave our journey halfway. At this stage we need a Guru, who can constantly guide us and encourage us to move on this path.

Spirituality under the guidance of a Sadguru; with complete surrender and a determination to remain happy 24/7, one can proceed on this path and be equipoise. One can by practice attain a stage, where he will not have any hatred or jealousy for anybody. He will be able to see that he is never getting angry and feeling hurt. He will remain the same in success and failure. No success or adversary will be able to effect his balance of mind and his mind will always remain silent and he will be happy all 24/7.

You cannot learn swimming in the ocean in one day. One has to have patience to move on this journey. We take medicine everyday to control our blood pressure, sugar, fat, cholesterol and all the other parameters of our body. Similarly we will have to take the guidance of our Guru with full faith and surrender to control our emotions. Then gauge them every day and adjust doses as per your requirement but you can't leave it half way to die.

We have to introspect whether the way we live our life is a conscious way of living? We live in a mechanical life propelled by our habits. It is the easiest way to live, but it makes our life dull. We do feel cozy and comfortable but our level of consciousness starts going lower. The sharpness of our life comes when we bring more and more awareness to each moment. Then we can get out of the vicious circle of habits and liberate ourselves from karmic bondage.

Peace for many is the mere absence of conflict. The peace they long for is a gentle retirement in old age; a simple cottage in the mountains or by the sea; a secured income; and the certainty that any crisis that may come their way will be met with a minimum of efforts and worry.

Yet, often, when we retire from a life of intense activity, without continued challenges we succumb to the perils of old age. Something similar happens in the absence of conflicts. What begins as peace soon gives way to boredom.

The dream cottage is idyllic perhaps for a weekend. Then it becomes a dreary prison. Peace is a goal of *Yoga*. The longing for peace is instinctive, but the peace of the soul, dynamic expanding to the consciousness, the very opposite of stagnation, is too easily mistaken by the worldly mind for sleep and other negative states of being.

Bhagwat Gita describes the spiritual path as a battle between the forces of light and darkness in our consciousness. The battlefield where the discourse between *Krishna* and *Arjun* takes place is, in fact, the field of man's inner consciousness.

It is not a wall placed protectively around one to shut out the horrors of life; it is a blinding light, banishing those horrors into non-existence. No man ever slides downhill into heaven. The path has been described as an ascent up to a mountain, to be achieved only after hardship.

The theory of *Karma* exists, but only for those who live life without full awareness. For a man of awareness, a *Buddha*, this theory has no relevance. We are victims of our habits. Hindus call it the theory of *Karma*, each action that we repeat or each thought we create is also a subtle action in mind; it becomes more and more powerful. Then we are in the grip of it.

We are imprisoned in the habit. When we get angry, we rationalize and say that the situation demanded it. That's how our ego goes on thinking that we are still the Boss, but we are not. Anger comes out of old patterns, out of the past. And when anger comes, we try to find an excuse for it.

Osho points out. Nobody is responsible except you. Nobody can make you angry and nobody can make you happy. You become happy on your own. You become angry on your own, and you become sad on your own. Unless you realize this, you will always remain a slave. Therefore become more and more conscious to make life blissful.

There are times we feel joyous, enthusiastic and full of energy. And there are times we feel low and lethargic drained of energy. This is due to the interplay of our bio rhythm and Nature's rhythm. When we feel low, we may attribute it to many things, over load of responsibility, financial challenges, injustice of life and so on. When we feel good; we attribute it to success, achievement, love, and suddenly a stream of joy fills us.

The truth is; we seek our peace in others, their behaviors towards us. We seek peace in our fast-escalating technological carriers and lifestyle without creating that beautiful motion of love based emotions. We lack connecting the self with the external environment of Nature.

Creating harmony requires smooth flow of self-energy and not rush- rush that takes us away not only from nature but also from life also. The same feeling of rhythm comes when we do selfless service, because we bring positive vibrations within, arising out of annihilation of ego. Take some time off to connect with nature; feel its rhythm. Being linked with nature brings joy and peace as it is the acknowledgment of the Law of Nature.

Spirituality is not to be confused with religion. Religion refers to one type of belief, one sect and one philosophy. Those who are governed by religion create a theocratic state; historically most theocratic states have developed into narrow confines of human faith and behavior. Theocratic states seek conformity to one belief and to meet this end, individual freedom of faith and expression is curbed, thereby creating an 'US' versus 'THEM" divide.

Spirituality is a fundamental shift to bring out the best in an individual and in a Government. Spirituality refers to a finer response, a wiser and more just behavior of inclusion and empathy. Spirituality is also discipline of body, mind, response and approach. It is a controlled approach rather than an approach to control others.

Spirituality's very foundation is respect for self and others. From this spring a host of virtues – fairness, spirit of service and the goal of achieving a prosperous and peaceful world. It would engender empathy, patience and acceptance of the different.

Rooted in respect for self and others, the spiritual approach seeks to unify and harmonies. Anything that disrupts, divides and furthers disharmony is negative and so is not spiritual. The motto for spirituality is *"Sarvjan Hitaye, Sarvjan Sukhaye"*, all about working for common good.

Spirituality is mind full governance–mindful of consequence, impact and mindfulness beyond the immediate result and reward. The spirituality teaches working hard in the spirit of mindfulness with the right intent and will to persist in the face of inevitable obstacles, opposition and criticism.

Spirituality provides an environment free from corruption and the desire to amass wealth by any means, whatsoever. An important characteristic of spirituality is individual freedom even as it seeks to harmonize the diverse and the different. It is never violent in spirit and deed. It allows for free dialogue but fair in meeting justice as appropriate and visible. It bars one from exploitation of people and natural resources.

Many prayers in India sum up this spiritual intent with an invocation for peace and harmony throughout the world; that is prayers for *Vishwa Shanti*, world peace and *Vishwa Kalyan* for the welfare of humanity.

It is the time for change in politics of India as well. We have to create spiritual politics free of cast and religion barriers. Politics should be based on honesty secularity and spirituality. Spirituality in any field including politics means fair and just behavior.

The approach of spiritual governance has been advocated by *Mahatma Gandhi*, Emperor *Akbar* and *Ashoka*. The intent of spiritual Governance is so far as to bridge the divide between existing religions and to reduce interfaith conflicts. The need is to bring, positive social change. Present Government's '*Sabka Saath, Sabka Vikas*' initiative is also moving towards this end.

Bhagwat Gita explains the kind of education which is the essence of all doctrines and philosophies. There is no dearth of knowledge in the field of philosophy or transcendental knowledge. The most confidential or transcendental knowledge involves understanding the difference between the soul and the body.

Generally people are not educated in this confidential knowledge. They are educated in external knowledge. As far as ordinary education is concerned, people are involved with so many departments; politics, sociology, physics, chemistry, mathematics, astronomy and engineering etc. There are so many departments of knowledge all over the world and many huge universities, but there is unfortunately, no university or educational institution where the science of the spirit soul is instructed. Yet the soul is the most important part of this body; without the presence of the soul, the body has no value. Still people are placing great stress on the bodily necessities of life, not caring for the vital soul.

Bhagwat Gita especially stresses the importance of the soul. It is said that this body is perishable and that the soul is not perishable. This is confidential part of knowledge because it does not give positive information about the soul. Sometimes people are under the impression that the soul is different from the body and that when the body is finished or one is liberated from the body, the soul remains in a void and becomes impersonal. But actually that is not the fact. How can the soul, which is so active within this body, be inactive after being liberated from the body? It is always active. It is eternal, then it is eternally active, and its activities in the spiritual kingdom are the most confidential part of spiritual knowledge.

It is said that execution of spirituality is so perfect that one can perceive the results directly. This direct result is actually perceived and we have practical experience that any person who is trying to move on the path of spirituality; in course of time feels some transcendental pleasure and very quickly becomes purified of all material contamination. Furthermore, if one engages not only in hearing but in trying to broadcast the message of spiritual activities as well or if he engages himself in helping the missionary activities, he gradually feels spiritual progress. This advancement in spiritual life does not depend on any kind of previous education or qualification. The method itself is so pure that by simply engaging in it one becomes pure.

Devotional service is so potent that simply by engaging in the activities of devotional service, one becomes enlightened without a doubt. *Narada*, who happened to be the son of a maid servant, had no education, nor was he born into a high family. But when his mother was engaged is serving great devotees, *Narada* also become engaged and sometimes in the absence of his mother, he would serve the great devotees himself. *Narada* personally says, "Once only, by their permission I took the remnants of their food, and by doing so all my sins was at once eradicated. Thus being engaged, I became purified in heart, and at that time the very nature of transcendent tales became attractive to me".

Thus by associating with the sages he developed a great desire for devotional services. If one is engaged simply in the acts of devotional service, everything is revealed to him automatically. It is said that religious people generally do not know that the highest perfection of religion is the attainment of the stage of devotional service. This process is so potent that even without performing the religious process regularly one can be raised to the highest perfection. One who is in association with great *Acharyas*, even if he is not educated or has not studied Vedas can become familiar with all the knowledge necessary for realization.

Story in the present context

Man creates society as he pursues his imagination of Paradise, a place where all creatures are safe. However, in this process, he creates a world where some are safer than others. Human society invariably favors a few over others. Culture is thus, always imperfect. So controlling material reality will never be satisfactory.

For building a city in the forest, the only way to do this is by burning down the forest. As the forest burns, the birds and the beasts of the forest try to run away to save themselves. This seeks of cruelty until one realizes that until the forest is burnt a field cannot be established. Culture is built on destruction of a natural ecosystem.

Humans can never include everybody. Plants and animals are excluded, if they do not serve the needs of society. People whose points of view align with ours are included; the rest are excluded. This is what happens when human society becomes so focused on itself that it loses touch with the rest of nature, when culture expands at the cost of everything else, when the needs of culture override the needs of nature.

Every action has a reaction that one is bound to experience. This is Law of Karma. Just as society is created by an act of compassion, it is destroyed when the compassion becomes exclusive and fails to include all of nature.

---

8. TREE WITHOUT ROOTS LIFE WITHOUT LOVE

"No one can teach you how to love. It is easy to hate, and hate brings people together, as in war. But love is more difficult. You cannot learn how to love, but what you can do is to observe hate and put it gently aside. Let hate drop away; brush it aside, it is not important. What is important is not to let hate take root in your mind. Then you will find that your mind becomes very sensitive without being sentimental, therefore it will know love".

J Krishnamurti

Live life not as a curse rather as a blessing. Let life flow. Don't live like a tree that has lost its roots

The modern man feels too alienated feels too much an outsider, does not feel at home, at ease with life, existence, and the world. He feels almost if he has been thrown into it, and it is a curse rather than a blessing. A man who becomes too head oriented goes farther away from the heart. Heart being the centre which responds to the call of love, he is deprived of the sap of life. Life is no more flowing. Being a head oriented man he is cut off from the universe. He lives in the universes but lives as a tree that has lost its roots. He lives only for the namesake. He has lost contact; he is unconnected.

It happens because people give too much importance to head orientation, too much training of the head and in this process they cut all the roots from heart. They forget what the heart is. They see that their heart is functioning but the energy no longer moves via it. They bypass it and go directly to the mind. They use heart only for living alive.

Even when they love, they think and then love. When they feel, they think that they feel. People don't do anything without thinking. Actually, thinking is the great falsifier, because thinking is man's effort to understand the universe and love is God's effort to understand man.

One forgets that his existence has come through love only. Love has found your existence. It has happened only when God's hand was searching you via love. When one tries to understand existence or truth, it is one's effort - a part, a very tiny part trying to grasp the whole, the infinite whole. The effort is bound to be doomed. It's impossible. It cannot happen in the nature of things.

One cannot manage love. One can manage logic. One can be very efficient as far as logic is concerned. But the moment love arises he becomes very inefficient. Love does not know any logic; one does not know where he is, what is he doing, where he is moving and so he has no control.

Logic is controlled; love is uncontrolled. Logic is manipulated; love is a happening. Logic gives a feeling that you are somebody; love gives a feeling that you are nobody. When you look through the eye of logic; you will know a few things but those few things will not give the vision of reality. They will be only abstractions.

Love is one of the most significant words in human languages, because love is an existential language. When one looks through love, he knows the reality as it is. Love is falling with the universe together .But somehow now from the very childhood, we are being crippled. Our roots with the heart are cut. We are forced towards the head and we are not allowed to move towards the heart. The man has not yet become capable of living love.

Love is risky. To love is to move into danger, because it cannot be controlled. When one moves in love, he cannot calculate the possibilities, he cannot calculate the results. One cannot be result oriented. For love, future does not exist. Only the present exists. One can be in that moment only; he cannot think anything about the next moment. No planning is possible in love.

One cannot feel in love, if one is aware, then falling in love is a sin. If one is aware then one can love, but it will not be like a fall, it will be like a rise. We all use the term falling in love; if it is falling; one is falling not rising. When one is aware, falling is not possible – not even in love. With awareness it is impossible, you rise in love. Rising in love is a totally different phenomenon from falling in love. Falling in love is a dream state. That's why people who are in love, they are more a sleep than others, intoxicated and dreaming. People who rise in love are totally different. It can be seen they are no longer in a dream, they are facing the reality and they are growing through it.

Falling in love; one remains a child, rising in love one matures. By and by love becomes not a relationship, but it becomes a state of one's being. Then it is not that you love this and you don't love that, no – you simply love. Whatsoever comes near you, you share with them. Whatsoever is happening, you give your love to it. You touch a rock and you touch as if you are touching your beloved's body. You look at tree and you look as if you are looking at your beloved's face. It becomes a state of being. Not that you are in love – now you are love. This is rising, this in not falling.

Love is beautiful when you rise through it and love becomes dirty and ugly when you fall through it. Sooner or later one will find that it proves poisonous, it becomes bondage. One is caught in it, he loses his freedom. His wings are cut, he remains free no more. Falling in love one becomes a possession. One is simply possessing and allowing somebody else to possess him.

Mostly it happens so between husband and wife. They both try to possess each other. Only the things can be possessed. How can one possess a person? How one can dominate the other person. A person cannot be converted into possession. But the husband is trying to possess the wife; the wife is trying to possess the husband. Then there is a clash.

Love should give freedom; love is freedom. Love will make the beloved more and more free. Love will give wings, and love will open the vast sky. It cannot become a prison, an enclosure. Such love can happen only when one is aware; that quality of love comes only when there is awareness.

Love cannot be controlled. Control is a poor substitute for awareness, a very poor substitute. It does not help much. If one is aware, he need not control love, in awareness he will always love. Awareness is what makes you a master and by master I don't mean a controller. When I say be a master, I mean be a presence – a continuous presence. Whatever, may happen, you be constantly in your consciousness that you love.

The female mind has grace, the male mind has efficiency. And of course, in the long run, if there is constant fight, the graceful is bound to be defeated and then efficient mind will win, because the world understands the language of mathematics, not of love. But the moment your efficiency wins over your grace, you have lost something tremendously valuable; you have lost contact with your own being. You may become very efficient but you will no longer be a real person. You will become a machine, a robot like thing.

Because of this there is constant conflict between men and women. They cannot remain separate, they have to get into relationship again and again, but they cannot remain together either. The fight is not outside, the fight is within you.

So unless one resolves his inner fight between the right and the left hemispheres, one will never be able to be peaceful in love never because the inner fight will be reflected outside. If you are fighting inside and you are identified with the left hemisphere, the hemisphere of reason, and you are continuously trying to overpower the right hemisphere, you will try to do the same with the woman you fall in love with. Similarly, if the woman is continuously fighting her own reason inside, she will continuously fight with the man she loves.

People wish to go deep in a relationship but unless one is resolved within himself, he will create more problems than they already have, if they move into relationship. The greatest and the most beautiful thing in the world is love, but if we mess it; nothing is more ugly, more hell creating.

People go on avoiding marriage; people go on putting it off. When someday they find it impossible to get out of it, only then they relax. If one is outside of it, it may look like a beautiful oasis in the desert, but as one comes close, the oasis start drying and disappearing. Once one is caught in it, it is an imprisonment, but imprisonment does not come from the other; it comes from within him only.

There is a way to follow life through arithmetic and there is another way to follow life through dreams and through visions. They are totally different. One can create his own world of fairies all around, but if you think and find them stupidity then they just remain shadows. You will start forgetting all poetry of the life and will learn mathematics. One who lives through the imagination, which lives through the dreaming quality of his mind; that looks through visions - then trees are greener than they look to you, then birds are more beautiful. Ordinary pebbles become diamonds. Everything becomes divine and sacred.

A man sitting with his friend drinking tea said, "Life is like a cup of tea". The other friend asked, "But why? Why is life like a cup of tea"? Later that person saw a lotus flower and said beautiful, the friend again asked why? The person replied, "Am I a philosopher. Actually there is no reason behind it; it is a simple statement of fact as he felt. *Upanishads* say. "God is –don't ask why? They say God is beautiful God is near, closer than your heart – but don't ask why? In gospels Jesus says, "My God is in heaven, I am his son, he is my father- Don't ask why".

The right hemisphere is the hemisphere of poetry and love. A great shift is needed, that shift is inner transformation. *Yoga* is an effect to reach the oneness of being through the left hemisphere using logic mathematics, science and trying to go beyond. This can be easily explained through stories rather creating theories and doctrines.

There is a story explaining the whole thing.

A son of a burglar, when noticed that his father is getting old asked him to teach him the trade so that he can carry on the family business after his father retires.

The trade of a burglar is not a scientific thing, it is an art. Burglars are as much born as poets, one cannot learn, learning won't help. A burglar is born burglar. He lives through intuition. He is not a businessman. He is a gambler. His whole trade is danger and risk. It is just like a religious man. They are also burglars; in search of God. There is no way to reach God through logic or reason or accepted society, culture, civilization. They break the wall somewhere they enter the backdoor. If in the day light it is not allowed they enter in the dark. If it is not possible in the crowded place they go to the forest.

Opening a large chest, the father told his son to go in and pick out the jewelry. As soon as the boy was inside, the father looked the chest and then made a lot of noise so that the whole house was aroused. Then he slipped away quietly.

Locked inside the chest, the boy was angry, terrified and puzzled as to how he was going to get out. The father was trying to teach him to leave logic and find out some out of box idea. If burglar goes by logic, then anybody who follows the logical method can catch him anywhere. A burglar has to be unpredictable; logic is not possible. He has to be illogical, so much so that nobody can predict him.

How! It is a logical question? Hence, he was terrified because there was no way – As it has no answer. When how does not have answer and one feels defeated then it says why not give a chance to the oppressed, to the imprisoned part of the mind? Let that take a chance. May be there can be no harm.

Then an idea flashed to him - to make a noise like a cat. Now this is not logical. Making a noise like a cat, simply an absurd idea. But it worked. The family told a maid to take a candle and examine the chest. When the lid was unlocked, the boy jumped out, blew out the candle pushed his way past the astonished maid and ran out.

This too is not of the logical mind. Details are useless as far as intuition is concerned because intuition is never a repetition. Details are meaningful as far as logic is concerned; so logical people go into minute details, so that if the same situation happens again, they will be in control and they will know what to do. But in the life of the burglar the same situation never happens again.

In real life to the same situations never come again. If one has conclusion in their mind, they will become almost dead, you will not be responding. In life response is needed, not reaction. You have to act from nowhere, with no conclusions inside.

Whenever, you are in such a corner that your logic fails, don't be desperate, don't become hopeless. Those moments may prove the greatest blessings in your life. The heart is feminine and the head or mind is manly. People miss a lot in their lives because the head goes on talking; it does not allow the heart. And the only quality in the head is that it is more articulate, cunning, dangerous, and violent. Because of its violence it has become the leader inside and that leadership has become an outside leadership. So grace is dominated by violence.

The mind is a trouble making phenomenon, hence it overpowers and dominates. But deep down although, you may attain power, you miss life and deep down the heart continues.

Unless one falls back on heart and surrender, your resistance and struggle become surrender. You will not know real life and the celebration of it. Your life will be without love like a tree without roots.

When something comes from the inner, it comes from your heart. You can feel the flow, the warmth coming from the heart. Whenever your mind thinks, it is just on the surface, in the head

9. REALIZATION OF GOD

Oh when will that time come?
When in a beautiful full-moon night,
Sitting on the banks of some river,
And in a calm, yet high notes repeating
"Shiva! Shiva! Shiva!"
All my feeling will come out through the eyes
In the form of tears?

The field of religion is beyond our senses, beyond even our consciousness. We cannot sense God. Nobody has seen God with his eyes or ever will see; nobody has God in his consciousness. Consciousness is only one of the many planes in which we work; one has to transcend the field of consciousness, to go beyond the senses, approach nearer and nearer to your own centre and as one do that, he will approach nearer and nearer to God.

There is no proof of God or direct perception, *Pratyaksha*. The proof of everything is that we perceive it. God has been perceived that way by thousands before, and will be perceived by all who want to perceive Him. But this perception is no sense-perception at all; it is super sensuous, super conscious and all this training is needed to take us beyond the senses.

The first thing required of the aspirant for wisdom is to learn to keep the organs in their own centers, without allowing them to stray out. Let us talk of eyes.

Eyes are not the organs of vision, but only the instruments. Unless the organs are also present, one cannot see, even if he has the eyes. But given both the organs and the instruments, unless the mind attaches itself to those two eyes, no vision takes place. So in each act of perception three things is necessary- first the external instruments, then the internal organs, and lastly, the mind. If any one of them is absent then there will be no perception. Similarly, when we look at somebody and speak, both the organs and instruments are active. But when we close the eyes and don't speak but begin to think, the organs are active, but not the instruments.

We must bear in mind that by the word 'Organ' is meant the nerve centre in the brain. The eyes and ears are only the instruments of seeing and hearing, and the organs are inside. If the organs are destroyed by any means, even if the eyes or the ears be there, we shall not see or hear. So in order to control the mind, we must first be able to control these organs i.e., the nerve centre in the brain.

The second thing required is not thinking of things of the senses. Most of our time is spent in thinking about sense objects, things which we have seen or we have heard, which we shall see or shall hear, things which we have eaten or are eating, or shall eat, places where we have lived and so on. We think of them or talk of them most of our time. For God realization we must give up this habit.

The next is preparation. It starts with the idea of forbearance. 'Resist not the evil'. We may not resist an evil, but at the same time we may feel very miserable. A man may say very harsh thing to me, and I may not outwardly hate him for it, may not answer him back, and may restrain myself from apparently getting angry, but anger and hatred may be in my mind and I may feel very badly towards that man. That is not non-resistance; one should be without any feeling of hatred and anger, without any thought of resistance; my mind must then be calm as if nothing had happened.

The next qualification required is '*Shraddha*', faith. One must have tremendous faith in religion and God. Until one has it, one cannot aspire to be a *Gyani*. It is said that hardly one in twenty millions in this world believe in God. We may have faith in God, may be knowing Him as the greatest source of happiness and bliss but still we don't struggle to reach to him.

It can be explained by a little story "Suppose there is a thief in this room, and he gets to know that there is a mass of gold in the next room, and only a very thin partition between the two rooms, what will be the condition of thief?" Everybody will reply; "He will not be able to sleep at all; his brain will be actively thinking of some memos of getting at the gold, and he will think of nothing else". The reply comes, "Do you believe that a man could believe in God and not go mad to get him? If a man sincerely believes that there is that immense infinite mine of Bliss, and that it can be reached, would not that man go mad in his struggle to reach it" strong faith in God and the consequent eagerness to reach him constitute *shraddha*.

Then comes *Samadhana* or constant practice i.e., to hold the mind in God. Nothing is done in a day. Religion cannot be swallowed in the form of a pill. It requires hard and constant practice. The mind can be conquered only by slow and steady practice.

Next is *Mumukshutra*, the intense desire to be free.

All the misery we have is of our own choosing. Such is our nature. We run headlong after all sorts of misery and are unwilling to be freed from them. Every day we run after pleasure and before we reach it, we find it is gone; it has slipped through our fingers. Still we do not cease from our mad pursuit, but on and on we go, blinded fools that we are.

We are just moving blindfolded like bullocks, looking forward stretching our necks to get at the straw. It never catches the straw but goes round and rounds in the hope of getting it, and in so doing goes on grinding out the oil. Similarly we are all born slaves to nature, money and wealth, wives and children, are always chasing wisp of straw, and are going through an innumerable round of lives without obtaining what we seek.

Thus, the world is going on, society goes on and we, blinded slave, have to pay for it without knowing, chasing happiness. We have to study our lives and find how little of happiness there is in them and how little truth we have gained in the course of this wild goose chase of the world. Such is the tremendous power of nature over us. It repeatedly kicks us away, but still we are always hoping against hope, this hope maddens us, we are always hoping for happiness.

We always feel 'Hope' is the most wonderful thing in the world. The whole world is surviving on 'Hope'. Day and night we see people dying around us, and yet we think we shall not die; we never think that we shall die or that we shall suffer. Each man thinks that success will be his hoping against hope, against all odds, against all mathematical reasoning. Nobody is ever really happy here. If a man be wealthy and have plenty to eat his digestion is out of order, and he cannot eat. If he be rich, he has no children. If he be hungry and poor, he has a whole regiment of children, and does not know what to do with them.

It is so because happiness and misery are the two sides of the same coin. We all have this foolish idea that we can have happiness without misery and it has taken such possession of us that we have no control over the senses.

There are two extremes into which men are running; one is extreme optimism, when everything is rosy and nice and good; the other extreme pessimism, when everything seems to be against them. Naturally we run into extremes. When we are healthy and young, we think all the wealth of the world will be ours and later when we get kicked about by society like footballs and get older, we start throwing cold water on the enthusiasm of others.

Few men realize that with pleasure there is pain, and with pain, pleasure; and as pain is disgusting, so is pleasure, as it is the twin brother of pain. It is derogatory to the glory of man that he should be going after pain and equally derogatory, that he should be going after pleasure. Both should be turned aside by men whose reason is balanced. Why will not men seek freedom from being played upon?

Have a faith and belief – The moment we are whipped, and when we begin to weep, nature gives us a dollar; again we are whipped and when we weep, nature gives us a piece of ginger-bread and we begin to laugh again. It is the heart which takes one to the highest plane, which intellect can never reach; it goes beyond intellect and reaches to what is called inspiration. Intellect can never become inspired; only the heart when it is enlightened becomes inspired. An intellectual heartless man never becomes an inspired man.

It is not at all necessary to be educated or learned to get to God. A sage once told, "To kill others one must be equipped with swords and shields, but to commit suicide a needle is sufficient; so to teach others, much intellect and learning are necessary, but not so for your own self illumination. Are you sure? If you are pure, you will reach God. "Blessed are the pure in heart, for they shall see God".

Bondages will fall off by themselves and we shall go up beyond this plane of sense – perception to which we are tied down and when we shall see hear and feel things which men in the three ordinary states viz., waking, dream and sleep neither feel nor see nor hear. Then we will speak a strange language, as it were and the world will not understand us, because it does not know anything but the senses.

We know there is no progress in a straight line. Every soul moves, as it were in a circle, and will have to complete it, and no soul can go low but there will come a time when it will have to go upwards. No one will be lost. We are all projected from one common centre which is God. This is highest as well as lowest life. God ever projected, will come back to the Father of all lives, "From whom all beings are projected in whom all live, and unto whom they all return; that is God".

10. FIRST STEP TOWARDS GYANA AND BHAKTI

I have crossed oceans to find wealth.
I have blasted mountains to get jewels.
I have spent whole nights in graveyards repeating Mantras
And have obtained – not the broken cowries' of
blessedness
Ah, Desire, give me up now.

The word *Gyana* means knowledge. What is the object of the *Gyana*, *Yoga* and Freedom? Freedom from what? Freedom from our imperfections; freedom from misery of life. Why are we miserable? We are miserable because we are bound. What is the bondage? The bondage is of nature. Who is it that binds us? We ourselves.

Now this bondage in which we are is a fact. It need not be proved that we are in bondage. For instance; I would be very glad to get out of this room through this wall; but I cannot; I would be very glad if I never became sick; but I cannot prevent it; I would be very glad not to die, but I have to; I would be very glad to do millions of things that I cannot do. The will is there, but we do not succeed in accomplishing the desire. When we have any desire and not the means of fulfilling it, we get that peculiar reaction called misery. Who is the cause of desire? I am myself. Therefore I myself am the cause of all the miseries I am in.

Misery begins with the birth of the child weak and helpless, he enters the world. The first sign of life is weeping. Now how could we be the cause of misery when we find it at the very beginning? We have caused it in the past. It gives rise to the very interesting theory of 'Reincarnation'. For explaining our present existence we have to see whether we existed previously? We see lots of things in child, which can never be explained until we grant that child has had past experience for instance, fear of death – instinct to survive and a great number of inmate tendencies.

Who taught the baby to drink milk and to do so in a particular fashion? Where did it acquire this knowledge? We know that there cannot be any knowledge without experience. Why should it have fear of death if it never saw death? If this is the first time it has ever born how it knew to suck the mother's milk.

It is out of habit. Habit is one's nature. All that is in your nature is result of habit and habit is the result of experience. There cannot be any knowledge but from experience.

So this body must have had some experience too. This fact is granted even by modern materialistic science. It proves beyond doubt that the body brings with it a fund of experience. It does not enter into this world with a blank mind upon which nothing is written ready equipped with a bundle of knowledge.

Each one of us reaps what we ourselves have sown. These miseries, under which we suffer, these bondages under which we struggle, have been caused by ourselves and none else in the universe to blame. God is the least to blame for it. We normally say, "Why did God create this evil world? Why did God create me so miserable? Actually he did not create this evil world at all. We have made it evil, and miserable. We have to make it good and happy. He has given same powers to every being.

His mercy is always the same his sun shines on the wicked and the good alike. His water, his earth gave the same chances to the wicked and the good. God is always the same external, merciful father. The only thing for us to do is to bear the results of own acts.

We must learn that in the first places we have existed eternally; in the second place that we are the makers of our own lives. There is no such thing as fate. Our lives are the result of our pervious actions, our *Karma*. And it naturally of our *Karma*, we must also be able to unmake it.

The whole gist of *Gyana Yoga* is to show humanity the method of undoing this *Karma*. We, with our bondages are going round and round through countless ages. We feel miserable and cry over our bondages. But crying and weeping will be of no avail. We must set ourselves to cutting these bondages. The main cause of all bondages is ignorance. Man is not wicked by his own nature; not at all. His nature is pure, perfectly holy. Each man is divine. Each man that we see is a God by his very nature. This nature is covered by ignorance and it is ignorance that binds us down. Ignorance is the cause of all misery. Ignorance is the cause of all wickedness, and knowledge will make the world good.

Knowledge will remove all misery. Knowledge will make us free. This is the idea of *Gyana Yoga*. But question is what knowledge? Chemistry? Physics? Astronomy? Geology? They help us a little, just a little. But the chief knowledge is that of your own nature. "Know yourself". You must know what you are, what your real nature is. You must become conscious of that infinite nature within. Then your bondage will burst.

Knowledge is power. It is through knowledge that power comes. The more one becomes conscious of his own self the more he manifests this power, and his bonds break and at last he becomes free. How to know yourselves? The question remains now. There are various ways to know this self. *Gyana Yoga* takes the help of nothing but sheer intellectual reasoning. Reason alone, intellect alone, rising to spiritual perception, shows what we are.

There is no question of believing. Disbelieving everything is the idea of the *Gyani*. Believe nothing and disbelieve everything – that is the first step. Dare to be a rationalist. Dare to follow reason, wherever it leads you. We say we believe in reason only but we are bound to follow superstitions all the time – old hoary superstitions all the time , either national or belonging to humanity in general; superstitions belonging to family, to friends, to country, to fashion, to books to sex and to what not.

We talk of reason, but very few people reason. We hear lots of people saying, "They do not believe in anything; they don't like to grope through darkness, they must reason." And so they reason but when their reason smashes to pieces, they say 'No more'. The reasoning is all right until it breaks my ideas. Stop there. Such man would never be a Giyani. That man will carry his bondages all his life and his lives to come. Such men are not made for *Gyana*.

It is very hard to believe in reason and follow truth. This whole world is full either of the superstitions or of half hearted hypocrites. Superstition and ignorance are much better to half hearted hypocrites. They are no good. These half hearted hypocrites stand on both sides of river.

Take anything up fix your ideal and follow it out boldly unto death. That is the way to salvation. Half heartedness does not lead to anywhere. Be superstitious, be a fanatic, if you please, but be something. Be something, show that you are something; but be not like these hypocrites with truth, these jack of all trades who just want to get a sort of nervous titillation, a dose of opium, until this desire after the sensational becomes a habit.

The obstructions to our following reason are:-

The first obstruction to our following reason is our unwillingness to go to truth. We want truth to come to us. People normally complain that the following religion is not comfortable.

They want comfortable religion. There is nothing such as comfortable religion. Religion is based on truth, whether it is comfortable or not. Why should truth be comfortable or not. Why should truth be comfortable always? Truth many times hit hard. We understand what people mean by comfortable religion.

Once Swami Vivekananda met a lady who was very fond of her children and her money, as usually people are, while preaching her Swami said to her, "The only way to God is by giving up everything", after hearing this that lady stopped coming to him. When enquired she said the religion preached by *Swamiji* is very uncomfortable to her. She wanted to see God in her Children in her money and in her diamonds.

We are slaves in the hands of nature – slaves to a bit of bread, slaves to praise, slaves to blame, slaves to wife, to husband , to child, slaves to everything. We want to do anything, beg, steal rob anything to make happy a boy, because he is your son. We just don't care about millions of boys in this world dying of starvation – boys beautiful in body and in mind. We let them die to save our son only because one has given him birth. This is being called love. Actually this is brutality.

The first step towards *Gyan* is to give up desires, even the desire to getting heaven. All desires of enjoyment in this life, or in the life to come should be given up. We should make goal of our life not the enjoyment of our senses but knowledge. Man is not born to have pleasure or to suffer pain knowledge is the goal. Knowledge is the only pleasure.

True civilization does not mean congregating in cities and living a foolish life, but going God ward, controlling the senses and thus becoming the ruler in this house of self. Think of slavery in which we are bound. Every beautiful form I see, every sound of praise I hear, immediately attracts me; every word of blame I hear immediately repels me. Every fool has an influence over my mind. Every little movement in the world makes an impression upon me. Is this a life worth living? So when one realizes the misery of this physical existence- when you have become convinced that such a life is not worth living – one has made the first step towards *Gyana*.

Now let us talk of our first step towards Bhakti.

The philosophers of the world have defined *Bhakti* as extreme love for God.

Why a man should love god is the question to be solved; and until we understand that, we should not be able to grasp this subject at all. There are two entirely different ideals of life. A man of any country who has any religion knows that he is a body and spirit also but there is a great deal of difference as to the goal of human life.

In western countries, as a rule people, lay more stress on the body aspect of man but in India a man give up his body .The one idea is that man is a body and has a soul, the other that man is a soul and has a body. More intricate problems arise out of this. It naturally follows that the ideal which holds that man is a body and has a soul lays all the stress on the body. If you ask why man lives, you will be told it is to enjoy the senses, to enjoy possession and wealth.

He cannot dream of anything beyond even if he is told of it; his idea of further life would be continuous of his enjoyment. He is very sorry that it cannot continue all the time here, but he has to depart; and he thinks that somehow or other he will go to some place where the same thing will be renewed. He will have the same enjoyment, the same senses, only heighted and strengthened. He wants to worship God, because God is the only means to attain this end.

On the other hand there is an idea that God is the goal of life; there is nothing beyond God, and the sense enjoyments are simply something through which we are passing now in the hope of getting better things. Think of the power of hearing in lower animals, power of seeing: all their senses are highly developed. Their enjoyment of senses is extreme. They simply become mad with delight and pleasure.

In sense satisfaction we behave like little boys. In school we remember we used to fight for some sweetmeats and the stronger boy used to snatch from the weak boy. The feeling week boy used to have that when he would grow up and become strong would punish that boy. But later on when we grow up become good friends.

The love for our children and our wives is mere animal love; that love which is perfectly unselfish, the only love and that is God. It is very difficult thing to attain to. The wife says she loves her husband and kisses him; but as soon as he dies, the first thing she thinks about the bank account, and what she shall do the next day. The husband loves the wife; but when she becomes sick and loses her beauty, or becomes haggard or makes a mistake, he ceases to care for her. All the love of the world is hypocrisy and hollowness.

We say that a wife loves her husband. She thinks that her whole soul is absorbed in her husband; but as she has a baby half of this love goes out to the baby. She herself will feel that the same love for husband does not exist now. Same is with the father. We always find that when more intense objects of love come to us, the previous love slowly vanishes.

The love presents to us manifold stages of love. We have first to clear the ground. Upon our view of life the whole theory of love will rest. To think that this world is the aim and end of life is brutal and degenerating. Any man who starts in life with that idea degenerates himself. He will never rise higher, he will never catch this glimpse from behind, and he will always be a slave to the senses. He will struggle for the money that will give him bread to eat. Better die than live that life. Slaves of this world, slave of the senses, let us raise ourselves; there is something higher than the sense life.

Bhakti is a religion. Religion is not for the many that is impossible. The chief thing is to want God. We want everything except God, because our ordinary wants are supplied by the external world; it is only when our necessities have gone beyond the external world that we want a supply from the internal, from God. It is only when we have become satiated with everything here and we look beyond for a supply.

It is only when the need is there that the demand will come. Have done away with the child's play of the world, as soon as you can and then you will feel the necessity of something beyond the world and the first step in religion will come. When a man loves a woman in this world, there are times when he feels that without her he cannot live although that is a mistake. When a husband dies, the wife thinks. She cannot live without him; but she lives all the same. This is the secret of necessity; it is that without which we cannot live; either it must come to us or we die.

There comes a time when we feel the same about God, or in other words, we want something beyond the world, something above all material forces, then we may become *Bhaktas*. What are our little lives, when for a moment the cloud passes away and we get the one glimpse from beyond, and for the moment all these lower desires seen like a drop in the ocean. Then the soul grows, and feels the want of God and must have him.

The first step is; what do we want? Let us ask ourselves this question every day, do we want God? When we begin to talk religion, and especially when we take a high position and begin to teach others, we must ask ourselves, the same question. *Bhakti* is the highest ideal. I don't know whether we shall reach it or not in millions of years to come, but we must make it our highest ideal, make our senses aim at the highest. If we cannot get to the end, we shall at least come nearer to it. We have slowly to work through the world and the sense to reach God.

11. LIVE IN PRESENT- BE POSITIVE

As far as the human mind is concerned, the past is something which exists only in the form of a memory – it does not exist in reality anymore. When you say yesterday I did such a thing, the act is over, finished, there is nothing left of it. What I can see is only the present reality. The future I cannot see, I can only speculate. This is limitation of human mind. It cannot live in the past, the present and the future at the same time. It can think of past, but thinking of the past is not living in the past. It is only a mental process, a memory.

The only thing one is sure of is present. One is not sure of the future because it is speculation. Based on the past, through the present, one speculates on what the future could hold. One can only project the present into the future and say, this is what could be; which may or may not be. The only certainty that the human being can experience is the present. And every second, every moment of the present is going into the past. I am going to think of something and the moment I have thought about it, I store it in my memory. It has gone into the past. All of us live in this flow of the past through the present and into the future. This is the movement through which we live, and this is what gives us hope.

Normally when we say past we think something that happened before, and when we think of the future, we think of something that is going to happen later. As far as the Supreme power; what has happened, what is happening and what is going to happen; is all known at the same time. We cannot conceive of such a situation. The human mind is simply incapable of it. We can only think of life and experience in terms of past, present and future.

The *Upanishads* deal with common experience of all human beings, irrespective of caste, creed or religion. We don't have to believe in God to know that we are awake, we dream and we have deep sleep. These three experiences are common to all. Deep sleep helps us to relax and forget everything about this world, which is why we feel refreshed when we wake up. The second part is dream state. It is like a light that shines in a closed place. In a dream our eyes are closed and so we don't see the outside light; but we do see light, we see the day, night and various other things. All this is illuminated by the second part of the, 'Supreme Being'.

These dream experiences need not be dismissed as unreal. In fact when the dream takes place, at that moment the dream state is as real as the waking state. Only when we wake up from the dream does it become unreal; otherwise it is as real as the reality of the outside world. When you are chased by a tiger in a dream you are actually being chased by the tiger in that state. It cannot be doubted. When you wake up your heart still beating fast, you are sweating, your body is trembling. It has the same effect on the mind and physical body as in the waking state. So it is as real in the dream state as it would be in the waking state.

This is how the dream state is; it is real and it is an experience of the subtle world, the inner world of imagination and thought. Many a times, what is not fulfilled in our waking state may be fulfilled in the dream. Sometimes, bottled up emotions and desires, long forgotten or suppressed, may surface in the form of dreams.

This dream state has a way of inventing its own world which is similar to daydreaming. Sometimes in the waking state we sit down and imagine various things. At that time, most of our mind is in the Jagriti Awastha and so we are able to recognize this activity as an imagination or visualization, but in dream this is held in abeyance. It is closed 'So the Swapna becomes real.

The third part of that Supreme Being is identified with the last sound sleep where in everything is closed and absorbed in itself. So it represents the closing up or the end of all activity, where both the waking activity and dream state are in abeyance. They are all drawn in like a tortoise pulling in its head and limbs. The energies that are operating, both in the physical world and the dream or the subtle world, have ceased to function, everything is closed and absorbed in itself.

In that state when one is fast asleep, one has no desire. One does not have any desire since there is nothing and nobody existing in that state to desire or to be desired. Everything is rolled up, coiled up. It does not see any dreams. There is not even a desire for dreams.

So, absolute bliss is being enjoyed in deep sleep. The only difference is that one is not even aware of the enjoyment of that supreme Bliss. But there is enjoyment going on because, when we wake up, we always feel, AH! I had a wonderful sleep, it was very restful.

Deep sleep is the greatest blessing that has been given to us. It is in this '*Sushupta Awastha*' that we go to rest finally, after a whole day of activity, and even after the dream state has ended. And because there is no outward or inward movement, there is no wastage of energy of any kind.

There is also no differentiation between 'me' and 'you', because in deep sleep I am not aware of anything. Since, there is no 'I' and 'you', there is no duality, there is no tension, no insecurity, no friction. As long as there is duality, there is no rest, no peace.

I might go to sleep clutching my safe keys in my hand because I am afraid someone may come and rob my safe, but when I am in deep sleep it does not matter because there is no discrimination and duality, there is no fear but absolute rest. So, when I wake up from deep sleep, I feel absolutely *Jagrita*, Swapna and *Sushupti* are all parts of that Supreme Being.

That 'Being', who is in absolute bliss that is free from all dualities, who is now in the state of *Sushupti*, that 'Being' is beyond the mind, so we cannot conceive of it with our brains? But that does not mean that it is an abstract entity. A Lord cannot be abstract entity. It is a 'Being" and that is why the word, *Sarveshwara*, the 'Lord' is used.

The *Sarveshwara* knows everything; he is the knower of all. It is omniscient, It also means that when we say, "I Know' we are mistaken. It is only the Supreme Being who knows, and it is because our consciousness is an *Ansha*, a part of the 'Supreme Being' that we know 'I'. Therefore, when we say, 'I' Know' it is wrong. *Upanishads* say, "He who thinks he knows, knows not, and he who knows not, knows. This is not a riddle. It is to indicate that with our limited intellect, if we think we know the 'Supreme Being', we are still growing in darkness. When it is completely understood that it cannot be known, then it comes as a flash which is beyond our understanding. So, it is this 'Supreme Being', who is 'Lord of all' – the knower of all. It is also *Antaryami* – our inner controller.

The tendency to enjoy and move towards happiness is an essential part of our soul of our Being. The only problem is that the search for this happiness is in the wrong or different direction. If only the direction can be changed and brought back to the source of all happiness, which is the 'Supreme Being', then all problems and doubts will be resolved. The fragrance is in all of us. It is the source of all creation. We humans have become evolved; we can search and find the source of this fragrance. But we search for happiness in the material world until somebody points out. Now watch it! Halt turn back! To find the source from which all this comes, turn within! And to reach that aim; one has to change direction.

Like every high aim, the search for happiness within oneself requires *Sadhana*, practice and hard work, because nothing can be achieved without that. Sadly, it is only in religious and spiritual matters that people, want a short cut. For everything else, like making money or gaining fame, we are ready to work hard without any problem.

There is no shortcut in spiritual matters. For spiritual development one does not have to run away from day to day life. One can remain in the material world. With proper guidance, one can also advance in spiritually. The search must be done with humility, because if we think we already know, then we are not going to learn anything. Soon, everybody can become a teacher.

One has to realize that he has learnt different things from different people and also from other beings, including bees, the honey bee who teaches us to save for a rainy day. We should have an attitude that anybody who is in touch with us is not hungry. It is such a principle when realized we will see that the 'Divine Supreme Being' is innate in all beings. Then the whole world becomes our family.

Past is impressions, future is expectations and present is realization. Delete the impressions and do not live in expectations as one is past and another is uncertain. Realize the present, enjoy what is happening. Many a times we are not able to forget the past; constantly we are invoking it and then begging for love and compassion for the whole life. Supposing one has lost his dearest one, may be wife or husband, mother or father and constantly feel their deficiency in their life, go on keeping the grief in their memory, go on invoking the pain again and again. In this process we always remain in a position where we are missing that love and compassion and start deriving pleasure in begging for love and compassion.

A beggar cannot be chooser and as such where he gets love and compassion he is impressed and where he doesn't get develops hatred. In this process we lose our sense of discrimination in seeing the real and unreal. Thus, we take real as unreal and accept unreal as real and many a times we are lost in this so much that we add to our pain, instead of reducing it.

So actually to get rid of our pain we have to delete our past impressions and whatever, is coming should accept it as real. Similarly for transforming our dark side into a positive one we need to forget the past and move ahead. Everyone gets disturbed with incidents of genocide, abuse, perversion, destruction and corruption. We hear big talks of changing this outward grim reality. But no one cares to look within.

There is a dark side within us that puts up a fierce resistance to change. The instinctive life nature consisting of energy, desires, emotions, impulse and passions is marked by hedonism –ferociously pleasure – seeking and with a resolute wish to ward off even the most minor frustrations. Under the influence of this part, we develop troublesome habits, negative emotions, base indulgences, self destructive behaviors and disturbed relational patterns.

The dark part forces our mind to come up with reasons that uphold its feelings and demands consequently. We disregard the voice of reason and the voice of conscience. When we gain some self awareness we develop an aversion towards this shadow part. We decide to bring in a transformation. Despite best efforts, either the change does not take place or we fall back into the old trap after making some progress. During these moments, we often speculate on what is a miss.

Analytical Psychologist Carl Jung believed that although this shadow contains several undesirable elements, it also holds potential positivity. What matters is whether we are following a correct approach to reform it or not. According to integral psychology, this dark side need not be looked at just an impediment that has to be kicked away. It has fierce capacity of evolving into something beautiful, pure and blissful and of eventually becoming divinized. The mother maintains that the best way to transform the shadow part is through love, discrimination, nurturance and robust faith.

The dark side cannot stand boredom and constantly seeks excitement. When catering to it, we normally deteriorate in consciousness and find comfort in thing that we otherwise despise. We overlook the fact that sensory delight can also be obtained from higher sources. Our shadow part has the ability of becoming attracted to something beautiful, heroic and divine and can open itself up and surrender unconditionally. Therefore, we should fully employ it in different creative and spiritual pursuits that have a higher vibration. Consequently, the dark side will gradually accept and relish this refined joy and give up its crude pursuits.

The next step, the most important is aspiration, which means creating a steady will to transform the shadow part. It is a position of conviction where one sees the necessity of transcending better tendencies. When this aspiration is made strong it serves as a constant guide. It is best to create three layered aspiration. Firstly one must endeavor to restrain the expression of negative and to restrain the expression of negative in one's actions, feelings and thoughts. Secondly, besides deciding to subdue the negative, we must also strive to nurture the reciprocal positive within us. Thirdly, our aspiration must not be restricted to just growing into a better person, but to prepare oneself in such a manner that each cell in our body vibrates with divine love.

This ensures that we are not content with a minor degree of self advancement, but to continue to march forward in our evolution till the time we are able to embrace the divine light into our being. Soon the reformed dark side will take great pleasure in being the instrument of the divine.

We have to learn from our experience how to get a positive meaning from the experience. Then even through failure, we become richer. Also one has to learn the art of ending one's past and not constantly fret and fume over it.

We are full of cunning, are not we? My mind is such a problem. I am not able to decipher how mind is working. Mind is nothing but thoughts and thoughts repeat themselves. Ask yourself "Why are my thoughts repeated? Then you will see it is because you have not digested the experience of life. If you eat an apple and don't digest the apple, the undigested apple creates stomach disorders. Similarly if experiences are not digested they repeat themselves.

Some person went through a divorce and that pained him very often. Somebody advised, "Learn to end that incident in your mind, instead of carrying it. You are carrying the burden of yesterday. And hence you are not alert to the present and not sensitive to the present. The dissatisfaction of the past is polluting the present. Teach your mind to leave the past, let go of the past, learn from past failures. Let it teach you the right lessons.

True education enables you to not be doormat in your office. Learn to be creative. Learn to grow in your life. Watch your mind deceiving you, and then the mind will learn to be creative. Education is just not for giving you livelihood but giving you the art of living wholly and joyously.

We are normally victim in life to the fact that we do not like when someone disagrees with us. Learn to connect to people despite difference so that you don't get trapped in differences. If you can still bond with the person you disagree with, then you are a mature person. Then you are bigger than the differences. Such a person will be effective, and he is truly an educated person.

Seers and teachers in Indian traditions, while imparting their knowledge to the students tell them: I have seen, I have realized and you also can see and you also can realize. The idea behind this assertion is that the knowledge being provided by the teacher is not only bookish or theoretical knowledge; it is also something of which he has direct experience.

Seers ask people to accept what is being taught to them as a hypothesis to begin with but the pupils are asked to authenticate it with their own experience. It is not that important reason, like the scientific temper of which it is a synonym, was unknown to Indian thinkers. They accept only those doctrines that stand the scrutiny of analysis, tests of proof and satisfy intellectual understanding. Nothing is regarded as gospel truth; therefore there is no place for dogmatism here. Only that has to be accepted as knowledge which stands the scrutiny of reason, the experience of the teacher and the taught.

Classical literature of India, namely the *Upanishads, Bhagwat Gita, Mahabharat* and the *Bhagwat* too lay emphasis on reason, as the source as well as foundation of all knowledge. However it asserts that in case experience and logic contradict each other, experience has to be given priority. History of Indian thought is a history of relentless spirited debates and rigorous discussion which are strictly logical, even in the western sense of the term.

The education imparted thus was both knowledge leading to emancipation and the knowledge required for dealing with arts and crafts and day to day affairs of the world we live in.

When we have attained *Vidya*, we have unshakable calm. That is why *Krishna* says in *Gita* 5.18, "The learned ones, the ones endowed with *Vidya*, look with equanimity as a learned person, a cow and elephant and a dog as well as an eater of dog's meat". Again, in 3.26 & 27 *Gita* emphasizes that the *Vidyavan*, the enlightened person, acts without attachment. He does not create disturbance in the beliefs of the ignorant.

It is possible to dispel the darkness of despair with the light of the *Guru's* compassion and his teachings. The path of spirituality is like that of a river. There are ups and downs; sometimes swift, sometimes slow. Accept them all. Do not hurry or despair. Be extremely earnest in your spiritual pursuit. Pursue with great zeal. Let it not be half hearted attempt.

Initially, one may feel baffled. It can be disconcerting when you cannot discern the right means to practice or having practiced the right means, you don't get the desired results. At this point it is natural for one to feel discomfort. We have to make a diligent effort to understand the nature of the self.

A seeker in desperate moments may feel, "I have heard so much about the self. Yet I fail to experience the bliss of the self. I feel despondent for I neither experience the inner bliss, nor do I find the world comforting. A sincere seeker has not to give up and with great patience he has to endeavor to go deeper within.

Wishing of quick results without putting in the required amount of efforts does not bear fruits in spirituality. The conscious and blissful self cannot be realized by mere wishful thinking. The path is easy. However, it cannot be attained by unnecessary haste. One must bear in mind that he is faltering in his efforts and is stuck somewhere and so by turning inwards, he must vigilantly pursue till the end. But the condition is that without being obstinate that it must happen now only he has to pursue. Haste is waste.

What you are today is the result of what you have desired for and thought of many times in the past. Pessimism creates negative thoughts, feelings and an inner state that can only generate despair. It is very difficult to free oneself from the iron chain of despair because despair does not let the hope of freedom rise.

We have to rise above our despair to take on the mammoth task. Those who have realized the self too had undergone much unfavorable circumstance. Even if circumstances are unfavorable, they are never so unfavorable that they become an obstruction to self-realization. That is impossible. There are no hindrances other than despair and pessimism.

The reason for despair is that the mind is over ambitious. It wants to accomplish more and more in shorter period of time. And when the mind tries to hurry, it experience despair. The task of self-realization will not be achieved through haste or needlessness. It needs patience, earnestness, enthusiasm, attentiveness and freedom from tension. Everything moves at its specific pace seasonal flowers grow fast but wither away soon too, while the tall trees of deodar grow slowly. Progress too has its pace.

A seeker peacefully accepts all phases and pursues his goal without any expectation of fruits. Success will come but at its own time. When desire and passion surface, the seeker becomes weak and gets disturbed. But if one faces bravely, accepts all ups and downs with peacefulness, he creates positivity by not identifying with them and watching them from a distance.

Those who, while in this world, had purified themselves will gain entrance to paradise. Everybody is born with an upright nature, but due to the influence of his environment he adopts an unnatural life. Purification is for one to properly understand this problem and to de-condition himself and thereby make himself once again a person in true nature. It is this personality that would be regarded as purified personality.

De-conditioning is in other words, the name for the process of self correction. This task of self correction or de-conditioning is not something that someone else can do for another. It is each one's own responsibility. The first duty of every person is to engage in introspection and carefully search out every notion that was not present in them by birth but later become part of their personality because of the conditioning of their environment.

If one seriously engages in this sort of conditioning, one's natural personality will emerge having been purified. This is meaning of a purified personality.

Ethics as efficiency for rapid growth has been accepted by all as the first step. We cannot achieve without ambition. But unless ambition is translated into specific goals and general principles of advance are identified, progress would be limited. How old do you think you are? You are as young as your faith, as old as your doubt; as young as your self confidence, as old as your fear, as young as your hope, as old as your despair.

Death is essential fact of life which makes no exceptions. It comes to kings as well as beggars, to the rich, and poor, to saints as well as sinners, the aged and the young. One cannot simply turn a blind eye to it and fool himself into believing that death comes to other people but will spare you. It will not. It is best to prepare our self for it and when it comes, welcome it with a smile on lips.

As a rationalist it is hard to believe in unproven, the ones of life-death-rebirth in different forms as an unending process till our beings mingle with God and we attain Nirvana. But it is sure that death is the finality of every being. We do not know what happens after one dies. Very few people have dates with death apart from those who take their own lives or are convicted by courts to hang.

The old and ailing may sense the day drawing near but never know exactly what day or time it will be – we must always bear in mind that death is inevitable, so without brooding over it be prepared for it.

Positive people always do what they say and mean what they say. There are three principles in a man's being in life; the principles of thought, speech and action. The origin of all conflict between me and my fellow men is that I do not say what I mean, and I don't do what I say.

---

12. BE DIFFERENT

In the story of *Markandeya*, Shiva asks a young couple if they want an intelligent child who will die young or a dull child who will live long. And the parents choose the intelligent child. When faced with the imminent death of their child, they do not know what to do.

Let's ask ourselves what kind of life we want to live-do we want a short meaningful life or a long life, full of struggles. Does quality matter or quantity? Perhaps a short, meaningful life makes sense to old suffering souls and a long meaningless life makes sense to youth facing imminent death.

So is life about length or quality? Given a choice what would we prefer a short successful life or a long mediocre one? The next dimension that one has to see is whether one is restless or restful in one's daily activities of life. Being restful, calm, inwardly silent and not noisy is indispensable to spiritual health. If one is restless, mind pollutes perception. If the mind is calm, one sees situations objectively. If disturbed, one sees things in a distorted way. Hence, it is said, we don't live in the objective world; we live in our subjective world. We don't live in GOD's world; we live in our private world of hurts and upsets.

A washer man was going along with his donkey. In the dark, the donkey fell in a pit. So the washer man could not stand the noise and cry of the donkey and decided to bury it. He started to put mud to cover the pit. After sometime the washer man was shocked to see the donkey coming out of the pit. What had happened was – Whenever the mud was put, it used to shake it off, and the mud became steps from which it came out. In the same way if people throw muck at you, shake it off and go up. If the content of consciousness is superior, every difficulty will be an opportunity for you to grow.

To live a life of gratitude is an enlightened way of living. Be grateful and not greedy. If one is grateful one is sensitive to life, and if one is not grateful, one is sentimental to life. Being grateful one will not be egoist and being sentimental one becomes egoist. Sensitive is experiencing what is and sentimental is reacting to what is. To drop the arrogant self is truly being spiritual. When you are successful be grateful and see that the success is not due to me ('I') but caused by some higher operating force. So work towards reducing this egoistic 'I' and see the greater force operating. Then one will be grateful and not arrogant.

Education gives rise to the action and activities that shape the direction of society overtime. Education for global citizenship, in particular, can provide the conditional context that enables people to reframe events, whenever they may occur, through a shared human perspective and to foster action and solidarity. It can encourage people to consider global issues in terms of their own lives and lifestyles, thus bringing forth the inner capacities we all possess.

When youth make the determination to illuminate the corner of the world they inhabit now, it brings into being a space of security in which people can regain hope and power to live. The determination to live together that is ignited in this space of security shines as an embodiment of the global society in which no one is left behind, inspiring courage in people living in other communities who confront similar challenges.

Actions and renunciation go together. Renunciation has been misunderstood as giving up the good things of life to adopt a life of deprivation and misery. Hence, people shun spirituality and do not benefit from the power of renunciation. Renunciation is not giving up things you enjoy. It is moving up to far more fulfilling avenues. Renunciation is not dispossession. It is all possession. Renunciation is not giving up action. It is performing dynamic action in a spirit of renunciation. Action and renunciation go together. They are not mutually exclusive.

Renunciation is shedding weakness for strength. It is asserting oneness and rising above difference. Exuding warmth and shunning bitterness creating goodwill and giving up ill will. Renunciation is giving up the residue of grudges, prejudices and hatred to live a life of freedom and happiness. Renunciation is growth when a caterpillar transforms into a butterfly, its erstwhile life of darkness and limitation vanishes. Similarly you experience freedom, joy and cheer and live a life of effortless excellence with renunciation.

Sri Ramakrishna spoke of four types of fish that a fisherman encounters. The wise fish never gets caught. It sees the net coming and swims away. The second gets trapped but manages to break free. The third is ensnared but struggles to get out of the net. The fourth oblivious to the life threatening situation, bites the net and feels all is well. The fifth chapter of the *Gita* speaks of four types of people – the *Bhogi, Yogi, Sanyasi,* and *Gyani.*

The *Gyani* is ever free never bound by the world. The *Sanyasi* understands the danger of worldly entanglement and manages to steer clear. The *Yogi* is bound but endeavors to escape. The *Bhogi* is blissfully ignorant of the risks of worldly involvement and is content with instant pleasures that his life affords. The *Bhogi* looks outward for happiness and gets only sorrow and disappointment. He is full of desires for objects of the world. The *Yogi* has understood that happiness is a commodity not available in the world and begins the journey inwards. He tries to reduce and refine his desires. A *Sanyasi* is an evolved soul knocking at the doors of enlightenment. The *Gyani* has readied the destination of infinite bliss.

As you move up you become more successful, experience greater happiness and gain more power. A *Gyani* has the option of operating with the body, mind and intellect when needed. He retreats into the world of infinity when not required. The other three are struck in the world.

As soon as you embark on the spiritual journey you become free from agitation and sorrow. Then you get released from the baggage of the past. You develop equality of vision towards all beings. You remain unaffected by fluctuation in the world.

As long as you look outward for happiness you remain unhappy. The moment you turned inward you experience peace; when you get to *Atman* you gain infinite bliss. Pleasures that arise from sense contact are wombs of sorrow. They yield continuing misery. They are transient. The wise do not revel in them. Endure the force born of desire with the intellect. Reduce the number of desires, improve the quality of desires and change their direction. Then you are ready for meditation.

An intention is an idea, vow, promise, yearning or intense aspiration that you intend to carry out. We announce our intention to marry, to take legal action or say that it was not our intention to hurt someone's feelings. But just having an intention or stating it is no guaranteeing of auctioning it; so many forces are at work, which may delay or derail the final result.

The word *Sankalp* has several connotations but mainly – an orientation of the mind or heart; intentions, determination, decision, wish, resolve and will power. Why will power? Because even your will weakens over time; whereas *Sankalp* acts as a strengthening element. The yogic views see *Sankalp* as resolve or promise to oneself, embedded in the subconscious mind, repeated frequently so that it becomes a reality.

From intention to find action, there are certain phases. Many intentions remain unfulfilled because there is no resolve, the drive, zeal or will power to activate them. Even after activation one needs to sustain the flow to have stamina, to not be discouraged, to see it through. Additionally, there is need for conviction and discipline and all this depends on one's character. Most early enthusiasms wane in the absence of discipline to carry things through.

Sankalp finally refers to sincerity of promise. To most it sounds like a determination. The moral goodness of a deed comes from goodness of intention. Integrity has largely to do with purify our intentions.

Whatever, you do with your body; mind or energy leaves a certain residue. When you gather a huge volume of impressions, these slowly shape themselves into tendencies.

These tendencies have been traditionally described as *Vasanas*. *Vasana* literally means smell. Depending upon the type of smell you emit, you attract certain kinds of life situations to yourself. *Vasanas* are generated by a vast accumulation of impressions caused by your physical mental, emotional and energy actions.

It is possible for us to choose not to be victims of our *Vasanas* or puppets of our pasts. We can choose the fragrance we leave behind for the world. Any conscious thought, emotion or action has the potential to endure. Aware that every action has a consequence, they choose to live consciously and attain a certain kind of morality that others of their time never did.

Those in position of power need to realize that they can leave behind enduring beneficial legacies to the world, if they lead lives of greater responsibility and awareness.

To day we have technologies at our disposal that could either create phenomenal well being or destroy the planet several times over. If the ignorant are empowered they could sabotage humanity entirely. It does not take a nuclear holocaust. We are capable of gassing ourselves without any nuclear assistance, as we know from the current predicament in our capital city.

When those in positions of power realize the enormous consequences of their thoughts and actions and invent an inner *Sadhana*, it could be the dawn of a great possibility. We could now turn not merely into the architects of our own destiny but be collaborators in the collective destiny of the human race.

Young people have immense amount of feelings and enthusiasm in the blood. Each one of you has a glorious future if you dare believe in yourselves. Have tremendous faith in yourselves that eternal power is lodged in every soul and you will revive the whole of humanity.

It is the young, the strong and healthy of sharp intellect that will reach the Lord. This is the time to decide your future, while you possess the energy of youth, not when you are worn out and jaded, but in the freshness and vigor of youth. Work this is the time; for the freshest, the untouched and un-smelled flowers alone are to be laid at the feet of the Lord.

Raise yourselves, therefore for life is short. A far greater work is this sacrifice of yourselves for the benefit of your race, for the welfare of humanity. We can understand in plain language that you work best when you work for others. The best work that you ever did for yourselves was when you worked for others. This life is short, varieties of the world are transient, but they alone live who live for others, the rest are more dead than alive. Be not afraid of anything become fearless. You will do marvelous work. The moment you fear, you are nobody. It is fear that is the great cause of misery in the world. It is the fear that is the greatest of all superstitions. It is fear that is the cause of our woes, and it is fearlessness that brings heaven even in a moment.

All power is within you, you can do anything and everything. Believe in that do not believe that you are weak. Stand up and express the divinity within you. Therefore, arise awake and stop not till the goal is reached.

Napoleon said that the word impossible is found in the dictionary of fools. By impossible Napoleon meant that certain goals or accomplishment, which we normally consider out of reach, may be capable of being achieved if only one was daring enough to entertain them and determined enough to go after them. One might have considered it impossible of France to achieve the kind of military victories that Napoleon achieved for his county.

This idea of impossible becomes even more relevant when we come to the individual, who might consider certain accomplishments impossible without realizing that with persistent efforts and determination they could be achieved. Perhaps, in such a context the word 'impossible' is best understood as really denoting the improbable, which our imagination consider impossible.

Swamy Vivekananda once asked his *Guru Sri Ramakrishna*, "How does one achieve the impossible". The *Guru* told him, "By treating end as the means" One hesitates to offer an interpretation of such as oracular pronouncement and reader may have his own understanding of it. But what was perhaps meant was that when we think of achieving something we tend to focus on the end product more, rather than how that end product might be actually achieved in terms of the concrete steps required to accomplish it.

So, we should focus our attention on the means with the same passion with which we covet the goal itself. That would be one way of treating means as the end. And then once such a concrete step is realized, similarly, the success we have achieved should be considered only a step in relation to what remains to be achieved to accomplish the goal. This would be one way of treating the end as the means.

One should begin by doing the necessary; then one should do the possible, and then he adds that. If, one does so one would find oneself accomplishing the impossible.

13. NATURE THE ENJOYER AND CONSCIOUSNESS

This body is called the field and that one who knows this body is called the knower of the field. This body is the field of activity for the conditioned soul. The conditioned soul is entrapped in material existence and he attempts to Lord over material nature. The body is made of senses. The conditioned soul wants to enjoy sense gratification and according to his capacity to enjoy sense gratification, he is offered a body or field of activity.

It is not very difficult to understand difference between the field and its knower, the body and the knower of the body. Any person can consider that from childhood to old age he undergoes so many changes of body and yet is still one person, remaining. Thus, there is a difference between knower of the field of activities and actual field of activities. A living conditioned soul thus can understand that he is different from the body. A curator of a cricket pitch may know everything about the pitch but he does not become the owner of the pitch. Still he does not know how the pitch will behave in case of change of weather, temperature, watering, etc. We all know our body but since, body consists of senses we do not know how and when it will behave in what way as per the dictate of the senses. Similarly we are the part of the super power and we know about our body only whereas the super power knows about all the bodies.

One must thus have firm conviction that GOD will take care of the soul surrendered to Him. "I shall never be alone", one should think all the time. Even if I am in the darkest region of a forest I shall be accompanied by GOD and he will give me all the protection. The conviction is called *Abhayam*, without fear. This state of mind is necessary for a person in the renounced order of life. Then he has to purify his existence.

For purifying life charity is the best mean for householders. The householders should earn a livelihood by an honorable means and spend some percentage of it to propagate good social work all over the world. Thus, a householder should give in charity to such institutional societies that are engaged in the way. Charity should be given to the right receiver.

The householder should exercise sense control. Although he has a wife, a home; holder should not use his senses for sex life unnecessarily. Sacrifice is another item to be performed by the householder. The best sacrifice in this age is called *Sankirtana*, the chanting of *Hare Rama Hare Rama Rama Rama Hare Hare, Hare Krishna Hare Krishna Krishna Krishna Hare Hare.* This is the best and most inexpensive sacrifice; everyone can adopt it and derive benefits. So these three items namely, charity, sense control and performance of sacrifice are best for householder. .

It is also said that for purification of one's life one should follow *Satyam* meaning, one should not distort the truth for some personal interest. One should not construe some interpretation for his personal interest. One should learn to check his Anger. Even if there is some provocation one should be tolerant for once one become angry his whole body becomes polluted. Anger is the product of the modes of passion and lust. One should not find fault with others or correct them unnecessarily. Of course to call a thief a thief is not fault finding, but to call an honest person a thief is very much offensive for one who is making advancement in spiritual life.

One should be very modest. One should have firm determination meaning thereby that one should not be agitated or frustrated in some attempt. There may be failure in some attempts, but one should not be sorry for that, we should make progress with practice and determination. One should also try to be strong enough to give protection to the weak. They should not pose themselves as non-violent. If violence is required they must exhibit it.

All these qualities mentioned are transcendental qualities. They should be cultivated according to different status of the social order. The purport is that even though material conditions are miserable, if these qualities are developed by practice, by all classes of men, then gradually it is possible to rise to the highest platform of transcendental realization.

Arrogance, pride, anger, conceit, harshness and ignorance, these qualities belong to those of demonic nature. The demoniac want to make a show of religion and advancement in spiritual science, although they do not follow the principles. They are always arrogant or proud in possessing some type of education or so much wealth. They desire to be worshiped by others and demand respectability, although they do not command respect.

Such people do not know what should be done and what should not be done. Over trifles they become very angry and speak harshly not gently. They do everything whimsically according to their own desire and they do not recognize any authority. These demoniac qualities are taken on by them from the beginning of their bodies, in the womb of their mothers, and as they grow they manifest all these in auspicious qualities.

The conditioned living entities are divided into two classes in this world. Those who are born with divine qualities follow a regulated life that is to say they abide by the injunctions in scriptures and by the authorities. One should perform duties in the light of authoritative scriptures. This mentality is called divine. One who does not follow the regulative principles as they are laid down in the scriptures and who act according to his whims is called demoniac or *Asuric*. There are no other criteria but obedience to the regulative principles of scriptures. Both the *Demigods* and demons are born of the GOD, the only difference is that one class obeys the injunctions and the other does not.

In every civilized human society there is some set of spiritual rules and regulations which are followed from the beginning. Those who follow them are known as the most advanced civilized people. Those who do not follow the scriptural injunctions are supposed to be demons. It is said that demons do not know the scriptural rules, nor do they have any inclination to follow them. Most of them do not know them and even if some of them know, they have not the tendency to follow them. They have no faith, nor are they willing to act in terms of the scriptural injunctions. The demons are not clean either externally or internally.

The demoniac conclude that the world is phantasmagoria. There is no cause no effect, no controller, no purposes; everything is unreal. They say that this cosmic manifestation arises due to change material actions and reactions. They do not think that the world was created by GOD for a certain purpose. They have their own theory; that the world has come about in its own way and that there is no reason to believe that there is a GOD behind it. For them there is no difference between spirit and matter, and they do not accept the supreme spirit. Everything is matter only for them. According to them everything is void, and whatever manifestation exists is due to our ignorance in perception. The demons say that life is a dream and they are very expert in enjoying this dream. They conclude that as a child is simply the result of sexual intercourse between man and women; this world is born without any soul.

The demon's lust is never satiated. They will go on increasing and increasing their insatiable desires for material enjoyment. Although, they are always full of anxieties on account of accepting non permanent things; they still continue to engage in such activities out of illusion. Accepting non-permanent things such demoniac people create their own GOD, create their own hymns and chant accordingly. The result is that they become more and more attracted to two things – Sex enjoyment and accumulation of material wealth. Such demoniac people are always attracted by wine, women, gambling and man eating; those are their unclean habits induced by pride and false prestige. Although they are gliding towards hell they consider themselves very much advanced.

Such demon people believe that to gratify the senses is the prime necessity of human civilization. Thus there is no end to their anxiety. Being bound by hundreds and thousands of desires by lust and anger, they secure money by illegal means for sense gratification.

We experience every day such people whose plans for life are never finished and they go on preparing plan after plan, all of which are never finished. Such people even at the point of death request their physicians to prolong their life for a few more years as their plans are still incomplete. They do not know that a physician cannot prolong life even for a moment.

The demoniac person, who has no faith in GOD or the super soul within himself, performs all kinds of sinful activities simply for sense gratification. They do not know that there is a witness sitting within their hearts. The super soul is observing the activities of the individual soul. Such people have no knowledge or any faith; therefore they feel free to do anything for sense's enjoyment, regardless of the consequences.

The demoniac person thinks, "So much wealth they have today and will gain more according to their schemes. So much is mine now and it will increase in the future more and more. He thinks I am the lord of everything. I am the enjoyer. I am perfect, powerful and happy. I am the richest person, surrounded by aristocratic, relatives. There is none; as powerful and happy as I am. I shall perform my sacrifices. I shall give some charity and then I shall rejoice. In this way such persons are deluded by ignorance.

The demoniac man knows no limit to his desires to acquire money. That is unlimited. He only thinks how much assessment he has just now and scheme to engage that stock of wealth further and further. For that reason he does not hesitate to act in any sinful way and so deals in black market for illegal gratification. He believes in his own strength and he does not know that whatever he is gaining is due to his past good deeds.

He simply thinks that all his mass of wealth is due to his own endeavor. A demoniac person believes in the strength of his personal work not in the law of *Karma*. A man takes his birth in a high family, or becomes rich or very well educated or very beautiful because of good work in the past.

The demoniac thinks that all these things are accidental and due to the strength of his personal ability.

Each demoniac person thinks that he can live at the sacrifice of all others. Generally, a demoniac person thinks of himself as the supreme GOD and he preaches his followers: why are you seeking GOD elsewhere? You are all yourself GOD, whatever you like you can do. Don't believe in GOD. Such demoniacs continue to be envious and they are always full of lust, always violent and hateful and always unclean. They are just like so many beasts in a jungle.

The material energy is always giving us trouble in the shape of three fold miseries. This material energy is constituted of the three modes of material nature. One has to raise himself at least to the mode of goodness before the path of understanding the supreme can be opened. Without raising oneself to the standard of the mode of goodness, one remains in ignorance and passion, which are the cause of demoniac life. Those who are in the modes of passion and ignorance deride the holy man and deride the proper understanding of the spiritual master. In spite of hearing the glories of devotional services, they are not attracted. Thus, they manufacture their own way of elevation. These are some of the defects of human society, which lead to demoniac status of life. If however, one is able to be guided by a proper and bona fide spiritual master, who can lead one to the path of elevation, to the higher stage, then one's life becomes successful.

Those who are situated in goodness generally worship the *Demigods* like *Brahma*, *Shiva* and others. Similarly those who are in the mode of passion worship the demons. A man in Calcutta worshiped Hitler because thanks to the war he had amassed a large amount of wealth by dealing in the black market. Similarly, those who are in the modes of passion and ignorance generally select a powerful man to be GOD. They think that anyone can be worshiped as GOD and that the same results will be obtained.

There are persons who manufacture modes of austerity and penance for some ulterior motives. Fasting for some purpose to promote is a purely political and is not in accordance of goodness. Actually such acts are out of pride, false, ego, lust and attachment for material enjoyment. But such activities; not only are the combination of material elements of which the body is constructed and disturbed but also the supreme personality of Godhead living within the body. Such unauthorized acts of fasting for some political end are certainly very disturbing to others. If however such persons are fortunate enough to be guided by a spiritual master who can direct them to the right path, they can get out of this entanglement and ultimately achieve the supreme goal.

The general tendency is to offer sacrifice with some purpose in mind, but it is stated that sacrifice should be performed without any such desire. It should be done as a matter of duty. Take for example the performance of rituals in temples or churches. Generally they are performed with the purpose of material benefit, but that is not the mode of goodness. Some people think that there is no use in going to the temple just to worship GOD. One should go simply to offer respect to the deity. That will place one into the mode of goodness.

To make the mind austere is to detach it from sense gratification. It should be so trained that it can be always thinking of doing well for others. The best training for the mind is gravity in thoughts. Satisfaction of the mind can be obtained only by taking the mind away from thoughts of sense enjoyment. The more we think of sense enjoyment the more mind becomes dissatisfied. In the present age we unnecessarily engage the mind in so many different ways for sense gratification and so there is no possibility of the mind becoming satisfied. The mind should be devoid of duplicity, and one should think of the welfare of all. Silence means that one is always thinking of self realization. Control of the mind means detaching the mind from sense enjoyment. One should be straight forward in his dealings and thereby purify his existence. All these qualities together constitute austerity in mental activities.

Sometimes penance and austerity are executed to attract people to receive honor, respect and worship from other persons in the mode of passion arrange to be worshipped by subordinates and let them wash their feet and offer riches. Such arrangements artificially made by the performance of penances are considered to be in the mode of passion. The results are temporary; they can be continued for some time, but they are not permanent. There are instances of foolish penance undertaken by demons like *Hiranyakasipu*, who performed austere penances to become immortal and kill the Demigods. He prayed to GOD for such things but ultimately he was killed by the Godhead. To undergo penances for something which is impossible is certainly in the mode of ignorance. The gift which is given out of duty, at the proper time and place to a worthy person and without expectation of return is considered to be charity in the mode of goodness.

14. MAKE LIFE SIMPLE

"Life is really simple but we insist on making it complicated"
Confucius

"The body is temporary. We are actors, paid according to our performance. Play your part well in Vraja Lila, Shaking off desires and obsessions. Our duty is to watch this divine play as witness. Be always in a natural state of oneness, free of all sense of want"
- Dada Amiya Roy Chowdhary

Chinta or worrying, are not about money, family, fame, power and possessions all the time. We worry so much because we are so attached to the body and material possession. *Chintan* or introspection brings us in a state of awareness. *Atma Chintan* is just knowing that, "I am a Soul", with immense energy, that I am not just a body. It is contemplating with detachment about the impermanence of the body and related things and the misery they cause.

Life is a gift, appreciate it and live it to the fullest. Most of us don't understand this simple fact and we complicate even the simplest of things. On the one hand we have simplified life with advance in technology and modernization, on the other we have yet to meet our truest needs. Perhaps it is the time to relearn the basics.

Your attitude is the key as to how life treats you. If you want to play the *'Victim'* you will become one. If you want to be a winner, act like one and see the difference. Have the fearless attitude of a hero and loving heart of a child.

Our love for food makes us who we are. We should not lose track while we eat and that everything works best in moderation. Overreacting makes us uncomfortable and unhealthy.

Watch what you say, and whatever you say practice it. It is always easier to give advice than take it. Never say things that you would not follow yourself. Your words are powerful. So use them wisely and mean what you say.

The past can always return to haunt you if you have painful memories. Do not regret the past. Look to live in the present. When an opportunity presents itself, learn to make the best of it. However, in the heat of the moment don't act hastily. Weigh the pros and cons and then take the step.

In the *Bhagwat Gita, Krishna* emphatically declares there is no place for grief in life. We invite grief into our lives by unintelligent identification. We further compound the problem by suffering in anticipation of pain, anguish during the experience and agonizing in memory of past trauma. The root cause is ignorance.

Gita says the word is a mix of pairs of opposites; is ever changing and in unpredictable. Understand the world as it is. Enjoy it, but never depend on it. Then the same world that now gives stress will become pleasurable and you will be happy.

Grief and delusion come from identification with body, mind and intellect – the little self. When you view everything from a personal angle, there is grief. View the same thing from larger perspective; there is peace.

Arjuna, the mighty prince and warrior, is reduced to tears when he looks at the entire scenario from his personal view point. He lays down his bow and arrow and refuses to fight. He surrenders to *Krishna* and says, "I am your disciple. Please teach me" *Krishna* does not comfort *Arjuna*. He speaks Truth

– uncompromising and forthright. It removes the despair and prepares *Arjuna* for the philosophy that is to come.

Krishna's opening words are- *Arjuna*, you speak words of wisdom but you mourn for those that should not be mourned for. The wise grieve neither for the living nor for the dead. From verses 11 to 53 *Krishna* presents *Arjuna* with the highest knowledge - indestructibility of the soul.

Arjuna is worried about dying. So are we all. *Krishna* explains what happens at death. Atman, the real you, never dies. Even the mind and intellect do not perish. You only leave behind the body and environment and no longer meet with your needs and move to another body and circumstances more suited to the fulfillment of your desires just as man gives up tattered clothes to lease new ones. Thus, your journey to truth continues.

Krishna says there was never a time when you and I did not exist nor will there ever come a time when we shall cease to be. Everything around us changes. One who is not troubled by these fluctuations and remains steady, equal to joy and sorrows is fit for immortality.

In the midst of this cycle of birth and death – it is your duty to act as warrior in the battle of life. Each one has obligations to perform. Do what you have to do without attachment. Your right is to action only, not to its fruits.

Perfection in action is *Yoga*. Also serenity is *Yoga* and excellence is peace in the midst of intense exertion. When the mind is calm the intellect is sharp and action is brilliant. If the mind is disturbed, thinking gets fuzzy and action becomes flawed.

Every person is born with an upright nature, but due to the influence of his environment he adopts an unnatural life. In this context, purification is for one to properly understand this problem and to de-condition himself and thereby make himself once again a person of true nature. It is this personality that would be regarded as purified personality.

De-conditioning is, in other words, the name for the process of self correction. This task of self-correction or de-conditioning is not something that someone else can do for another. It is each one's own responsibility. The first duty of every person is to engage in introspection and carefully search out every notion that was not present in them by birth but that later became part of their personality because of the conditioning of their environment.

If one seriously engages himself in this sort of reconditioning one's natural personality will emerge having been purified. This is the meaning of a purified personality.

We all have lions in our worlds. If you panic and run away from your fears, nobody can save you, but if you charge towards them, the whole world will be right behind you. Miracles happen when fears are faced without thinking about, "What will happen". Always choose what you want to do instead of being defeated by your own limiting thoughts that keep telling you why or what you can't do.

The basic purpose of body and mind tells one that he has to grow out of this roller coaster ride of success, failure, happiness and sadness. Everyone thinks he needs to be human and serve mankind in which there is happiness for one and all, that in itself is experiencing and realizing GOD. Awareness within tells me these are nothing but two sides of the same coin, inherent and intrinsic to one another. One has to stand up as rebel supporting his own thoughts and humaneness, in the midst of those who are weak, dependent and conditioned.

Life has become one gigantic game; to succeed in this game we have to struggle. This struggle is consuming our life silently. One should not discard success because of the simple reason that the creative process which is installed in our DNA has to be allowed. Being creative has to be encouraged. But in this process, if one is not alert, our inner joy will be destroyed. Hence, we have to make sure that our commitment for excellence is based on ethics. Ethics is based on goodness and it is not bound by any definition, but it is intrinsic wisdom.

The focus should be on spiritual health which involves operating from right values. This involves self discipline; one has to learn to drop self love. Self love is the mother of all conflicts. When you are addicted to your point of view and your dogma, then you are in conflict with the other. By self one constructs consciousness of the self and hence will be in conflict with the other. One should love the whole and such should be inclusive and not exclusive. So such love should include the self and not get imprisoned by the self.

First of all it is necessary for us to understand the place where we are now. It is a necessity to know the actuality first in order to realize the possibility. To know what you can be, it is a necessity to first know what you are. We are standing in sex, and lust. We have to take future steps towards spirituality beginning our journey from here. So, in order to understand the last step, it is necessary to understand the first because it is the first step that is going to pave the way for the last step of the journey.

---

15. DUTY IS DIVINE CONSCIOUSNESS

O ne should perform his duties in Divine consciousness. There are two classes of men, some of them are full of polluted material things in their hearts, and some of them are materially free. Divine consciousness is equally beneficial for both of these persons. Those who are full of material things can take to the line of Divine consciousness for a gradual cleansing process, following the regulative principles of devotional service. Those who are already cleaned of the impurities may continue to act in the same Divine consciousness so that others may follow their exemplary activities without having knowledge of Divine consciousness.

Arjuna's desire to retire from the activities on the battlefield was not approved by the Lord. One needs only to know how to act. To retire from the activities and to sit aloof making a show of *Krishna Consciousness* is less important than actually engaging into the field of activities for the sake of *Krishna*.

Action in *Krishna Consciousness* has to be executed in accord with the bona fide devotees. The intricacies of action are very hard to understand. Therefore one should know properly what actions are forbidden and what action is inaction. One has to apply oneself to such an analysis of action, reaction and perverted actions because it is a very difficult subject matter.

To understand *Krishna Consciousness* and action according to the modes one has to learn one's relationship with the supreme i.e., one who has learnt perfectly knows that every living entity is the eternal survivor of the Lord and consequently one has to act in *Krishna Consciousness*. *Krishna Consciousness* teaches us values of truth, peace, harmony, compassion towards all living beings. It teaches "***Vasudeva Kutumbkam***" the whole world is one family. We treat all living being at par with humans as well as we believe, in presence of a soul which exists in every living organism right from plant to animals.

Furthermore, we also believe that the soul is the integral part of the supreme soul or the highest one. At the same time human beings have a mind of their own, which is subject to wrong influences, which may lead to certain wrong actions.

The sun, moon, trees and mountains do not have any caste; – human values a strong character and extraordinary dedication of upholding values of truth, peace, harmony in all; that matters to human being.

It is a blunder to accept (assume) a thing, which is not one's own, as one owns a thing which is one's own. Only the things, which may ever live with us and with which we may ever live can be our own. The body in the same state does not stay with us even for a moment while GOD ever lives with us. The reason is that the body belongs to the class of the world, while the self belongs to class of GOD.

Hence, it is the greatest blunder to assume the body as one's own and not to assume GOD as one's own. In order to rectify this blunder, we have to understand that we are not the entity which dies i.e., we are not the body. We are a resident of the divine world while the body is a resident of the matter (mortal) world. We are fragment of GOD while the body is a fragment of *Prakrati* (Nature). We ever live in immortality. By the decay and death of the body we don't decay and die in the least. Therefore, we should not be obsessed by grief, worry and fear, etc.

In human life there is predominance of discrimination. Therefore 'I am not body this discrimination is possible in the human body. The sense of 'I' and 'mine' in the body is not the work of human intellect but that of beastly intellect. So now give up this beastly intellect that you will die. As the body was nonexistent in the past, it was born afterwards and will die in future, it is not the case with you (the self) that you were nonexistent in the past, were born afterwards and will die in future.

Every person is born with an upright nature, but due to influence of his environment, he adopts an unnatural life. In this context, purification is for one to properly understand this problem and to de-condition himself and thereby make himself once again a person of true nature. It is this personality that would be regarded as a purified personality.

Reconditioning is in other words, the name for the process of self correction. This task of self correction or de-conditioning is not such a thing that someone else can do for another. It is each one's own responsibility. The first duty of every person is to engage in introspection and carefully search out every notion that was not present in them by birth but that later became part of their personality because of conditioning of their environment. If one seriously engages in this sort of de-conditioning, one's natural personality will emerge, having been purified. This is the meaning of a purified personality.

The difference between material and spiritual life is our perception; how we see the reality around us. According to our conditionings, the species of life we are in the various designations we have identified with, our desires and our ego, everything is being filtered and creates a perception.

If you wear rose-colored glasses, everything looks rosy, so we, the soul, are perceiving life through the ego, then intelligence, mind and the five senses do not see what is real. Spiritual life is not about interpreting reality according to our different conceptions and conditionings. Real spiritual life is about waking up to the internal underlying substance of truth that is within everything.

Therefore, if you want to look for real substance, meaning the truth in life, then you have to come out from amongst men and be separate and understand that, "I am not this body but the consciousness, the life force within this body" seeing through the eyes, tasting through the tongue and loving through the heart.

If you examine every motivation that every human being has, it is desire for pleasure or the reaction to the frustration of not getting pleasure. Yet there is only one pleasure that can truly satisfy the heart and that is pleasure of love. So this is reality and why do we all have that in common? Because our nature is to love God and we are seeking that love in everything at all the times and that love is within our own hearts. So reality is on the spiritual platform to see everything in relationship to the truth in relation to God.

So we need to transform our conditioned habits to spiritual habits and the most powerful way is to chant the names of God. Don't be exploited by the propaganda of the illusions of this world. Search for light, truth and real love.

How often do we read in the papers these days that some person or the other in one of our bigger cities was mugged, beaten or raped in the presence of dozens of other people who didn't lift a finger to help? Or how a hit and run victim is carefully avoided by passing vehicle's don't stop, while pedestrians walk around the body taking care not to step on the blood? Similar incidents don't just happen in India but they do happen across the world.

The reason for people not coming for help to the victim has been examined by many psychologists. It has been found that many a times if there is an alone person he comes out to help but when there are other people also, only 40 percent offer any help. The reason for this include that onlookers (a) see that others are not helping either (b) that onlookers believe other will know better how to help (c) that onlookers feel uncertain about helping while others are watching. In other words, being with a lot of people around the same emergency situation; it creates diffusion of responsibility so the question is who is your real neighbor; one who is moved with compassion and starts taking care without waiting for anything else. Such people are those on whom God shows mercy.

One should look into every single layer of his life. He should try to search within himself to find out why some of his habits just as anger, hatred or jealousy cannot bring joy. Simple thinking or saying that anger, hatred or jealousy is bad is not going to help. We have to experience on its own that these things are poisonous and they simply bring misery and pain; and we are filled with the anguish of suffering and the poison of these habits we will feel scorched in the burning fire of anger, hatred or jealousy. The moment we are able to see the whole burning sensation, all the pain and hell would become clear to us. We will understand how bad these emotions are. Then we can repent our emotions. But this repentance is meaningless because afterwards there is no way we can see those emotions again so if we watch these emotions with wisdom and thoughtfulness, that seeing would give birth to the experience of knowing them.

Simply repentance, vows and oaths are all substitutes for the ego; they serve no purpose. They are utterly fake and pseudo. Certainly, something can happen, not by just repentance, but by being aware. Whatever situation grips your mind, be alert, wake up and try to look at the situation, try to identify what is happening. If you see pain and suffering, ignore it.

All sins are committed in a state of unconsciousness. We find this more than surprising; how a person attains such a state that anger disappears from his life? That no fire of lust burns inside him? That not hatred or jealousy arises in him? Osho says it all can happen in everyone's life provided we are not guided by other people's thoughts; start observing our conduct, watch it; be alert and aware of it.

When a man rises, after a sound sleep, he says that he slept soundly and he was not aware of anything. It means that he knows that he was not aware of anything during sound sleep. This knowledge of nothingness by the self proves that the self existed, even during sound sleep. Thus, his own self existed before his sleep, during his sleep and also after his sleep i.e., the self (soul) exists continuously.

The intellect which determines only one thing and remains unshakably fixed to it and cognizes only one entity i.e., GOD, the embodiment of truth, knowledge and Bliss, the various forms of sensuous enjoyment and the means of attaining them fall entirely beyond the range of its cognition. It is referred to as a stable mind or equipoise mind.

Freedom of will is allowed to a human being alone. Man has a right to action alone, not to the renunciation of action. If out of egoism one forcibly tries to renounce all action, he will not succeed in the attempt; for his nature will compel to act. In this way he will be abusing his authority, and by refusing to perform an obligatory duty he will also have to bear the evil consequence of violating his duty. Therefore, it is obligatory for every human being to perform his duty resolutely and not to renounce it.

When we say that man has no right to the fruits of his actions, it is intended to bring out that man is not free in the matter of obtaining the fruit of his actions. He does not knows what action of his will bear what type of fruit nor how and when he will get that fruit; one cannot get that fruit when he desires to get it; nor can he avoid it. One desires one thing; and gets something else in return.

Many men crave to obtain various forms of enjoyment but it is not in their hands to get an opportunity for such enjoyment. They do not seek separation from or contact with certain people; but they are forced on them. Dispensation of the fruits of action is wholly under the control of Providence and man is totally helpless in this matter.

It is nothing but ignorance to be obsessed by desire for the possession of wealth, power, honor, fame and prestige etc., in this life. Entertaining a desire, attachment, hope or craving for actions with the body, mind and intellect as well as for their fruit is what is meant by becoming instrumental in making ones action bear fruit, for the alone who gets attached to actions and their fruits reaps their fruit, and not he who renounces all his desire for, and attachment to actions as well as their fruit.

Renunciation of an obligatory duty is in no way justified without performing one's allotted duties; one cannot reach the end of path of *Karma Yoga*. One should avoid attachment to inaction or non-performance of prescribed duties. One should perform his duties renouncing attachment and even tempered in success and failure; evenness of temper is called *Yoga*. It will bring a man to a stage where mind will remain unperturbed amid sorrows, thirst for pleasure altogether disappeared and become free from passion fear and anger and his mind becomes quite stable.

So passion, fear and anger have no place in the mind and speech of such people. No occurrence of any kind can ever induce the least attachment, fear or anger in his mind. Therefore his speech also will be free from passion, fear and anger and will exhibit both tranquility, guileless and simplicity. He may at any time for the sake of world give expression of attachment, fear and anger through action of body and speech, yet they never be swayed by any morbid feeling.

It may be possible for a clever man possessing exceptional self control to use words which are altogether free remaining unaffected by such feelings. But merely external speech and exhibiting self control and stability in speech is not sufficient to have a stable mind; but to possess a stable mind one should be faithful to the state of his mind, wholly pure and entirely free from passion, fear and anger.

One who is unattached to everything; meeting with good and evil neither rejoices not recoils; his mind is stable. A person can bodily renounce objects of enjoyment but mentally goes on enjoying the same; but in as much as such mental enjoyment presuppose attachment for the objects of senses can be avoided even before GOD realization with the help of a recourse of reason; whereas the realization of GOD lays the axe at its very roots.

Turbulent by nature, the senses even of a wise man practicing self control forcibly carry away his mind. One who merely renounce enjoyment of sense – objects; only sense objects withdrew but not the taste for their enjoyment. We may think that what is the harm or may find it difficult; if the taste for enjoyment does not disappear. But it should be clearly understood that so long as attachment for the enjoyment of sense objects remains embedded in the heart of the man, his senses will on account of that attachment forcibly lead him to the enjoyment of sense objects; hence, his mind and intellect cannot remain stable. Thus, senses forcibly carry away the mind of man. So, having controlled all the sense and collecting the mind one should engage him in the practice of meditation.

After subduing the senses, if the mind is not brought under control it will dwell on objects of the world and bring about the fall of the person, mind and intellect. That is why it is advised that one should sit for the practices of meditation of GOD, collecting his scattered mind and devoting himself heart and soul to GOD. One who having subdued mind and senses engages himself in practice of meditation will soon attain stability of intellect, which will bring him within easy reach of GOD-realization.

With the attainment of such placidity of mind, all his sorrows come to an end and the intellect of such a person of tranquil mind, soon withdrawing itself from all sides becomes firmly established in GOD; his heart becomes pure and he succeeds in attainting the joy of the spirit, his mind will not give up joy and tranquility even for a moment. All the distractions of his mind therefore disappear and his intellect soon gets firmly established in GOD, the embodiment of Truth, Knowledge and Bliss.

Story regarding belief in God

There was a swami who was learned and highly intellectual. He did not believe in the existence of God. Whatever someone believed in he would try to undermine with devilry formulated arguments. He did not believe in God, yet he was a monk. He used to say that he became a monk to refute and eliminate the order of monks. They are all fake, just showing to be monks. They are a burden on society. He used to say that "I have found out there is nothing genuine in it, and I am going to tell world".

Swami had a friend. He told his friend to go to mountains in summer. They are beautiful and we will enjoy there. Why we need God to enjoy. His friend was born in Himalayas and had resistance for cold. He readily agreed.

While they were moving on mountains they reached to a height of 14000 feet. After 14000 feet swami started feeling breathing problem swami used to teach philosophy every day. So his friend told him not to accept defeat. The friend would say to swami, what a beautiful thing, to go so close to nature.

After they had been walking in the mountains four days, it started snowing. They camped at a height of 15000 feet. They had only a small tent-four foot by five feet. When it had snowed up to two feet, the friend said that it may snow seven to eight feet and our tent may be buried and we will be buried inside the tent.

Swami was worried and expressed desire to go back but it was not possible to go back. Swami asked his friend what we will do now. The friend told 'I will pray God' Swami said, "I believe in facts; I don't believe in the silly things, you are talking of".

The friend said 'I will pray and hope that by the grace of God, the snow will stop. If you want to use your philosophy and intelligence to stop it, you are welcome, just try". Swami said "how will he know if prayers work. Suppose you pray and the snow stops. Even then I will not believe in God because snow might have stopped any way".

The snow was soon four feet deep on all sides of the small tent, and swami started to feel suffocated. The friend knew something was sure to happen either they would die or God will help. Finally Swami was trembling by the fear of death and asked his friend, "Do something. Your God is a great man and I have insulted him many times. Perhaps, that is why I am now being put through this torture and danger.

The friend told him to pray God and snow will stop in a few minutes. If you don't you will die and you will kill me too. God has just whispered this to me". Swami asked "Really, How are you hearing this?" The friend replied, God is speaking to him.

Under pressure of the fear of death, such a man reverses himself and quickly acquires great devotion. Swami started praying with tears in his eyes. Suddenly snow stopped and swami asked his friend, "Will we live". The friend replied, "Yes God wants us to live. Swami replied, "Now I realize that there really must be something which I did not understand".

After we have gone through intellectual gymnastics, we find something beyond the intellect. A stage comes when intellect cannot guide us, and only intuition can show us the way. Intellect examines calculates, decide accepts and rejects all that is happening within the sphere of mind, but intuition is an uninterrupted flow which dawns spontaneously from its source, deep down within. It draws only when mind attains a state of tranquility, equilibrium and equanimity.

That pure intuition expands the human consciousness in a way that one starts seeing things clearly. Life as a whole is comprehended, and ignorance is dispelled. After a series of experiences, direct experience becomes a guide and one starts receiving intuition spontaneously.

It flashes a thought into our mind, the famous saying of a great sage *Tulsidas*, "Without being God fearing, love for God is not possible and without love for God; realization is impossible". The fear of God makes one aware of God consciousness and fear of the world creates fear and thus danger. This atheistic Swami became God fearing when he experienced God- consciousness. Intellectual gymnastics is a mere exercise which creates fears, but love of God liberates one from all fears.

16. MATERIAL AND SPIRITUAL REALITY

Material reality is tangible reality that can be perceived through the senses. Spiritual reality is intangible reality that cannot be perceived through the senses. Material reality is known as *Prakrati* and spiritual reality is referred as *Purusharth*. *Prakrati* means nature and *Purusharth* means human.

Humans are accorded a special place in nature over minerals and animals because only humans have the ability to imagine, observe, reflect and introspect. All these qualities make it possible for humans to rise above physical limitations, transcend the boundaries of nature and discover infinity. Human life is special.

Material and spiritual realities are interdependent. Without material reality spiritual reality cannot be discovered and without spiritual reality material reality has no purpose. This idea of complementary realities is expressed as a human couple. The interdependence of material and spiritual reality is best expressed through the interdependence of women and man. *Prakrati* e.g., material reality is called *Lakshmi* and *Purusha* e.g., spiritual reality is called *Vishnu*. *Vishnu* sustains the world and *Lakshmi* is wealth personified. He cannot perform his role without her and she has no role without him. He gives her purpose and she gives him wherewith all. Thus, *Lakshmi* and *Vishnu* validate each other one cannot exist without the other.

Material reality is represented by red color of blood that sustains life as it flows through the veins; spiritual reality is represented by white the color of bones that uphold life by being still.

What does material growth mean? It means access to all the wonderful things, the material world has to offer to please the five senses; food, clothing, shelter, music, dance, art, entertainment, relationships, peace, pleasure and prosperity. But material things are impermanent, sooner or later; they wither away or cease to pleasure the mind. This causes pain, frustration, anxiety, stress, insecurity and fear; emotions that are most undesirable. Left unchecked, they can evoke in the mind greed and jealous, rage and attachment.

Spiritual growth is the ability to overpower these emotions so that one has the wisdom to appreciate and enjoy all things material without getting needy or clingy. One is happy when the material world favors us and not unhappy when it does not. This can only happen when material growth is accompanied by intellectual growth i.e., spiritual growth. Only spiritual growth can control emotional turmoil caused by dependence on material things.

Human being is blessed to understand both material and spiritual realities. Only the body can sense material reality and only human consciousness can fathom spiritual reality.

The human mind observes that nature is never still. As one moves from place to place turn into deserts, cold icy mountains turn into vast oceans. Even when one sits in a place, one observes nature restless, changing with times. Everything that is born eventually dies.

Maya is an aspect of material reality. But while *Prakrati* is physical *Maya* is mental. Unfortunately *Maya* is not static. It is continuously informed and colored by experiences and expectations. *Maya* recalibrates himself with the changes in experience and expectations. As a result what was right in the past may be wrong in the future. What one person may find beautiful may be ugly for another. This confuses and confounds and leads to conflict between the persons; one wonder what the perfect truth is. One starts questioning reality and wonders what the point of life is. This amplifies fear.

Maya often is taken to mean delusion. A world seen through a measuring scale is a delusion, because it is a perception, dependent on a measuring scale. It is a delusion because it comforts as well as perplexes. Nature treats man no differently from any other living creature, but human being has been given different set of strengths and cunning to survive. Human can imagine, and this gives him the right to domesticate nature and create culture of his own. But human can create this world of his own with the help of *Maya*

Without *Maya*, man would be at the mercy of nature; with *Maya* man is able to dominate nature and establish culture. Maya thus elevates man from being an animal. Life is no longer about survival alone; it is about meaning. The quest for meaning provokes man into action and he creates society.

Maya creates measuring scales and subjective realities. One forgets all about them as soon he experiences material pleasure – home, family, children and village. Then some things happen and they disturb the equilibrium of a happy material life, spreads turmoil through comparison and gossip. This ignites a conflict. Conflict stems from material things and measurable, hence in the realm of *Maya*.

Most people get embroiled in the conflict and pay no attention to them; the few who do think of self surrender to a power that is indifferent to *Maya* i.e. spirituality. This results in peace, realization of self and GOD.

The larger brain, especially the frontal brain, enables humans to imagine. Imagination allows human being to conjure up a better world where we are not at the mercy of the elements. Imagination inspires us. We are driven to realize what we imagine. We inquire about the elements, and the means to control it or improve upon it. We work towards creating to chorologist that will empower us to look beyond survival. In other words, it is the larger brain that compels us to create culture.

Of all living creature only humans can imagine a world where might is not right. Where the tiger and goat live in harmony where the hawk and serpent are friends. From this imagination comes the notion of heaven – the paradise of perfection. Desire to create this paradise of perfection provokes man into creating culture.

Manu does what no other creature can do. He responds to the cry of little fish, collects it in the palm of his hand and puts it in a small pot. In other words, *Manu* interferes with nature. This interference has the roots in empathy. The presence of Manu transforms nature. The little pot in which the fish is kept represents culture, a man made creation, where the little fish is safe from the big fish.

Human property is not just about need. At one extreme, human property is based on compassion - to provide for more and more people, even unrelated people. This compassion stems from empathy, imagination of other people's fear. At the other extreme human property is based on greed- to hoard more and more for one-self, even when there is no immediate need. This greed stems from fear, an imagination of scarcity that is unique to humans.

Animals give up territory only when forced to but humans have the ability to give up property voluntarily. This is made explicit in *Ramayana*, where *Ram* is more than willing to let his brother, *Bharat*, become king of his kingdom, *Ayodhya*, when asked by his father to give up his claim to the throne in favor of his younger brother.

Man creates society as he pursues his imagination of paradise, a place where all creatures are safe. However, in the process he creates a world where some are more, safe than others. Human society invariably favors a few over others; culture is thus always imperfect. This is true; the control of material reality will never be foolproof and satisfactory. To build new cities forests have to be burnt down. As the forest burn, the birds and beasts of the forest try to run away to save themselves. This reeks of cruelty until one realizes that until the forest is burnt, a new city cannot be established. Culture is built on the destruction of a natural ecosystem.

In this process, fish gets bigger and bigger utilizing all the resources. A point comes when the dark clouds gather overhead and it rains relentlessly. The sea begins to swell and swallow the earth. It is *Pralaya*, death of the world.

This is what happens when human society becomes so focused on itself that it loses touch with the rest of nature, when culture expands at the cost of everything else, when the needs of culture override the needs of nature. Eventually something will snap and nature will strike back.

Many a times there is a debate why should we read our scriptures which are thousands of years old. We all think that old things tend to lose their relevance when new things are invented or come in use. So, the question arises why old texts are still revered. What could they possibly tell us that which can be relevant today? No doubt, life has changed so much that now many old values are not practical in today's context.

A society needs periodically to discard its old values and get new, relevant ones. To place this in perspective one needs to understand the concept of *Shruti* and *Smriti*. *Shruti* refers to what is heard. *Shruti* refers to those principles and values that are true for all people at all times. They are not dependent on time or space. They are eternal laws of life. Take for example the Law of gravity. This is an example of an eternal law from science. It will always hold true. It does not depend on who you are or where you are on earth.

Smriti is what is remembered. They are the personal opinions of sages and saints who gave out for the welfare of the people. It is like the prescription of a Doctor for an individual. These opinions of the prophets were no doubt very useful for the people they spoke to. But to assume that they will be relevant to all is asking to believe that a good doctor's prescription will be relevant to all sick persons. *Smriti* contains the opinions and instructions the great men gave to benefit their particular people. This instruction may or may not be relevant to other people at other time or other places.

When *Krishna* tells *Arjuna* to fight or Christ says if someone hits on one cheek, lend him the other, may not be applicable to all in different situations but when *Krishna* says, "The kingdom of heaven is within", this is true for all people for all the times.

Humanity needs "*Sanatan Dharma*", the rest we can check for continued relevance. Some may or may not be relevant any more. But to discard the eternal principles would be like re-inventing the wheel. These principles are very useful to humanity. They function as the manual for life. They help us understand our world and ourselves in it.

Every being in the cosmos has boundaries and limits. Humans are restricted to the earthly realms, Human personality has two aspects – need for stability and our need for growth. The former makes us either insecure or complacent. The latter makes us frustrated and restless. We crave for *Lakshmi* mostly. Sometime we crave for *Saraswati*, with the sole pursuit of obtaining *Lakshmi*; for when *Lakshmi* arrives we ignore *Saraswati*. That we experience these emotions is an indicator that we have not yet realized or experienced spiritual reality.

We in life experience victory, sometimes spiritual victory and sometimes material victory. At any moment of life, things either go our way or the other way. When things go our way, we are happy. In the state of material victory, for we have got what we wanted, often at the expense of others. When things do not go our way, we are unhappy. But unhappiness propels us to introspect on the nature of material things, and question the reason for our emotions. This introspection and questioning reveals to us mysteries of the world; we realize the true nature of the world. It is the state of spiritual victory for we have learnt something vital.

Equanimity is the dominant note of the *Gita* and all religions. The test of God realization lies in the attainment of equanimity in all the three paths of knowledge, Action and Devotion. Cultivation of equanimity has been pointed out as distinguishing mark of those who have realized God through any of the three paths.

He who lacks equanimity cannot be called a realized soul. In the path of knowledge, *Yoga*, action or devotion, it is only he who is possessed of equanimity is eligible for immortality or liberation.

One who looks upon well wishers and neutrals as well as mediators, friends and foes, relatives and objects of hatred, the virtuous and the sinful, with the same; ever stands supreme. One who is alike to friend and foe, as well as honor and ignominy, who remains balanced in heat cold, pleasure and pain and other pairs of opposites and is free from attachments is said to have reached near to God.

In this way he who looks on all with the same eye, who, though entertaining the feelings of 'I' and mine only in name in his dealings with the world is even minded towards all, who sees unity in the whole world; such a man is possessed of equanimity and he alone is an advocate of equality in the real sense of the term.

There is a world of difference between the cult of equanimity preached by spirituality and the doctrine of the so called equality preached by modern socialism. Modern socialism is anti-theistic in its outlook, whereas the cult of equanimity preached by spirituality sees God everywhere and in everything.

One uproots Religion, while the other upholds Religion at every step; one is violent in its conception, while the other establishes the principle of nonviolence; one is based on self-interest, while the other has no room for selfishness. One, though abolishing all distinctions in the matter of intermingling and social intercourse etc., maintains disunion in spirit; while the other, though maintaining due discrimination in the matter of inter dining and social intercourse according to the bounds prescribed the *Shastras*, does not admit any disparity in spirit and exhorts us to perceive the Supreme Spirit as the same in all. The goal of one is man-worship, while that of the other is God-realization. In one there is identification with one's party and disrespect for others; while in the other there is complete absence of pride, and respect for all which comes from a sense of the immanence of God. In one, there is emphasis on external behavior, while in the other it is the spirit which matters; in one it is material happiness which is of primary importance, while in the other it is spiritual happiness that counts; in one there is want of tolerance for others wealth and others views, in the other there is equal respect for all; one is dominated by partiality and prejudice, while the other prescribes conduct which is free from partiality and prejudice.

In material victory *Lakshmi* walks in our direction and in spiritual victory *Saraswati* can walk in our direction. But the point of life is to experience the two states together. *Lakshmi* and *Saraswati* need to arrive simultaneously, not subsequently. Only when both material and spiritual victory come together the gateway to Vaikuntha opens up in our lives.

Indian mythology has well defined the meaning of spiritual and material reality.

Shiva, who emerged from the limitless pillar of fuel-less fire, is therefore visualized sitting under the pole star on a snow capped mountain, in the shade of banyan tree. Through this form, the idea of spiritual reality is communicated.

At every Hindu ritual, "Shanti, Shanti, Shanti" is chanted. Humans yearn to come to terms with the three worlds. Realization of the true nature of Tripura reveals their material nature and the futility of clinging to them. Shiva is Tripurantaka, who reveals this reality and hence destroys Tripura. Shiva chases Triputra and destroys with one arrow and collects the ashes and smeared them across his forehead as three parallel lines. It communicates to the world that the body, the property and this rest of nature, the three worlds created by Brahma, are mortal. When they are destroyed, what remain is Purushartha, the soul

17. DHARMA AND ADHARMA DEVA AND ASURAS

Dharma is the underlying principle that enables man to realize his Divine potential through social behavior. Words like justice, righteousness and goodness do not adequately explain the term *Dharma* because notion of justice, what is right and what is good, change over time and are different in different parts of the world.

To understand the words *Dharma* and *Adharma*, we have to realize the stark divide between humans and the rest of nature. Only humans have the ability to reject the Law of Jungle, both positively and negatively. Positive rejection of the Law of Jungle means that we empathize and include others in our quest for security and growth. This is *Dharma* Negative rejection of the Law of the Jungle means that we exploit others and include all in our quest for security and growth. This is *Adharma*

Dharma manifests as rules that seek to provide for and protect all creatures. This means actions that help the helpless, where the mighty care for the meek. *Adharma* is very opposite; taking advantage of the Law of the jungle for the benefit of a few at the cost of the rest. *Adharma* is about domination, territoriality, hoarding, attachment and power. *Dharma* is about outgrowing these cravings.

This is not easy, it must be remembered. Because human life is validated when there is growth. Animals have no such desire to grow. Growth of human civilization involves the domestication of nature, the uprooting of forests and destruction of ecosystems. This material growth can destroy the world if unchecked. The only way to check it is by tempering it with intellectual growth and emotional growth, which are the two limbs of spiritual growth.

Dharma balance nature and culture between the needs of animals and the needs of humans. As human society creates settlements, forests are turned into fields and animals are domesticated. This gives man extra resources- more food and time. This enables man to move from material pursuits to other pursuits, such as art and philosophy. But to ensure that there is no excessive material exploitation of earth, rules are put in place. Only this would ensure peace and prosperity.

But in material world nothing is permanent. As faith is spiritual reality collapses, fear resurfaces, duty gives way to desire, ambition raises its ugly head, and eventually rules are compromised. Humans refuse to function as per their station in society and stage in life.

Animals are governed by their sexual and violent instincts. Human can overpower these instincts because of their larger brain. Hanuman, though animal, practices celibacy and fights only for the benefit of others and that is why he is transformed and even being beast; he comes to be equated with GOD. *Ravana* has ten heads and twenty hands. He is described as the son of a priest. He is also described as a devotee of *Shiva*. Despite all this knowledge, and all the powers bestowed upon him, he does not display wisdom.

While, the monkeys have transformed themselves into humans, Ravana descends from being human to animal. In fact he is worse than animal, for his actions are not motivated by self delusion and self importance and that is ultimately his downfall.

As the people of Ayodhya find *Sita* women of tainted reputation because she spent several months as *Ravana's* captive,

Rama, the king of *Ayodhya* chooses to be king first, sacrificing personal joy abandoned *Sita*. This draws attention to the limitations of rules and traditions. But while *Rama* abandoned *Sita*, the queen, he does not abandon *Sita*, the wife. He refuses to remarry. Instead he places beside him on his throne the golden effigy of *Sita*, a reminder that none can take her place.

The final chapter of *Ramayana* draws attention to the difference between *Dharma*, *Niti* and *Riti*. *Niti* means Law and *Riti* means tradition. Laws and traditions are created in full earnestness to help the helpless. Sometimes they can end up being unfair and cruel. *Sita*'s abandonment is a case in point. When law and tradition fail to uphold the principle of *Dharma*, they need to be abandoned or changed.

While material reality is bound to transform its transformation is predictable by anticipating the changes and acting accordingly. Thus, over time all organizations and systems, processes and codes lose their relevance. This inevitable and gradual collapse of all systems is expressed in the concept of Yuga. Just as human life has four phases; childhood, youth, maturity and old age, every organization or system goes through four phases; *Sadyug*, *Treta*, *Dwapara* and *Kaliyag*.

In *Bhagwat Gita Krishna* says, "Whenever *Dharma* is threatened, I descend to set things right". The time does not stop. Any *Yuga* does not restore the ideal *Dharma*, because there is no ideal *Dharma*. The *Dharma* is redefined for a particular Yuga. *Dharma* of *Sadyug* is not the *Dharma* of *Treta Yuga*, times are different needs are different, and hence the code of civilization is different. One can look it as a doctor, who appears whenever there is a disease. He restores health but does not stop aging. Eventually a patient will die. The doctor's duty is to help the patient live a full and healthy life.

So there is a vast difference between *Ram* and *Krishna*. Though they are both *Avatars* but since one belongs to *Treta* and the other belongs to *Dwapara* they have to be different. While *Ram* is called

Maryada Parushottam, he who upholds rules of society at any cost, and *Krishna* is called *Leela Purushottam*, he who enjoys the game of life. Unlike *Rama*, who is serious and serene and evokes respect, *Krishna* is adorable and evokes affection.

Ram was in *Treta* and *Krishna's* stories are of *Dwapara Yuga*. *Krishna* world is thus closer to the world we live in. It shares the lazy morality and ethics we encounter today. In this world, the concept of *Dharma* becomes even more difficult to express and institute.

What seems a good thing in *Ram's Yuga* becomes a bad thing in *Krishna Yuga*? Ram's unquestioning obedience of his father transforms him into GOD. While, in *Dwapara Yuga Yayati*, an ancestor of *Krishna* is cursed by his further in law to become old and impatient when he is discovered having a mistress. Yayati begs his sons to suffer the curse on his behalf so that he can retain his youth. *Yadu*, the eldest son, refuses to do so because he feels his father should respect the march of time. *Puru*, the youngest son, however, agrees to accept his father's old age. *Yayati* was so happy that he declared that the younger *Puru* will be his heir and not the elder *Yadu*.

Later on, history tells that *Puru's* unquestioning obedience results in collapse of society. The difference is while, *Dashratha* requests *Ram's* obedience so that he can uphold his word, while, *Yayati* however, demands the obedience of his children for his own pleasure. Yayati exploits the rule for his own benefit whereas *Dashratha* enforces the rule so that royal integrity is never questioned. The rule obey the father resonates *Dharma* in *Dashratha's* case but not so in *Yayati's*.

Yayati's conduct results in a society where the letter of the Law becomes more important than the spirit of Law. This is world of *Krishna* a world where that matters more than the deed is; the thought behind the deed.

We are all combination of what we are born with as well as what we are raised to be. Our natural disposition is known as

Varna (Jati) while, the cultural indoctrination is known by our work. Our behavior towards others is based on what we see and how we process our observation. But not all things can be seen. Culturally we can be seen but not Varna, the originality. One can see behavior but has no access to beliefs. A man can dress as cow herd (*Krishna*) and talk like a cow herd, but he may at heart be a prince. We will never know unless we open our eyes to this possibility.

Krishna BAL Leelas of Makhan Chori & *Vastra-Haran* depict that he wanted a free flow out of love. It depicts hearts resist and tongues complain, "Don't steal our butter; don't steal our clothes". The reason being no one wants to be free with love. No one wants to expose the vulnerable heart. Love does not flow like butter unless there is an open invitation to heart without any Pot (conditions) and Clothes (ego).

When the heart is opened up, when love flows into it and from it a sense of security prevails. With security comes freedom. There is no need to pretend. We can be ourselves. There is no desire to force our wills on anyone. We accept and embrace everyone. We include people; we allow them to be themselves, because we are accepted and embraced by GOD.

Krishna acknowledges the violence that is implicit in human survival. More than the act of violence, what matters is the thought behind the violence? The violence for creating fear in other's mind is *Adharma* but violence in self defense rooted in the human need to survive and thrive, not wanted to hurt or exploit anyone; this violence is therefore '*Dharma*'.

The Killing of *Kansa* is unique, because it is the only story in Hindu mythology where a father figure is killed. This tale makes a shift in thinking where the younger generation refuses to suffer the tyranny of the older generation. This makes *Krishna* a radical hero in Hindu spiritual landscape.

Krishna encourages the Pandavas to declare war on the Kauravas. This war is not for property. This war is about *Dharma* and *Adharma* is about outgrowing the animal instinct of territoriality and discovering the human ability to share and care. Likewise the MAHA-RAAS is not about sex. MAHA-RAAS is the absence of desire for any physical conquest; it is about perfect love and absolute security that allows married women to dance and sing all night in the forest with Divine. Before the start of war it is clear to Pandavas that war is not about property or vengeance. It is about restoring *Dharma* and *Dharma* is about sharing; about giving, not taking. It is about realizing spiritual reality through material reality.

It is the Divine wisdom which realizes that there is more to life than material reality that is perceived through the senses. It is wisdom that liberates us from the limitations of nature. It enables man to break free from *Prakrati* and realize *Purushartha*. *Prakrati* makes us mortal and restless, *Purushartha* makes us immortal and serene.

The notion of property is not an objective reality, but a subjective truth, a cultural construction of human beings, not a natural phenomenon. If man does not exist, there would be no property to possess. Nature does not need man, man needs nature. It is delusion of man that it is the master of nature, and the owner of nature's wealth and information.

When we are self-aggrandize ourselves by being territorial and dominating other human beings, wisdom reminds us that we are still animals, displaying animal instincts of survival, and that we have not evolved despite a larger human brain. This wisdom is that which enables man to break free from the animal and discover the human. To break free from fear and discover faith, we have to surrender to the idea of spiritual reality to *Purushartha*, that which exists beyond *Prakrati*.

We all crave for material security. Even when we get it we become insecure. In security one transforms into complacency and cynicism as one finds our self bereft of any purpose. It becomes the sole purpose of existence. When we grow materially we become arrogant and feel invulnerable, until circumstances turn against us. In misery we thrash trying to get rid. No one comes to our rescue. We become restless and anxious. Liberation from this state will come only when we surrender to the wisdom, revealed through spiritual reality.

18. FEAR -EGO AND MAYA

Fear is well defined as false evidence appearing right

The greatest fear of all living creatures is death. Nobody wants to die. Everyone wants to survive. To survive, we need food but to get food we have to kill. The act of killing and the act of feeding are thus two sides of the same coin. Death ends up sustaining life. This is the truth of nature.

Fear of death leads to two kinds of fears as it transforms all living creatures either into predator or prey. The fear of scarcity haunts the predator as it hunts for food; the fear of predation haunts the prey as it avoids being hunted. Nature has no favorites. Both the lion and the deer have to run in order to survive. The lion runs to catch its prey and the deer runs to escape its predator. The deer may be prey to the lion, but it is predator to the grass. Thus, no one in nature is a mere victim.

Fear of death establishes the law of Jungle that might is right. Fear of death is what makes animals establish pecking orders and territories. Fear of death- makes animals respect and wish for strength and cunning for only then they can survive.

Such behavior based on fear is appropriate for beasts or *Pashu*, but not humans. Humans have imagination and hence are capable to break free from animal instincts. Humans need not be territorial or dominating in order to survive. Humans need not form packs or herds in order to survive. Humans can break free from the fear of death; shatter the mental modifications emerging from time. Humans need not be predator or prey, victim or victimizer.

Since, humans have the ability to imagine, humans stand apart from the rest of nature. On one side stands nature, the web of life, the chain of eaters and eaten. On the other stands the human being who can imagine a world where the laws of jungle can be disregarded, overpowered or outgrown. Humans therefore, experience two realities; the objective reality of nature and the subjective reality of their imagination. The former is *Prakrati*; the latter is *Purushartha*.

Prakrati is by nature has no favorites. *Purusharatha* is humanity that invariably favors a few over the rest. Nature creates and destroys life without prejudice. Human imagination is the seat of prejudice. It has two choices; to imagine a world without fear or to imagine a world with amplified fears. When the *Purusha* outgrows fear and experiences bliss, it is *Shiva*, the destroyer of fear. When *Purusha* amplifies fear and gets trapped in delusions, it is Brahma, the creator of fear.

One becomes immortal when outgrows the fear of death. Faith is not rational just as immortality is not natural. Immortality is an idea that appears in the human imagination in response to the fear of death. When one liberates oneself from the fear of death using faith, one becomes indifferent to death. Death then no longer controls us or frightens us. We are liberated. We achieve immortality.

Those are ignorant who derive identity from the temporary flesh (Body) the wise look beyond at the permanent soul. Flesh (Body) is tangible but the soul is not. Flesh (Body) is fact but soul demands faith. Atma follows no laws of nature – it has no form, it cannot be measured, it cannot be experienced using any of the five senses. It is a self assured entity that does not seek acknowledgment or evidence. One has to believe it. There is no other way to access it.

Brahma (*Prakrati*) has no faith. He refuses to look beyond the flesh (Body). He ignores Atma and so catalyses the creation of *Aham*, the ego. The ego is the product of imagination. It is how a human being sees himself or herself. It makes humans demand special status in nature and culture. Nature does not care for this self image of human beings. Culture, which is a man made creation attempts to accommodate.

Birth is not a choice and survival is a struggle, a violent struggle, plagued by fears of scarcity and predation. This is true for plants, animals and humans. But only humans can reflect on these fears and resent it and seek liberation from it.

Imagination makes human being think of scarcity in the midst of abundance, war in times of peace. Though he can rein in his fear, he ends up exaggerating fear. He assumes he has no choice in the matter. Unless he has faith he is not able to discover Atma, and finds himself alone and helpless before nature, a victim.

Human's expectation of *Prakrati* is imaginary. Nature has no favorites. All creatures are equal for nature. But as human can image, he imagines himself to be special and so expects to be treated differently by nature. This is because of the ego.

Yoga is a set of practice that stills the restless mind. The word *Yoga* comes from the root *Yuj*, meaning to align. Fear destroys the alignment of the mind; rather than accept the reality of nature, the mind seeks to change and control it. These attempts invariably fail; creating frustration, fear and confusion that blinds one to spiritual reality. *Yoga* restores mental alignment so that nature is seen for what it is.

Prakrati is nature. Human creates culture. *Prakrati* creates man. Man creates culture. *Prakrati* is objective reality. Culture is subjectively reality. Atma witnesses *Prakrati*, Aham constructs culture. Every human being has his own cerebrum, hence is subject to his own imagination of his self and the world around him, which is why every human being imagines himself to be special. Every human being is thus creator of his own fate. *Prakrati* and fate is unique to each human being.

Every human being compares his own reality with nature and finds nature inadequate. This dissatisfaction provides an opportunity to outgrow dependence on nature, hence fear. But instead of looking inwards, one looks outwards. Rather than taking control of nature. He proceeds to domesticate the world around him. Every person creates culture for his own pleasure or *Bhoga*, indifferent to the impact it has on others. The self indulgent act is described as pursuing one's own daughter. This is also called the pursuit of *Aham* over *Atma*, *Bhog* over *Yoga*.

Animals have territory but humans create property. Territory is held onto by brute force and cunning; it cannot be inherited; it enables animals to survive. Property on the other hand is created by manmade rules; take away the rules and there is no property. Rules also govern relationships in culture, creating families to whom property can be bequeathed. Neither wealth nor family a natural phenomenon, both are cultural construction, hence need to be codified and enforced through courts. A human being can die but his property and his family can outlive him.

There are three words known to the universe. Me, mine and what is not mine. The 'Me' is made up of the mind and body. 'Mine' is made up of property, knowledge, family and status. 'Not Mine' is made up of all other things that exist in the world over which one has no authority. Ever animals have 'me' but only humans have 'mine' and 'not mine'. Human self image is thus expanded beyond the body and includes possessions.

Humans identify themselves with other things besides their body; hence get hurt when those things get attacked. A man derives his self – worth-from his looks and his car. When his looks go or his car is damaged, his tranquility is lost. Tranquility is also lost when he yearns for things that are not his, things that belong to others. Anxiety and restlessness thus have roots in the notion of 'mine' and 'not mine', which depends on imagination for their survival.

Hence, 'Me', 'Mine' and 'Not mine', the three words i.e., body, the property and the rest of nature created by nature are mortal created by nature. When they are destroyed, what remains is the soul. As a matter of fact nothing needs to be done actively to destroy the three worlds. Eventually, inevitably, the body will die, the property will go and the divide between mine and not mine will collapse as *Prakriti* stakes her claim.

Ego is like dogs, which are attached to their masters; wagging their tail when they get approval and attention, and whining when they do not. Like the dog Aham blooms when praised and given attention and it whither when ignored. Ego or *Ahamkara* has no independent existence of its own but is contracted by human himself in attempts to outgrow fear. It ends up amplifying fear.

Dogs also remind us of the notion of territory. Dogs spray urine to mark their territory; even when they are domesticated and provided for, they mark territory indicating their lack of faith. They bark and bite to defend their territory. They fight over bones with other dogs. While dogs do it for their survival but humans behave similarly as they fight over their property and defend their rights. Humans seek the survival not of their bodies, as in the case of animals, but for their self-image, which a combination of body and property. Property includes not just wealth, but also family and status. Like dogs we cling to me and mine and are wary of what is not mine. We call this love, but it is in fact attachment as they give us identity and meaning.

One cannot seek freedom from fear by trying to control *Prakrati* rather than by seeking *Purushartha*. Wisdom, if divorced from the world is meaningless. If wisdom does not enable the liberation of those who are trapped in fear, has no meaning at all. In Indian philosophy, a thing exists when it is seen and a creative is alive when it sees.

When we genuinely look at others, we discover how the others react to us. If people around us behave like deer, it means we are behaving like lions, if people around us behave like lions, it means they see us as deer. If people around us behave like dogs, friendly or hostile, it means we matter to them.

Spirituality requires human to look at humans as humans. This will not happen as long as fear governs the relationship. True sacrifice is the sacrifice of one's animal nature and the realization of one's human nature; only then fear gives way to tranquility.

In life all circumstances are determined by *Karma*. Every event in our life is determined by past actions. So every moment is as it is supposed to be. But it is possible to change one's fate and fortunes. The dance of *Prakrati* can change if *Purushartha* intervenes. For that one has to invoke *Purushartha* through acts of determination that demonstrate desire and devotion.

The relationship between husband and wife should not be based on power. There is no conqueror and there is no conquest. Each one allows other to dominate neither seeks to dominate the other. This is love.

In nature, animals have sex in the mating season to procreate. It is an instinct that ensures survival, governed by hormones and an internal clock. It is not a choice and it is not accompanied by organism. Only in humans sex is a choice and pleasure seeking activity that need not culminate in procreation. One, whose mind is pure, untouched by demands of society and is in a state of eternal bliss and so does not seek pleasure seeking activities. He needs nothing and wants nothing. He is therefore autonomous, independent of nature.

Humans are the only creatures on earth, which can reflect on life. Humans wonder what the purpose of life is. Why do we live, why do we eat? Nature offers no answer. Humans are able to domesticate the earth, establish fields and orchards and gardens and grow abundant food. Surrounded by great wealth only humans wonder why they have such power over nature. Humans can build great walls and establish rules and make themselves secure. But the heaviest of security does not take away death. Human's feel invalidated, weak and helpless, and wonder what the point of human life is. When no answer is forthcoming, a frightened man starts hoarding things, not just to secure his future, but to create a delusion of immortality. Our wealth and family, our possession become an extension of our bodies. It is the fourth body – property that outlives the death of the other three. We hoard more and more property and thereby give ourselves meaning.

Humans desire life, fear death and construct three worlds because humans fear death more than any other living creature on earth. Our fear is greater because we can imagine. We imagine what happens after death, we imagine a world without death; we imagine a world without us and wonder what the point of life is. Unable to make a sense of things, we try to control life-we get attached to things, we resist change and we create property. Human civilization is thus rooted in fear. It is delusion or culture or *Maya*.

The first people who brought the word '*Maya*' into English were 18th century scholars who lived when Europe was in the throes of the scientific revolution. They used the word 'illusion' to translate the word '*Maya*'. For Hindus '*Maya*' is a constructed reality. More accurately *Maya* is the measuring scale that values and de values all things in *Prakriti* and by doing so gives rise to extreme pleasure, an individual's perception of the world. It is neither a bad thing nor it a good thing. It is just the way the human mind perceives reality. Animals do not live in *Maya*, because they do not possess imagination. Human beings do. Humans are therefore subject to *Maya*.

Although nature's truth is timeless, we forget it. We forget that what goes around comes around. As we suffer the winter cold, we forget that the previous year it was cold too but it did pass. As we suffer, we imagine the suffering will never end. We humans, forget what our mind was before it was contaminated by imagined amplified fear. We forget that only we can destroy this perception created, with its three constituent worlds of 'me', 'mine' and 'not mine', because we have the wisdom.

When two people meet, initially fear governs the relationship. This fear goes away when each one is convinced the other is no threat. This fear is amplified when one dominates the other. There is a way by which this fear can be outgrown. This is possible when one empathizes with the other, when there is love for the other, when one recognizes the autonomy of the other and neither seeks to dominate or be dominated or dependent in any way. But to empathize with the other, we have to look at the other, not in fear, but with genuine affection and sensitivity.

Human being has the option to spend their lives ignoring the reality of life, like monkeys spellbound by the rattle-drum. We can focus on meaningless activities that keep us busy, help us pass the time and prevent us from getting bored or distract us from introspecting and reflecting on life. The other option is to introspect and reflect on life. We can ask ourselves what shapes our decisions and where does our self image come from.

Why are we in certain situations like the petrified deer and in other situations like the dominant lion? We will realize that notions such as victim and villain and hero are all imaginary construction, stories within our head and stories that we receive from society. In other words they are *Maya*, constructions to fortify ourselves from fear, subjective realities that make us feel powerful.

Maya gives us meaning to survive this world until our consciousness gives us strength to outgrow fear and hence outgrow dependence on constructed reality that heroes, villains and victims are creation of fear. When fear is destroyed, there is no hero or villain or victim. This is liberation. This is *Moksha*.

19. MUKTI -LIBERATION

Quote by Maharshi Raman

"No one can be enlightened by anyone else- but sages inspire and give inner strength without which self enlightenment is impossible. Great sages are the source of inspiration and enlightenment"

Quote by SadGuru Rameshji

"Liberation is your nature. Bondage is your creation"

The concept of *Mukti-Liberation* or *Moksha* is commonly understood as to getting rid of all the 'miseries of the world'. We hear stories about *Swarg* and *Nark*. It is manifested that there are all kinds of pleasures and happiness in *Swarg* and all kinds of pains and miseries in *Nark*. We are also told that if we will remain in goodness, we will go to *Swarg* and if we act in the influence of senses to satisfy our senses only we will go to *Nark*. It is also told that to get rid of this re-birth we should seek for *Mukti-Moksha* or liberation.

As a matter of fact we have been listening this since ages and as such we have developed a belief in that. Actually, no one knows what is going to happen after death. Nobody has seen *Swarg* or *Nark*. Nobody has ever seen any life better than a human life.

We have born as a human being. We, no doubt listen lot of things but we do not know any specie better than 'Human being'. We instead of enjoying human life aspire for *Mukti* or liberations in the hope of getting something better. So, we are in the quest of *Mukti-Liberation*, running after expectation and leaving the present.

Liberation is an inner experience and expression of a state. It is beyond words, hence, inexplicable. Only subtle indication could be given about the state but most of the time it is not understood in its true sense. Various mental conditionings and impressions are the main cause for one's belief and bondage. Bondage as such is nothing. It is only due to ignorance of one's true state that one feels he is in bondage.

Bondage is nothing but a firm and constant thought in the mind and thereby need to get liberated. But if one allows himself to think that he is ever liberate, only under ignorance he was assuming himself to be in bondage, then he is liberated, he becomes free.

Bondage and liberation, both are mere thoughts in the mind and they have no existence as such. Contemplate and fix your mind on your consciousness and remain in an equilibrium state of mind without bondage or liberation thoughts. Finally, it is you alone who has to walk (contemplate) and reach the destination.

Liberation from ignorance is real liberation i.e., ignorance of being other than the self. One cannot be liberated by just following any rituals, doing virtuous deeds, loudly praying, crying emotionally or by bathing in Ganges or other sacred rivers.

As self, you are ever liberated. It is your nature. As self, even if it wants to get into bondage which you think you are in, is only your creation, created by the mind through various thoughts. Know this truth and enjoy your liberation.

As bondage is only an illusion and creation of the mind, there cannot be a better path than just removing the illusion and ignorance of the mind, which is possible thought the knowledge of self and realizing that you are the self (ever liberate) and not the ignorant human being.

Most of the people follow religious practices with the hope of liberation *Moksha* after death but they are under ignorance. How can the liberation take place after death when the bondage is while being alive? After death body has no meaning and the soul is already liberated from all the bondage. Liberation can take place only while being alive not after death. If you are in bondage while being alive then you have to liberate only while being alive.

Mind has doubts about liberation .What is liberation? Why liberation? What is experience of liberation? Etc. First step towards liberation is to still the mind through meditation. Liberation is purely an inner feeling. Liberation does not call for any physical effort and painful exercise. This ignorance can be removed only through right knowledge. As the knowledge of self increases; ignorance starts subsiding.

Liberation can be gained through contemplation on self. The more one is able to contemplate, the faster he will realize and establish in the self. To contemplate, one need not run away from the worldly duties. While performing normal duties one must be able to contemplate on self. One can liberate from the limitation and suffering of body through death. But death will not liberate from ignorance. Ignorance can be killed only through knowledge. Kill ignorance through the power of self.

Suicide is also an attempt to get rid of present miseries in the hope of some better life. The recent epidemic of reported suicides is cause of concern. "The myth of Sisyphus" talks about the absurdity, we all face – the feeling that life is meaningless.

Sisyphus was an evil king of ancient Greece, condemned by the GOD of death. Even as Sisyphus escapes death by sheer treachery, he is mortified by the GODs to the unrealizable task of rolling a huge boulder over to the top of a hill. The moment he reaches the top, he watches as it tumbles back to the bottom. He is cursed to repeat this cycle for eternity. So in popular parlance, the word 'Sisyphean' epitomizes any infinite and burdensome action that yields futile results.

But could this also have another, not so-negative connotation, the analogy of Sisyphus to the misery that man undergoes with 'absurdity'. At some point, people seek answers to the 'ideal' in this world, only to be confronted with unpleasantness and chaos everywhere. One gets the feeling that life is meaningless. In fact this is absurdity.

There are three philosophical responses emerging to this state of hopelessness – firstly an act of reposing faith in GOD or destiny, secondly suicide and lastly an act of defiance in continuing to live, despite understanding the futility of existence.

About the faith in GOD, if you become subjective, you will find it as an attempt to gloss over it as an illusion. Suicide is an escape route, without obtaining answers to the meaning of the 'ideal' in life, which one was craving all along. Now there is a third option, a life of subjugation to the misery of circumstance, with an attitude of acceptance.

We have to think can meaninglessness be justified? Embarking on futile labor, one is fully aware and conscious of his fate and that he cannot escape it, but he can endure it. With the, absurd there is no hope or faith. But by embracing hopelessness one is aware of the limitations in life. So, one is required not to contemplate suicide as an option; on the contrary, he should discerningly revolt against his fate. In doing so, one will gain inner strength and moral courage to rebel. One by his rebellion becomes free from the anxieties of life and chooses a life that is without appeal.

At this stage one is indifferent to the future and cherishes the present to the fullest, even if it is deplorable continuing a life in misery with a profound understanding of it, is more momentous than suicide, which serves no purpose. The situation is rather gloomy, yet one is thoughtlessly immersed in his task and thinks neither of hope nor of gloom. He is fully aware of the absurd, and is master of his fate.

By doing so one sees a small measure of gratification and also triumphs in tragedy. One will relish his surmounting response of resilience to a hostile environment and demonstrating that buoyancy in crisis as an admirable quality. It will be read with a positive connotation.

There is always a dialogue going on between religion and science. Both are crucial component of humanity's future. There are three different domains. A scientific one would cover the empirical descriptions of the outer world of matter and the inner world of the mind. A philosophical one would cover the efforts to ascertain the nature of ultimate reality and a religious one, which would refer to the practices of the tradition.

The interaction between science and religion in the Christian west has often been characterized by a measure of hostility, because their religion is based on revealed dogmatic truth and science on reason and experimentation. This however, need not necessarily apply as in the case of science and spirituality as in this case, one witnesses a broad methodological convergence. The reason is that while the ultimate goal of religious life in Christianity can only be achieved after death, the fruit of religious life in Buddhism can be experienced in this very life. Thus, the conclusions of Buddhism become as falsifiable and verifiable as those of science.

The enlightened view of reason treated the rational as representing the antithesis of the irrational so that this binary grid of the rational and the irrational has become the dominant modernity. Life, however, may be said to consist not just of the rational and irrational but also of the non-rational.

This category would cover such aspects of life as relate to our emotional attachment of our near and dear ones to the appreciation of the world of art, music and literature and humanity's urge for transcendence.

There is also a subtle issue involved science per se is not interested in human well-being but rather in the search for truth. Any benefit accrued is a foreseeable effect of science but not it's intended one whereas the intended goal of spirituality is to save humanity from sufferings. Hence, science, in view of its neutrality in terms of value, may be harnessed for either good or evil. By contrast, the sole goal of spirituality is the alleviation of human suffering which means that even its truths are meant to ensure human well-being and therefore are a means to an end and not an end in them.

In science, in strict sense, truth alone is the end. Science can explain the how of things but not their why whereas the reason of spirituality is the why of suffering.

Many a time people feel depressed and they seek for *Mukti-Liberation*. Depression is a prevalent psychological disorder that affects people of all age groups, across the world. The depressed individual feels low and sad most of the time and nothing seems to lift his mood. There are feelings of hopelessness, helplessness and worthlessness and the person has a strong belief that there will be no change in his inner state. Globally around 300 million individuals experience depression. While in India, there are more than 50 million people suffering from this debilitating condition.

The standard treatment for this condition recommended by medical science is a combination of medication, physic therapy and brain stimulation techniques. But in many cases depression becomes a chronic life long illness. When a person is suffering from depression & sadness is in the foreground of consciousness. But if we examine depressive feelings deeply at the root, there is hatred and anger.

These feelings come up because one feels disappointed with oneself, with significant others or with the world in general. As these feelings are difficult to deal with, they are often suppressed. But repressed emotions are not pacified and somehow, they find a way to direct their fury at the person and he becomes depressed.

One needs to have faith in the capacity to heal oneself. Now a day's people have become so dependent on mental health-professionals that they have forgotten the power within. *Zarathustra* revealed that powers of the Divine are latent in each one of us and we need to nurture them. When we have an intense aspiration and make a dedicated effort, the powers of hope, truth, good mind, the courage to destroy falsehood, love and devotion become manifest. These abilities help us overcome all deficiencies, disease and dysfunctions so that we become perfect and normal.

Hence, one should not lose hope; call upon the greatest force that can heal depression, which is love. Hatred and anger are overcome with love and when we learn to love deeply, depression terminates.

Just a mother would protect her only child at the risk of her own life; even so, let him cultivate a boundless heart towards all beings. Let thoughts of boundless love pervade the whole world, above, below and across, without any obstruction, without any hatred, without any enmity.

We need to forgive our own self, other people the whole universe and develop a deep encompassing love. It is important to acknowledge that no one, including ourselves is inherently bad; people behave harshly because they have been traumatized. Pain makes people turn selfish, cold and unforgiving to protect themselves. Rather than dwelling on their dark side, we must focus on the potential light and goodness within them.

This has a threefold benefit. Firstly we feel hopeful and peaceful. Secondly a change in our attitude encourages others to bring a change in themselves. Thirdly, as we send subtle positive vibrations and formations to others, these have a deep impact on their consciousness. In the long run, as we learn to love ourselves and love others deeply, they too reciprocate with similar positivity.

Then our being rejoices in boundless love. If any depressive thought or feeling comes up, we at once realize its falsehood and turn towards the truth. As a result the depressive movement ceases.

20. WHAT WE BELIEVE IN-SUPER CONSCIOUSNESS

We believe that every being is divine, is God. Every soul is a sun covered over with clouds of ignorance, the difference between soul and soul is owing to the difference in density of these layers of cloud of ignorance. We believe that this is the conscious or unconscious basis of all religions, and that this is the explanation of the whole history of human progress either in the material, intellectual or spiritual plane – the same spirit is manifested through different planes.

We believe that this is the very essence of the *Vedas*. We believe that it is the duty of every soul to treat, think of and behave to all souls as such i.e. as Gods and not hate or despise or verify or try to injure them by any manner or means. This is the duty act not only of the *Sanyansi*, but of all men and women.

We believe that no where throughout the *Vedas*, *Darshans* or *Puranas* or *Tantras*, it is ever said that the soul has any sex, creed or caste. Education is the manifestation of the perfection already in man. Religion is the manifestation of the Divinity already in man. Therefore, the only duty of the teacher in both cases is to remove all obstacles from the way. The Lord does the rest.

The Hindu theory is that religions do not come from without, but from within. The religious thought is in man's very constitution, so much so that it is impossible for him to give up religion until he can give up his mind and body, until he can stop thought and life. This, in fact is at the bottom of the whole universe – this rising from and this setting into the beyond, this whole universe coming up out of the unknown and going back again into the unknown, crawling in has child out of darkness and crawling out again as an old man into darkness.

So everything we have – our society, our relations with each other, our religion and what we call ethics. There are attempts at producing a system of ethics from mere grounds of utility. There cannot be any such rational system of ethics which don't say "Do well to others", as it is the highest utility. Suppose a man says, "I do not care for utility. I want to cut throats of others and make myself rich". What will you answer? But where is the utility of my doing good to the world? Am I a fool to work my life out that others may be happy? Why shall I myself not be happy, if there is no other sentiency beyond society, no other power in the universe beyond the five senses? What prevents me from cutting the throats of my brothers so long as I can make myself safe from the police and make myself happy? What will you answer? You are bound to show some utility. When you are pushed from your ground you answer, "My friend it is good to be good". What is the power in the human mind which says, "It is good to be good" which unfolds before us in glorious view the grandeur of the soul, the beauty of goodness, the all attractive power of the goodness, the infinite power of goodness. That is what we call God.

Thousands of means have been created everyday to conduce to the happiness of the world. But still the happiness in the world today is not more than what it was a century ago. Each wave that rises in the ocean is at the expense of a hollow somewhere. It is unreasonable to state that we can have happiness without misery. With the increase of all these means, we are increasing the wants and increased wants means insatiable thirst, which is never quenched.

It is very nature of life to be happy and miserable by turns. Then again is this world left to you to do well to it? This world is neither good nor evil. It is the Lord's world. It is beyond both good and evil, perfect in itself. His will is going on, showing all these different pictures; and it will go on without beginning and without end.

The world is the world, and it will be always so. If we open ourselves to it in such a manner that the action of the world is beneficial to us, we call it good. If we put ourselves in the position in which it is painful, we call it evil. So you will always find children who are innocent and joyful and do not want to injure anyone are very optimistic. They are dreaming golden dreams.

Old men who have all the desires in their hearts and not the means to fulfill them are very pessimistic. Religion wants to know the truth. And the first thing it has discovered is that without knowledge of this truth there will be no life worth living. Life will be a desert; human life will be vain if we cannot know the beyond. It is very good to say; be contended with the things of the present moment. The cows and dogs are, so are all animals and that is what makes them animals. So if man remains content with the present and give up all searches into beyond; mankind will have to go back to the animal plane again.

Throughout the world, wherever there has been a religion, and wherever will be religion, they have all spring and will all spring out of one source called 'Inspiration'. Inspiration is the only source of religious knowledge. We have seen that religion essentially belongs to the plane beyond the senses. It is where the eyes cannot go, or the ears cannot hear, where the mind cannot reach or what words cannot express. That is the field and goal of religion and from this comes that which we call 'Inspiration'. It is perfectly true that our reason cannot go beyond the senses.

I move my hand, and I feel and I know that I am moving my hand. I call it consciousness. I am conscious that I am moving my hand. But my heart is moving. I am not conscious of that; and yet who is moving the heart? It must be the same being. So we see that this being that moves the hand and speaks, that is to say, acts consciously, also acts unconsciously. We find, therefore, that this being can act upon two planes - one, the plane of consciousness, and the other, the plane below that. The impulsions from the plane of unconsciousness are what we call instinct, and when the same impulsions come from the plane of consciousness, we call it reason. But there is a still higher plane, super consciousness in man. This is apparently the same as unconsciousness, because it is beyond the plane of consciousness, but it is above consciousness and not below it .It is not instinct, it is inspiration there is proof of it. Socrates, while marching with the army saw beautiful sunrise, and that set in motion in his mind a train of thought: he stood there for two days in the sun in quite unconscious. It was such moment that gave the Socratic knowledge of the world. So with all the great preachers and prophets, there are moments in their lives when they, as it were, rise from the conscious and go above it. And when they come back to the plane of consciousness, they come radiant with light; they have brought news from the beyond, and they are inspired seers of the world.

But there is a great danger. Any man may say he is inspired; many times they say that. Where is the test? Sometimes fraudulent people try to impose themselves upon mankind. In these days it is becoming all too prevalent. A friend of mine had very fine picture. Another gentleman who was rather religiously inclined, and a rich man, had his eyes upon this picture; but my friend would not sell it. This other gentleman one day comes and says to my friend I have an inspiration I have a message from God. "What is your message?" my friend asked. "The message is that you must deliver that picture to me." My friend was up to his mark; he immediately added, "Exactly so; how beautiful! I had exactly the same inspiration that I should have to deliver to you the picture. Have you brought your cheque?" Cheque? What cheque? "Then", said my friend, "I don't think your inspiration was right. My inspiration was that I must give the picture to the man who brought a cheque for $100,000. You must bring the cheque first." The other man found he was caught, and gave up the inspiration theory. There are the dangers.

These are the two dangers always in this world- the danger from frauds, and the danger from fools. But that need not deter us, for all great things in this world are fraught with danger.

We find that this inspiration is the only source of religion; yet it has always been fraud with many dangers; and the last and worst of all dangers is excessive claims. If there is anything in the Universe, it must be Universal; there is not one movement hear that is not Universal, because the whole universe is governed by laws. It is systematic and harmonious all through. Therefore what is anywhere must be everywhere is atom in the universe is built on the same plan has the biggest sun and the stars. If one man was ever inspired it is possible for each and every one of us to be inspired, and that is religion.

In true religion there is no faith or belief in the sense of blind faith. No great preacher ever preached that. That only comes with degeneracy. Fools pretend to be followers of this or that spiritual giant, and although they may be without power, endeavor to teach humanity to believe blindly. Believe what? To believe blindly is to degenerate the human soul. Be an atheist if you want, but do not believe in anything unquestioningly. Why degrade the soul to the level of animals? You not only hurt yourself thereby, but you injure society and make danger for those that come after you. Stand up and reason out, having no blind faith. Religion is a question of being and becoming, not of believing. This is religion and when you have attained to that you have religion. Before that you are no better than animals. "Do not believe in what you have heard." says the great Buddha, "do not believe in doctrines because they have been handed down to you through generations; do not believe in anything because it is followed blindly by many; do not believe because some old sage makes a statement; do not believe in truths to which you have become attached by habit; do not believe merely on the authority of your teachers and elders. Have deliberation and analyze, and when the result agrees with reason and conduces to the good of one and all, accept it and live up to it."

21. THE GREAT ANCIENT EPICS RAMAYANA MAHABHARAT GITA

Ramayana – "The Life of Rama"

The sacred books of Hindus are written in a sort of meter but this book *Ramayana* is held by common consent in India as the very beginning of poetry. The name of the poet or sage was *Valmiki*.

There was a young man quite strong and vigorous, who could not in any way support his family and finally engaged himself in highway robbery. He used to attack persons in the street and robbed them to support his father, mother, wife and children. One day a great saint Narada was passing by and the robber attacked him. The saint asked the robber why you are doing this sin. The robber said to support my family. Saint asked, "Do you think that they take a share of your sin also. When robber asked his father, mother and his wife this question they all replied that you are my son or husband and it is your duty to support us but we can't share your sin.

The robbers' eyes were opened and he asked the saint, what I can do; the sage said, "Give up your present course of life. You see that none of your family really loves you, so give up all these delusions. They will share your property; but the moment you have nothing, they will desert you. There is none who will share in your evil but they will share in your good". This man left everything and went on praying and meditation until he forgot himself. He later was named *Valmiki* and became poet.

Valmiki, wrote the *Ramayana*. He described the whole life of *Rama* in it. I am not going in detail of the story of it, as it is known to everybody.

I will however, like to narrate some great incidents of *Ramayana* underlying the great principles of life.

When *Hanuman* reached to *Sita* and established his identity informed *Sita* that as soon as Rama would know her whereabouts, he would come with an army and conquer the giant and recover her. However, he suggested to *Sita* that if she wished it, he would take her on his shoulders and could with one leap clear the ocean and get back to *Rama*. But *Sita* could not bear the idea, as she was chastity itself, and could not touch the body of any man except her husband. So *Sita* remained where she was.

After *Rama* regained his kingdom, he took the necessary vows which in olden times the king had to take for the benefit of his people – The king was the servant of his people and had to bow to the public opinion as we shall see later on. *Rama* passed a few years in happiness with *Sita*, when the people again began to murmur that *Sita* had been stolen by a demon and carried across the ocean. They were not satisfied with the former test and clamored for another test, otherwise she must be banished. In order to satisfy the demands of people *Sita* was banished and left to live in the forest, where was the hermitage of the sage and poet Valmiki.

The Hindu householder has to perform hundreds of ceremonies, but not one can be duly performed, according to *Shastras*, if he has not a wife to complement it with her part in it. Now *Rama*'s wife was not with him then, as she had been banished. So the people asked him to marry again. *Rama* replied, "This cannot be. My wife is *Sita*". So a substitute, a golden statue of *Sita* was made, in order that the ceremony could be accomplished.

This is the great, ancient epic of India. *Rama* and *Sita* are the ideals of the Indian nation. The height of woman's ambition is to be like *Sita*, the pure, the devoted, the all suffering. When we study these characters, we can at once find out how different the ideal in India is from that of the west. For the East *Sita* stands the ideal of suffering. The west says, "Do! Show your power by doing". India says, "Show your power by suffering". The west has solved the problem of how much a man can have; India has solved the problem how little a man can have.

The two extremes we see. *Sita* is typical of India the idealized India. The question is not whether she ever lived, whether the story is history or not, we know that the ideal is there. There is no other *Pauranik* story that has so permeated the whole Nation, so entrenched into its very life and has so tingled in every drop of blood of the race as this ideal of *Sita*. *Sita* is the name in India for everything that is good pure and holy, everything that in women we call womanly. If a priest has to bless a woman he says," Be *Sita*". They are all children of *Sita* and are struggling to be *Sita*, the patient, the all suffering, the ever faithful the ever pure wife. Though all these sufferings and experiences; she uttered not one harsh word against *Rama*. She takes it as her own duty and performs her on part in it. Think of the terrible injustice of her being exiled to the forest. But *Sita* knows no bitterness. That is, again, the Indian ideal. Says the ancient Buddha," When a man hurts you and you turn back to hurt him that would not cure the first injury; it will only create in the world one more wickedness."

Sita was a true Indian by nature; she never returned injury. Who knows which is the true ideal whether the apparent power and strength as held in the west or the fortitude in suffering of the east. The west says," We minimize evil by conquering it." India says we destroy evil by suffering, until evil is nothing to us. It becomes positive enjoyment. Well both are great ideals. Who knows which will survive in the long run? Who knows which attitude will really most benefit humanity? Who knows which will disarm and Conquer animosity? Will it be suffering are doing? The intention of both is the same which is the annihilation of evil. Let west take their method and let us take our method; let us not destroy the ideal.

Mahabharat

Mahabharat is the story of a race descended from King *Bharata*, who was the son of *Dushyanta* and *Shakuntala*. *Maha* means great and *Bharat* means the descendants of Bharat, from whom India has derived its name, Bharat. The central story of the Mahabharat is of a war between two families of cousins, one family called the Kauravas and the other Pandavas – for the empire of India.

I will not go into the details of the story which are known to all. The greatest incident of the war was the marvelous poem of the *Gita*. It is the popular scripture of India and the loftiest of all teachings. I will describe about it separately. *Mahabharat* is one of the greatest books in the world and consists of about a hundred thousand verses in eighteen volumes. *Mahabharata* is a sublime poem describing the triumph of virtue and defeat of vice.

Mahabharat has presented the unending array of the grand and majestic characters of the mighty heroes depicted by the genius and mastermind of Vyasa.

The internal conflicts between righteousness and affection in the mind of the God fearing yet feeble old blind King *Dhratarashtra*; the Majestic character of the grandsire *Bhishma*; the noble and virtuous nature of the royal *Yudhishthra* and of the other four brothers as mighty in Velour as in devotion and loyalty; the peerless character of *Krishna* unsurpassed in human wisdom; and not less brilliant the characters of the woman the stately Queen *Gandhari*, the loving mother *Kunti*, the ever devoted and all suffering *Draupadi* – these and hundreds of other characters of this Epic and those of the *Ramayana* have been the cherished Heritage of the hole Hindu world for the last several thousands of years and form the basis of their thoughts and of their moral and ethical ideas. In fact the *Ramayana* and the *Mahabharat* are the two encyclopedias of the Ancient Aryan life and wisdom for portraying an ideal Civilization which humanity has yet to aspire after.

Gita

Gita is the compilation of truths described in details in *Upanishads*. They have been arranged together in their proper places like a fine garland or a bouquet of the choicest flowers. The *Upanishads* deal elaborately with *shraddha* in many places but hardly mentions Bhakti. In *Gita*, on the other hand, the subject of Bhakti is not only again and again dealt with, but in it the innate spirit of Bhakti has attained its culmination.

Though before the advent of *Gita*, *Yoga Gyana* Bhakti etc., had each its strong adherents, they all quarreled among themselves each claiming superiority for his own chosen path: no one ever tried to seek for reconciliation among these different paths. It was the author of the *Gita* who for the first time tried to harmonize these. He took the best form what all the sects then existing had to offer and threaded them in the *Gita*. But even where *Krishna* failed to show a complete reconciliation among these warring sects, it was fully accomplished by *Ramakrishna Paramahamsa* in the 19th Century.

The next theory of *Gita* is *Nishkama Karma* or work without desire or attachment. People now a day understand what is meant by this in various ways. Some say what is implied by being unattached is to become purposeless. If that were its real meaning, the heartless brutes and the walls would be the best exponents of the performance of *Nishkama Karma*.

The true *Nishkama Karma* is neither to be like a brute, nor to be inert, nor heartless. He is not *Tamas* but of pure *Sattva*. His heart is full of love and sympathy that he can embrace the whole world with his love. The world at large cannot generally comprehend his all embracing love and sympathy

Many others again give the example of *Janaka* and wish themselves to be equally recognized as past Masters in the practice of *Nishkama Karma*. *Janaka* did not acquire that distinction by bringing forth children but these people all want to be *Janakas* with the sole qualification of being the father of a brood of children. No! The true *Nishkama Karma* (performer of work without desire) is neither to be like a brute nor to be inert, nor heartless.

The world at large cannot generally comprehend all embracing love and sympathy. The reconciliation of the different paths of *Dharma* and work without desire or attachment are the two special characteristics of the *Gita*. *Krishna* painted the real position of *Arjuna* and then advised *Arjuna* to fight because it was not that the disinclination of *Arjuna* to fight arose out of the over whelming dominance of pure *Sattva Guna*; it was all *Tamas* that brought on this unwillingness.

In order to remove this delusion which had over taken *Arjuna* what did the *Bhagwan* say? As I always preach that you should not decry a man by calling him a sinner, but that you should draw his attention to the omnipotent power that is in him, in the same way does the *Bhagwan* speak to *Arjuna*. Hate not the most abject sinner. Look not to his exterior. Turn thy gaze inward where resides the *Parmatma*. Proclaim to the whole world with trumpet voices. There is no sin in thee, there is no misery in thee, and thou are the reservoir of omnipotent power. Arise awake and manifest the divinity within.

The reconciliation of different paths of *Dharma*, and work without desire or attachment – These are the two special characteristics of the *Gita*.

The nature of a man of *Sattva Guna* is that he is equally calm in all situations of life – whether it is prosperity or adversity. If one has the instinct and the inclination to fight but then out of fear he is overwhelmed by pity then it will not be said that he is not fighting as he is Sattvik but the fact is he is *Tamasika*.

Many people think they are *Sattvik* by nature but they are really nothing but *Tamasika*. Many living in an uncleanly way regard themselves as *Paramahansa*! Because the *Shastras* say that *Paramahansa* live like one inert or mad or like an unclean spirit. *Paramahansa* are compared to children, but here it should be understood that the comparison is one sided. The *Paramahansa* and children are not one and non- different. They only appear similar, being the two extreme poles, as it were. One has reached to a state beyond *Gyana* and the other has not got even an inkling of *Gyana*. The quicker and the gentlest vibrations of light are both beyond the reach of our ordinary vision; but in one it is the intense heat and in the other it may be said to be almost without any heat. So it is with the opposite qualities of *Sattva* and *Tamas*. They seem in some respects to be the same, no doubt, but there is a world of difference between them. The *Tamas* loves very much to array itself in the garb of Sattva. Here is *Arjuna*, the mighty warrior, has come under the guise of *Daya* (Pity). He came to the battle field with no other purpose than that to fight, but after seeing the army of *Kauravas* he was frightened and took the garb of *Daya* to not fight and become *Sattva*.

There is in the world neither sin nor misery, neither disease nor grief; if there is anything in the world which can be called sin, it is this 'fear', know that any work which brings out the latent power in you is *Punya* (Virtue); and that which makes your body and mind weak is verily sin. Shake off this weakness, this faint heartedness.

All these ideas of weakness will be nowhere. Now it is everywhere- this current of the vibration of fear. Reverse the current bring in the opposite vibration, and behold the magic transformation. Think we are powerful we don't fear to go to mouth of the cannon.

22. THE SUPREME WISDOM

Oh, when will that day come?
When in a forest, saying "Shiva, Shiva",
My days shall pass?
A serpent and garland the same,
The strong foe and the friend the same,
The flower-bed and the stone bed the same,
A beautiful women and a blade of grass the same.

Self surrender is the highest and fastest method for enlightenment. One who has surrendered himself is always protected by the divine power. One who possesses nothing and has no one to protect him belongs to God and is constantly under the protection of the divine.

We are all followed by the tiger of nescience, but the Lord is merciful upon human beings that they get some *Guru*, who can chalk out the plan of life and could act accordingly and perfect the mission of human life. We are all having constitutional position of the living entities but we are all controlled by somebody known as *Ishwara*. If a living entity says that he is not controlled by that; he is free, then he is insane. It is like saying that one has come on the earth without parents.

A master (*Guru*) bestows the divine experience of cosmic consciousness when his disciple, by meditation, has strengthened his mind to a degree where the vast vistas could not overwhelm him. The experience can never be given through one's mere intellectual willingness or open mindedness. The Lord, as the cosmic vision, is drawn by the seekers magnetic order into his range of consciousness.

One must not get over drunk with ecstasy. Much work yet remains for one in the world. It is the spirit of God that actively sustains every form and force in the universe; yet he is transcendental and aloof in the blissful uncreated void beyond the worlds of vibratory phenomena. Saints who realize their divinity even while in the flesh know a similar two fold existence. Conscientiously engaging in earthly work they yet remain immersed in an inward beatitude. The Lord has created all men from limitless joy of his Being. Though they are painfully cramped by the body, God nevertheless expects that souls made in his image shall ultimately rise above all sense identification and reunite with him. *Swamy Shivanand* has said "The aim of human life is not God-realization; rather, it is the cultivation of spiritual awareness". How far you are able to go does not matter. Don't think about one hundred percent; try to obtain even half a percent of spiritual awareness in your life and you will have obtained everything; when the mind is free from its sensorial mundane and external attachments, then it cultivates its own strength.

There are three strengths of the mind- will power, knowledge power and creative power *Ichha Shakti, Gyana Shakti* and *Kriya Shakti*. Everyone has these strengths within himself but however we don't utilize them, as there is dissipation of mental faculties and energies. If we are able to focus on mental perceptions we can lead to the development of will power and the mind gains its true strength and its true character. How the mind, the ego or intellect works we don't know and we should not bother about it. We must know how we can handle the situation, circumstances and condition that alter our perspective of ourselves.

We normally say, 'I think', who is it that says, 'I think? Who sits behind the mind and gives initial thought of, 'I think? Where does thought originate from? What is it that initiates the first movement of life, where does it originate from? What is it that makes me utter speech? What is the beginning of sound? What is this being that prompts me to see and who prompts me to hear? Or, what is it that sees and hears?

This roughly means, that which is the eye of eye, that which sees behind the eye, what is that? That is mind. The mind is the eye of eye. There is something behind the mind, which sees the mind also, which witnesses the mind. How blissful it is when I understand 'that' which is also the 'eye' of the mind is also 'I' my true self.

Even *Swami Chinmayananda* said, while understanding Upanishad from his *Guru Tapovan Maharaj*, said 'Sir please do not confuse me. Do not say this of this and that of that'. Maharaj kept quiet for some time and then said. "We will discuss this later". Afterwards he said, 'Go and get some water for me from the Ganges. Swamiji went with his Kamandalu, collected some water and returned. Tapovan Maharaj flew into rage and said, 'Who asked you to bring Kamandalu" Go get only the water, Swamiji Sir, how can I bring water without the Kamandalu? Tapovan then made this point.

When we say eye of the eye and 'ear' of the 'ear', we are talking about a 'Being' which cannot be grasped by the mind, which cannot be touched by the intellect. These are abstract truth, which require the use of some abstract to explain the idea; an instrument such as smile might be used.

We should understand that alone is *Brahman*, which is of great significance. *Vedanta* says it is not so, that there is no such reality but that reality has nothing to do with anything that you worship outside yourself. When you say worship, it is not only worshiping an image or a picture.

Upanishads are not saying, "Don't worship. Worship is required with a different level of understanding. Everyone cannot start swimming in the ocean right away, but have to be led to the stage gradually in steps, but when you begin to seriously understand the 'Supreme truth', these intermediate steps are not important.

This is very significant that which the mind cannot understand, grasp or express, but because of which the mind exists, 'That' alone is the Truth. "That which is not breathed by life, but by which life breathes."

Upanishads in its own way come from something very transcendental to something very real and actual. When I say, 'I know something, the 'I', the ego is getting strengthened. When this centre, the 'I' is gone, then what remains is the supreme Truth. In *Bhakti* there is not only singing of *Kirtans, Bhajans* and other acts of devotion. *Bhakti* is essentially an attitude by which a person begins to understand the limitation of the movement of the intellect.

Most of us feel that there are many other things to do, more important than the search of Truth. But we must realize that life can end at any moment, and therefore there is an urgency to know the reason why we live, what we live for and who we are. So urgency is required. It has to be now. *Ramkrishna Paramahansa* had given illustration to reveal great truths, "You cannot swim in the ocean straightway; first, you have to start in a little pool. Practice in the small pool. Start the practice now, with a sense of urgency.

We all desire happiness; every sane human being looks for happiness, not pain. Even if one goes through a lot of pain, one does so in the hope that at the end of it, there is happiness. The Vedas and *Upanishads* say that this movement of the mind towards happiness is actually a movement towards the Supreme self, which is within us, is the *Atman*. But not knowing the right direction, it goes in the wrong direction.

It can be steered in the right direction when one understands the importance of the world, when one sees the hollowness of existence. Then one begins to think, 'Maybe it is elsewhere that we should seek happiness'. Then one stops and turns around. It is difficult process. It is difficult because you become one of the few who turn around and go upstream while everyone else moves downstream.

It is because of the power of the self that the mind is able to remember. What we call will power, is also the power of the Supreme Being, although we would like to think that it is the power of our minds. It is said that when the mind moves towards happiness in the world, it is actually moving in the wrong direction. *Kabir Das* has this wonderful story about the musk deer. In the breeding season, the deer produces musk-*Kasturi*-in a little bag under its tail. When the fragrance begins to waft around it, the poor deer goes looking for the source everywhere, imagining that it comes from somewhere outside but not knowing that it emanates from itself. Similarly, we look for happiness all around us, everywhere but within us.

Shankaracharya has defined the word *Upanishad*. The word 'Shad' as, 'Shaking up', 'loosening the hold'. What holds the mind is mainly desire; desire by the senses to possess, sensual objects desired by imagination and other attraction. From high philosophy and abstract metaphysics, the discussion comes down to actually, the ego. But it comes down so gradually that one has to catch it. It requires a subtle mind. It is said in the *Gayatri Mantra* that we have all the time, to request God 'Stimulate my intellect; make my intellect subtle; may I understand the supreme wisdom.

To attain this we have to approach it with great humility and attention. This humility and attention is also a kind of affection, the love of knowledge. The love for knowledge and desire to understand must be there. When that kind of all consuming love comes, then one is not worried about anything else. Whole hearted attention is given because the seriousness of the problem is realized.

The mind always goes towards and moves towards the 'self' being attracted by it. It is also that which mind remembers constantly, i.e., Sankalp; the will to do something, the decision to do something, 'I want to do something'. This is part of the working of the 'self'.

The living being is controlled in every aspect, at least in his conditioned life. The cosmic manifestation is full of different activities. All living entities are engaged in different activities. We must learn what GOD is, that what the living entities are what *Prakrati* (nature) is, what the cosmic manifestation is and how it is controlled by time and what the activities of the living entities are.

When we see wonderful things happening in the cosmic nature, we should know that behind this cosmic manifestation there is a controller. Nothing could be manifested without being controlled. It is childish not to consider the controller. For instance a child may think that an automobile is quite wonderful to be able to run without a horse or animal pulling it, but a sane man knows the nature of automobile engineering arrangement. He always knows that behind the machinery there is a man a driver.

We all have original *Prakrati* (nature); the mode of goodness, the mode of passion and the mode of ignorance. Above these modes there is eternal time, and by combination of these modes of nature and under control activities which are called *Karma*. These activities are carried out from the times immemorial and we are suffering or enjoying the fruits of our activities.

For instance suppose I am a businessman and have worked very hard with intelligence and have amassed a great bank balance. Then, I am the enjoyer. But then say I have lost all my money in business, and then I am a sufferer. Similarly, in every field of life we face the results. This is called *Karma*. Many philosophers say that manifestation but according to *Bhagwat Gita* and many philosophers this is not so. Manifestation of world is not false. It is real but temporary. It is likened into a cloud which moves across the sky on coming of the rainy season which nourishes grains. As soon as the rainy season is over and cloud goes away, all the crops which were nourished by the rain dry up. Similarly, this material manifestation takes place at a certain interval, stays for a while and then disappears. Such are the workings of the *Prakrati*. But this cycle is working eternally. Therefore, *Prakrati* is eternal; it is not false.

When we are materially contaminated we are called conditioned. False contamination and false consciousness is exhibited under the impression that I am a product of material nature. This is called false ego. One who is absorbed in the thought of bodily conceptions cannot understand this situation. One, who wants to become liberated, must first of all learn that he is not this material body. *Mukti* or liberation means freedom from material consciousness. We are purified consciousness because we are part and parcel of the Lord, but for us there is affinity of being affected by the inferior modes.

The world revolves because every living being thinks that he is the Lord and creator of the material world. Material consciousness has two psychic divisions. One is that I am the creator and the other is that I am the enjoyer. But actually the supreme Lord is both the creator and enjoyer, and the living entity being part and parcel of the supreme Lord, is neither the creator nor the enjoyer, but a cooperator. He is the created and enjoyed .For instance a part of a machine cooperates with the whole machine; a part of the body cooperates with the whole body. The hands, feet, eyes, legs and so on are all parts of the body, but they are not actually the enjoyers. The stomach is the enjoyer. The legs move, the hands supply food, the teeth chew and all parts of the body are engaged in satisfying the stomach because the stomach is the principal factor that nourishes the body's organization. Therefore everything is given to the stomach. One nourishes the tree by giving water to its roots and we nourish the body by feeding stomach, for if the body is to be kept in a healthy state, then the parts of the body must cooperate to feed the stomach.

Similarly, the supreme Lord is the enjoyer and the creator and we are the subordinate living beings, are meant to cooperate to satisfy HIM. This cooperation will actually help us, just as food taken by the stomach will help all parts of the body. If the fingers of the hand think that they should take the food themselves instead of giving it to the stomach, then they will be frustrated. The central figure of creation and of enjoyment is the supreme Lord, and the living entities are cooperators. By cooperation they enjoy. The relation is like that of the master and servant. If the master is fully satisfied, then the servant is satisfied. Similarly the supreme Lord should be satisfied, although the tendency to become the creator and the tendency to enjoy the material world are there also in the living entities because these tendencies are there in the supreme Lord who has created the manifested cosmic world.

Ego is the end result of the fact that we are part and parcel of the LORD. It creates a feeling that we are the creators and enjoyer. This feeling of Ego comes when we forget that we are, no doubt, part and parcel of the LORD, but we are neither creator nor enjoyer, we are simply cooperator. The Lord has created and is enjoying; we as his part are simply cooperating with him to enjoy. If we will cooperate well he will enjoy and if we do not cooperate well he will suffer and as we are being his part will be fed with same enjoyment or suffering.

Bhagwat Gita's first *Sloka* starts with *Dharma*. Sometimes people confuse *Dharma* with religion. The English word 'religion' is a little different from *Sanatana Dharma*. Religion conveys the idea of faith and faith may change. One may have faith in a particular process, and he may change this faith and adopt another. But *Sanatana Dharma* refers to that activity which cannot be changed. For instance liquidity cannot be taken away from water, nor can heat be taken away from fire. Similarly the eternal function of the living entity cannot be taken away from the living entity.

As there is heat and light doing with the fire; without heat and light there is no meaning of the word fire. Similarly we must discover the essential part of the living being; that part which is his constant companion. The constant companion is his eternal quality and that eternal quality is his eternal religion.

As a matter of fact every living being is constantly engaged in rendering service to another living being. A living being serves other living being in two capacities. By doing so, the living entity enjoys life. The lower animals serve human beings as servants to their masters. We can see that one friend serves another friend, the mother serves the son, the wife serves the husband and the husband serves the wife and so on.

If we go on searching in this spirit; it will be seen that there is no exception in the society of living beings to the activity of service.

The shopkeeper serves the customer. The capitalist serves the family and the family serves the state in terms of the eternal capacity of the eternal living beings. No living being is exempt from rendering service to other living beings and therefore we can safely conclude that service is the constant compassion of the living being and that the rendering of service is the eternal religion of the living being.

Living being professes to belong to a particular type of faith with reference to particular type of faith, with reference to particular time and circumstance and thus claims to be a Hindu, Muslim, and Christian, Buddhist or any other sect. Such designations are not *Sanatana Dharma*. A Hindu may change his faith to become a Muslim or a Muslim may change his faith to become a Hindu or a Christian may change his faith and so on.

But in all circumstances the change of religion and faith does not affect the eternal occupation of rendering service to others. The Hindu, Muslim, or Christian in all circumstances is serving to someone. We cannot become happy otherwise. It is not possible to be happy independently, just as no part of the body can be happy without cooperating with the stomach. It is not possible for the living entity to be happy without rendering transcendental loving service into the supreme Lord.

Those whose minds are disturbed by material desires surrender into *Demigods* and follow the particular rules and regulations of worship according to their own natures. When we mention the name of *Krishna*, we don't refer to any sectarian name, *Krishna* means the highest pleasure. We are all hankering after pleasure. The living entities are full of consciousness and they all are after happiness. The Lord is perpetually happy and if the living entities associate with the Lord, cooperate with Him and take part in His association then they also become happy.

We are after designations. Someone wants to become a son, someone wants to become Lord, someone wants to become president or a rich man or a King or something else. As long as we are attached to these designations, we are attached to the body because designation belongs to the body. But we are not these bodies and realizing this is the first step in spiritual realization. Designations and attachments are due to our lust and desire. As long as we don't give up this propensity of lording it over this material nature, there is no possibility of returning to the kingdom of supreme the *Sanatana Dharma*. That eternal kingdom, which is never destroyed can be approached by one who is not bewildered by the attractions of false material enjoyments, who is situated in the service of supreme Lord i.e., mankind.

We are all forgetful living entities or conditioned souls and have forgotten our relationship with the supreme Lord and are engrossed in thinking of material activities. First of all we have to agree that we can separate ME from my body. We experience it many a times. It happens many times that we are present bodily somewhere but we actually do not listen or register anything which we are seeing or listening. So it is definite that we can separate ME from body.

It is advised that one should not give up his occupation but while he is engaged in his occupation he should remember *Krishna*. One can practice remembering the Lord by chanting the names of Lord always i.e., *Satat Jaap*.

It can be explained in simple worldly example. If a married woman is attached to another man or if a man has an attachment for woman other than his wife, then attachment is considered very strong one; with such an attachment he or she is always thinking of the loved one. The wife who is thinking of her lover is always thinking of meeting him, even while she is carrying out her household chores. In fact she carries out her household work even more carefully so that her husband will not suspect her attachment.

Similarly we should always remember the supreme *Lord Krishna* and at the same time perform our material duties very nicely. A strong sense of love is required here. If we have a strong sense of love for the supreme Lord then we can discharge our duties and at the same time remember HIM. But we have to develop that sense of love.

This human form of life is a most valuable asset for the living entity who can utilize it for solving the problems of life. Therefore one who does not utilize this opportunity properly is a miser. On the other hand there is one who is intelligent enough to utilize this body to solve all the problems of life.

Such miserly persons waste their time in being overly affectionate for family, society, county, etc in the material conception of life. One is often attached to family life, namely to wife, children and other members. He thinks that he is capable to protect his family members from all sorts of difficulties including death and he also thinks that his family or society can save him from all difficulties including death.

One should understand that his affection for family members and his wish to protect them even from death were the causes of his perplexities. In our hands there is only one thing and that to perform our duty. The definite solution to these perplexities is to perform your duties and surrender to *Krishna*

The problems of material existence birth, old age, disease and death cannot be counteracted by accumulation of wealth and economic development. In many parts of the world there are states which are replete with all facilities of life, which are full of wealth and economically, developed yet the problems of material existence are still present. They are seeking peace in different ways, but they can achieve real happiness only if they consult *Krishna* or *Bhagwat Gita*

One has to follow prescribed rules and regulations and religious and ethical principles in order to rise up to the platform of knowledge because by knowledge and devotion only can one liberate himself from the clutches of illusion.

There is no endurance of the changing body. That the body is changing every moment by the actions and reactions of the different cells as accepted by the modern science and thus growth and old age are taking place in the body. But the spirit soul exists permanently remaining the same despite all change of the body and the mind. That is the difference between matter and spirit. By nature, the body is ever changing and the soul is eternal. The living entities are bewildered by the influence of ignorance. Removal of ignorance involves the re establishment of the eternal relationship between the worshiper and worship able.

The individual soul is unbreakable and insoluble and it can neither be burnt nor dried. He is everlasting all pervading, unchangeable, and immovable and eternally the same. There is no doubt that living entities are all over GOD's creation. They live on the land, in the water, in the air, within the earth and even within the fire. It cannot be burnt by fire. Therefore, there is no doubt that there are living entities also in the sun planet with suitable bodies to live there. If the sun globe is uninhabited then the word GOD is living everywhere becomes meaningless.

23. SALVATION THROUGH KARMA NON ATTACHMENT

Quote from Swami Vivekananda

"*The highest idea of Karma yoga is non-resistance i.e, the power to renounce. We must first take care to understand whether we have the power of resistance or not. Then having the power, if we renounce it and do not resist, we are doing a grand act of love;*"

This is the one central idea in the *Gita*. Work incessantly, but be not attached to it. Every work that we do, every movement of the body, every thought that we think, leaves such an impression on the mind – staff, and even when such impression are not obvious on the surface, they are sufficiently strong to work beneath the surface subconsciously. What beneath the surface subconsciously. What we are every moment is determined by the sum total of these impressions on the mind.

If good impression prevails, the character becomes good; if bad, it becomes bad. If a man continuously hears bad words, thinks bad thoughts, does bad actions, his mind will be full of bad impression; and they will influence his thought and work without his being conscious of the fact. Similarly if a man thinks good thoughts and does good works, the sum total of these impressions will be good.

As the tortoise tucks its feet and head inside the shell and you may kill it and break it in pieces, and yet it will not come out, even so the character of that man who has control over his motives and organs is unchangeably established. He controls his own inner forces and nothing can draw them out against his will.

So the bad tendencies are to be countered by the good ones, and the bad impressions on the mind should be removed by the fresh waves of good ones, until all that is evil almost disappears, or is subdued and held in control in a corner of the mind; but after that, the good tendencies have also to be conquered.

Thus the 'attached' becomes the unattached. Work, but let not the action or the thought produce a deep impression on the mind. Let the ripples come and go, let huge action proceed from the mussels and the brain; but let them not make any deep impression on the soul.

Work as if you were a stranger in this land; work incessantly, but do not bind yourselves, bondage is terrible. This world is not our habitation; it is only one of the many stages through which we are passing. The whole of the nature is for the soul, not the soul for nature. We should know that nature is a book in which we are to read and that when we have gained the required knowledge, the book is of no more value to us.

The whole gist of teachings of *Gita* is that we should work like a master and not as a slave; work incessantly, but do not do slaved work. We normally see how everybody else is working. Nobody can be altogether at rest; ninety nine percent of mankind work like a slave, and the result is misery; it is all selfish work.

Work through freedom. Work through love. The word 'love' is very difficult to understand; love never comes until there is freedom. There is no true love possible in the slave. Every act of love brings happiness; there is no act of love which does not bring peace and blessedness as its reaction.

Suppose a man loves a woman; he wishes to have her all to himself and feels extremely jealous about her every movement; he wants her to sit near him, to stand near him and to eat and move at his bidding. He is a slave to her and wishes to have her as his slave. That is not love; it is a kind of morbid affection of the slave, insinuating itself as love. It cannot be love because it is painful; if she does not do what he wants; it brings him pain. With love there is no painful reaction; love only brings a reaction of bliss; if it does not, it is not love; it is mistaking something else for love.

When one succeeds in loving her husband, her wife, their children, the whole world, the universe, in such a manner that there is no reaction of pain or jealousy, no selfish feeling then one is in a fit state to be unattached. Working like slaves results in selfishness and attachment, working as master of our own mind give rise to the bliss of non-attachment.

There are two classes of men who realize the self. Some are inclined to understand by empirical, philosophical speculation and others are inclined to know by devotional work. There are people who want to make analytical study of the nature of spirit and matter. Such persons are inclined to speculate and understand things by experimental knowledge and philosophy. The other class of men work in *Krishna Consciousness* i.e., depending entirely on the Supreme and inner consciousness. In this way they are able to bring their all the senses in control and keep their mind cool and silent. Religion without philosophy is sentiment or sometimes fanaticism, while philosophy without religion is mental speculation.

Of these two paths, the path of *Krishna Consciousness* is better because it does not depend upon purifying the senses by a philosophical process; *Krishna Consciousness* is in itself a purifying process and by the direct method of devotional services it is simultaneously easy and sublime.

All men are forced to act helplessly according to the impulses born of the modes of material nature; therefore no one can refrain from doing something not even for a moment. It is not a question of embodied life, but it is nature of soul to be always active. Without the presence of the spirit soul the material body cannot move. The body is only a dead vehicle to be worked by the spirit soul, which is always active and cannot stop even for a moment. As such the spirit soul has to be engaged in the good work of *Krishna Consciousness* otherwise it will be engaged in occupations dictated by illusory energy.

There are many pretenders who refuse to work in *Krishna Consciousness* but make a show of meditation, while actually dwelling within the mind upon sense enjoyment. Such pretenders may also speak on dry philosophy in order to bluff sophisticated followers, but actually they are the greatest cheaters. For sense enjoyment one can act in any capacity of the social order, but if one follows the rules and regulations of his particular status, he can make gradual progress in purifying his existence. But he who makes a show of being a yogi, while actually searching for the objects of sense gratification, must be called the greatest cheater, even though he sometimes speaks of philosophy his knowledge has no value because the effects of such a sinful man's knowledge are taken away by illusory energy of the Lord. Such a pretender's mind is always impure, and therefore his show of yogic meditation has no value whatsoever.

On the other hand, he who controls the sense by the mind and engages his active organs in works of devotion, without attachment is by far superior. Perform your prescribed duty, for action is better than inaction. A man cannot even maintain his physical body without work. One should perform his prescribed duties for HIS satisfaction and in that way he will always remain unattached and free from bondage.

One should know, however, that all necessities of life that the human society requires for its survival are supplied by *Demigod* agents of Lord i.e. *Prakriti*. No one can manufacture them. Take for example, all the eatables of human society which include grains, fruits, vegetable, milk, sugar, salt etc for the persons who are vegetarians and eatables for the non-vegetarians like meats etc, none of which can be manufactured by the human society, without the supreme Lord, there can be no profuse sunlight, moonlight rainfall, breeze, etc; without which nobody can live.

Obviously, our life is dependent on supplies from the Lord. Even for our manufacturing enterprises we require so many raw materials like metal, sulphur, mercury, manganese and so many essential raw materials are supplied by the Lord only with the purpose that we should make proper use of them to keep ourselves fit and healthy for the purpose of self realization, leading to the ultimate goal of life, namely, liberation from material struggle for existence.

It is far better to discharge one's prescribed duties, even though they may be inferior to another's duties. Prescribed duties complement one's psychophysical conditions, under the spell of the modes of material nature. Spiritual duties are as ordered by the spiritual master, for the transcendental service of *Krishna*. But both materially and spiritually one should stuck to his prescribed duties even up to death, rather than imitate another's prescribed duties.

A living entity, as part and parcel of the supreme, is originally spiritual, pure and free from all material contaminations. Therefore, by nature he is not subjected to the sins of material world, but when he is in contact with material nature, he acts in many sinful ways without hesitation and sometimes even against his will. When a living entity comes in contact with this material creation his eternal love for *Krishna* is transformed into lust, as milk in contact with sour tamarind is transformed into yogurt. Then again, when lust is unsatisfied, it turns into wrath; wrath is transformed into illusion, and illusion creates the material existence.

Therefore lust is the greatest enemy of the living entity and it is lust only which induces the pure living entity to remain entangled in the material world. Wrath is the manifestation of the mode of ignorance.

The origin of everything is in the supreme. Therefore, the origin of lust is also in the supreme. If therefore lust is transformed into love for the supreme, in other words, desiring everything for *Krishna* then both lust and wrath can be spiritualized. *Hanuman*, the great servitor of *Lord Rama*, engaged his wrath upon the enemies for the satisfaction of the Lord. Therefore, lust and wrath, when they are employed in *Krishna Consciousness* become our friends instead of our enemies.

Thus a man's pure consciousness is covered by his eternal enemy in the form of lust, which is never satisfied and which burns like fire.

It is said in the *Manusmriti* that lust cannot be satisfied by any amount of sense enjoyment, just as fire is never extinguished by constant supply of fuel. In the material world, the centre of all activities is sex and thus the material world is called the shackles of sex life. In the ordinary prison house criminals are kept within bars, similarly the criminals who are disobedient to the laws of Lord are shackled by sex life.

The sense, the mind and the intelligence are the sitting places of the lust, which veils the real knowledge of the living entity and bewilders him. Mind is the centre of all activities of the senses and thus the mind is the reservoir of all ideas of sense gratification and as a result the mind and the senses become the repositories of lust. Next the intelligence department becomes the capital of such lustful propensities. Intelligence is the immediate next door neighbor of the spirit soul. Lusty intelligence influence the spirit soul and acquire the false ego and identify itself with matter and thus, with the mind and senses. The spirit soul becomes addicted to enjoying the material senses and misstates this as true happiness. This false identification of the spirit soul identifies this body as the mode of three elements with his self; senses mind and intelligence.

All the authoritative statements of the great sages, the *Vedic* hymns, the components of this world are earth, water, fire, air and either. These are the five great elements. Then there are false egos, intelligence and the un-manifested stage of three modes of nature. Then there are five sense for acquiring knowledge; the eyes, ears, nose, tongue and touch, then five working sense; voice legs, hands, the anus and the genitals. Then above the senses there is a mind, which is within and which can be called the sense within.

Therefore including mind there are 11 senses altogether. Then there are five objects of the senses; smell, taste, warms, touch and sound. Now the aggregate of these twenty four elements is called field of activity. Then there is desire, hatred, pleasure and pain, which are interaction, representation of the five general elements in the gross body. The living symptoms represented by consciousness and conviction are the manifestation of the subtle body, mind, ego and intelligence. These subtle elements are included within the field of activities.

It is true that none can ever remain inactive even for a moment; everyone is helplessly driven to action by nature-born qualities. The word '*Karma*" includes all activities of body, mind, senses such as movement, rest, satisfaction of hunger and thrust, going to sleep, walking ,thought reflection, dreaming, meditation and absorption in Samadhi. Therefore, so long as man carries his body he is bound to perform action in one form or the other according to his nature. This is what is meant by saying, "No one can remain wholly inactive even for a moment".

Human being has been given a special power of intellect, which no other specie possesses. So human being has the power to act rationally. Human being can think and plain his actions. He can renounce the sense of doer ship in action, give up the sense of possession, attachment and the desire for its fruits. To renounce these is to renounce action altogether.

When it is said that "No one can remain wholly inactive even for a moment" the obvious question comes to our mind that one could refrain from action by forcibly suspending the function of sense. Anyone who outwardly restrains the organs of sense and action sits mentally dwelling on the objects of senses, that man of deluded intellect is called a hypocrite. The external suspension of the function of the senses does not constitute renunciation of action.

Senses of *Karma* (*Karmandriyani*) mean all the ten organs of perception and action, with the help of which man carries on his external activities, i.e., perceives external objects – viz., the sense of hearing, touch, sight, taste and smell as well as the organs of speech, hands and feet, the organ of generation and the organ of defecation. The word *Karma* should not be interpreted to mean only the organs of action such as speech etc., Senses like the sense of hearing etc., are left unrestrained. *Karma Yoga* does not mean restraining of the organs of action such as speech etc alone, but the help of the senses of perception will also be required to be restrained for the practice of *Karma Yoga*.

In this connection it should be borne in mind that he who endeavors to restrain sense forcibly from running after sense – objects in order to bring them under control, so as to be able to concentrate his thoughts on GOD and yet owing to the wandering of his mind cannot help dwelling on sense objects, will not be classed as hypocrite. He is a spiritual aspirant; for like the hypocrite, it is not his objects to meditate on objects of enjoyment. He desires from the bottom of his heart to control the mind as well; but due to past habits, attachment for worldly objects and force of tendencies of past *Karma*, his mind reverts to worldly objects in spite of himself.

The practice of *Karma Yoga* does not mean stopping the function of the senses. It cannot be practiced when the sense have altogether ceased to function. The practice of *Karma Yoga* through the organs of perception and action consists in performing all actions such as sacrifice, charity austerity, study of and imparting instruction in the governance of kingdom, carrying on business transactions and menial service and carrying on all the function of the senses such as satisfaction of hunger and thirst, falling asleep and walking, movement and rest etc; enjoying the various sense objects such as sound, etc., through senses which are properly disciplined and controlled, maintaining an attitude of indifference to success and failure, and renouncing attraction for and conversion to one's prescribed duties as well as with regard to all enjoyment of this world.

There is a lurking misconception in the people's mind that, in the eyes of Lord Withdrawal from action was superior to participation in action; the Lord is seeking to dispel this delusion and asserts that action is superior to inaction. The performance of one's ordained duty leads to purifications of heart whereas, neglect of duty exposes to sins and makes him a victim of error, sloth and sleep etc., which brings about his fall. That is why it is said that performance of action in every way superior to its non-performance. Performance of duty even with some interested motives or with a view to expiating sin is far better than its non-performance.

It is impossible to live if one totally renounces all activities. One must do something at least for the maintenance of his body. It one renounces his prescribed duties his downfall is inevitable so from every point of view, performance of duty is always better than non-performance of the same.

Logically, somebody who never put effort into anything should be the master of effortlessness. But it is not so if you want to know effortlessness, you need to know effort. When you reach the peak of effort, you become effortless. Only a person who knows what it is to work understands rest. Paradoxically, those who are always resting know no rest; they only sink into dullness and lethargy. This becomes their way of life.

When someone is constantly giving a hundred percent, a point comes when one surpasses all limits, and reaches total effortlessness. Effortlessness does not mean becoming a couch potato. It means transcending the need for physical action. Only when you are able to stretch to your utmost and sustain the pack of effort do you reach this.

If we, as societies and individuals continue to allow every moment to pass by without setting the atmosphere for such a flowering, we have squandered a tremendous possibility. There is so much infantile talk about heaven and its pleasures only because the immensity of being human has not been exposed. If your humanity overflows, divinity will follow and serve you; it has no other choice.

So, one has the choice to perform actions. And how you perform those action is up to you. But the Lord says, you cannot dictate the fruits of those actions; it is not in your hands. Hence, do not perform actions for any desired fruits.

Furthermore, Lord adds that don't think on the lines of why I should perform any action if I am not going to receive the desired fruit of the action. This too is inappropriate. Just perform your duties without any expectation of appreciation and without any desire for the fruit – neither gross nor subtle. Failure and success should not stop you from doing your duty, your *Karma*.

Everybody in this country knows about the law of *Karma*. It means action, any action physical, verbal or mental-arising out of any positive emotion or sincere motivation. Like compassion and forgiveness is positive or good *Karma*. Since the motivation is good, there is a sense of concern for others well being, which as it benefits others and oneself, is considered positive. Otherwise there is not absolute positive or negative.

For example, anger, hatred and suspicion are considered negative. Suspicion may be positive or negative. Negative is that which is uncomfortable to oneself and or to others. Any such motivation will lead to physical, verbal or mental action that can produce negative *Karma*. Experience of pleasure, pain and the action that causes them constitute the law of causality.

Emotional trouble is essentially our own creation. It is largely due to two things. The first is lack of knowledge or reality due to absence of holistic view and the second is a self centered attitude. These two things create unnecessary problems. We can't blame our problems on anybody or anything else. Ultimately, we have to realize that the cause of these problems lies within ourselves. We may deal with them neither through prayer, nor through money nor through power but though understanding and awareness – what do we call wisdom.

It might be useful to know something about the system of our minds, just like pleasure, pain is also part of our experience. Usually, people are under the impression that the mind is independent, absolute. Science too is not yet clear about the distinction between the sensorial mind and consciousness.

It is important to understand distinction between sensorial mind and consciousness. When people seek pleasurable experiences, they rely mainly on the sensorial level to attain that pleasure – watching something beautiful, listening to music, tasting or smelling something. This includes tactile pleasures, including sex. These five are positive experience mainly at the sensorial level. They are temporary.

The object of beauty one behold or the beautiful music one hears is gone the moment one stops seeing or hearing it. Nevertheless, if one develops a mental level with certain positive experience, the experience of pleasure lasts longer. So a disturbing noise at the sensorial level will not affect this basic calmness. Even the pain of physical illness can be subdued in this state.

On the other hand no sensorial pleasure can be had if the basic mental state is that of fear, anxiety and stress. Obviously, mental level experiences are more important than sensorial ones. The mental level happiness need not be about pleasure. It is about mental satisfaction or fulfillment. Even physical suffering and pain can bring deep satisfaction at the mental level.

Happiness mainly refers to this feeling at the level of consciousness.

Various religions may have different approaches to many aspects of life but the fundamental purpose is the same; to enhance our ability to love and forgive and to be compassionate in day to day life. The greatest legacy one can pass on to one's children and grand children is not money or other material things accumulated in one's life, but rather a legacy of character and faith.

Knowledge meditation, devotion and selfless action are various prescribed paths of spiritual attainment. The mind would become one's strongest *Guru* and through the inner voice will tell us what is good and what is bad; what is beneficial for the self and the society and what is not. It makes sense to not only have deep understanding of the ground reality but also absolute selflessness.

It requires a great deal of courage and self confidence to select the path of selfless action to spiritual attainment. But this difficult path is the only solution and everyone must try to adopt it with sincerity. Becoming an ascetic even, while leading a worldly life is the greatest challenge. But that is what is required in this modern age.

Do virtuous deeds, as that will make your intellect pure and the supremely blissful *Sat-Chit-Ananda* will be reflected in this refined intellect. You will overflow with such joyous contentment that you will spontaneously share it with one and all. Perform your action deftly with an equally poised intellect, for it is this balance intellect which will liberate your from all bondage.

Karma Yoga means; even at the point of death to help anyone, without asking questions. Be cheated millions of times and never ask a question, and never think of what you are doing. Never expect gratitude from poor's for your gifts to them, but rather be grateful to them for giving you the occasion of practicing charity to them. Thus, it is plain that to be an ideal householder is much more.

God does not decide Karma each one of us should do, nor does he induce people to act, nor does he create fruits of any action. Each person acts according to his Vasanas (past and present perceptions of mind)

Any action or service done with a selfish motive to enjoy the results is far inferior to selfless service Nishkarmana. Those who act because they are motivated by desire for the fruits of actions are in truth very unhappy. A person who knows how to act this way gets rid of both good and bad karmic debt. Acting without becoming attached to the fruits of actions is called Karma Yoga

24. THE WAY OF
KNOWLEDGE

The great teachers do not lay claim to originality but affirm that they are expounding the ancient truth which is the final norm by which all teachings are judged, the eternal source of all religions and philosophies. *Sanatan Dharma*, "The wisdom that was not made, but is at this present as it hath ever been and so shall ever be".

The teaching is a renewal, a rediscovery, a restoration of Knowledge long forgotten. All great teachers like *Gautam* the *Buddha* and *Mahavira* are content to affirm that they are only restating the teachings of their former masters.

So long as the human heart has qualities of devotion and friendship, God will disclose his secrets to them. Divine self-communication is possible whenever we have sincerity and a sense of need.

Religious revelation is not a past event; it is that which continues to be. It is possible for all beings and not the privilege of a few. Everyone who is for the Truth; hearths my voice.

The embodiments of human beings are not voluntary. Driven by *Prakrati* through ignorance, they are born again and again. The Lord controls *Prakrati* and assumes embodiment through his own free will. The ordinary birth of creatures is determined by the force of *Prakrati*, while the Lord takes birth through his own power. *Avatara* means descent, one who has descended. The

Divine comes down to the earthy plane to raise it to a higher status. God descends when man rises. The purpose of the *Avatar* is to inaugurate a new world, a new *Dharma*. By his teachings and example, he shows how human beings can raise himself to a higher grade of life.

Dharma will conquer *Adharma*, truth will conquer false hood; the power behind death, disease and sin will be overthrown by the reality which is being, intelligence and Bliss. *Krishna* as an *avatar* or descent of the Divine into the human world discloses the conditions of being to which the human souls should rise. The birth of the birth less means the revelation of the mystery in the soul of man.

The avatar fulfils a number of functions in the cosmic process. The conception makes out that there is no opposition between spiritual life and life of the world. If the world is imperfect and ruled by the flesh and the devil, it is our duty to redeem it for the spirit. The *Avatara* points out the way by which men can rise from their animal to a spiritual mode of existence by providing us with an example of spiritual life.

The omnipresent Lord appears in the world not only for destroying the demoniac forces but also for teaching mortals. How else could the Lord, who is blissful in himself, experience anxieties about *Sita*? He knows hunger and thirst, sorrow and suffering, solitude and forsakenness. He overcomes them all and asks us to take courage from His example. He not only teaches us the true doctrine by which we can die to our separate temporal selfness and come to union with timeless spirit but He offers Himself to be a channel of grace. By inviting souls to trust and love Him, He promises to lead them to the knowledge of the absolute.

The *Avatara* helps us to become what we potentially are. We can all rise to the Divine status and the avatars help us to achieve this inner realization. The purpose of incarnation is not simply to uphold the world order but also to help human beings to become perfected in their nature. The freed soul becomes on earth a living image of the infinite. The ascent of man into Godhead is also the purpose of the descent of God into humanity. The aim of the *Dharma* is this perfection of man and the avatar generally declares that he is the truth, the way and the life.

God meets every aspirant with favor and grants to each his heart's desire. He does not extinguish the hope of any but helps all hopes to grow according to their nature. Name and form are used to reach the Formless. Meditation in any favorite form may be adopted. The Hindu thinkers are conscious of the amazing variety of ways in which we may approach the supreme of the contingency of all forms. The forms we worship are aids to help us to become conscious of our deepest selves. The Gita does not speak of this or that form of religion but speaks of impulse which is expressed in all forms, the desire to find God and understand our relation to him.

He who works without attachment is not bound. We are acting even when we sit quiet without any outward action. He who is devoid of existence and non-existence, who is wise; satisfied, free from desire, does nothing even if he may be acting in the eyes of the world. He who, without attachment to them, surrenders to God all religious practice ordained by the scriptures, obtains the perfection of non action, the promised fruit is only to attract us to action. Having no desires, with his heart and self under control, giving up all possession, performing action by the body alone he commits no wrong.

Wise men will teach us the truth, if we approach them in spirit of service and reverent inquiry. Until we realize the God within, we must act according to the advice of those who have had the experience of God. If we accept what is said in the *Shastras* taught by the teacher in unthinking trust that will not do. Reason must be satisfied, "He who has no personal knowledge but has only heard of many things cannot understand the meaning of scriptures even as a spoon has no idea of the taste of the soup". We must combine devotion to the teacher with the most unrestricted right of free examination and enquiry.

Blind obedience to an external authority is repudiated. Today there are several teachers who require their followers unthinking obedience to their dictates. They seem to believe that the death of intellect is the condition of the life of spirit. Such simple minded people are drawn to them not so much by their spiritual powers as by the publicity of their agents and the human weakness for novelty, curiosity and excitement. This is against Hindu tradition which insists on *Jigyasa* or inquiry, *Manana* or reflection.

We must open the whole of our inner being to establish personal contact. The disciple has to tread the interior path. The ultimate authority is the inner light which is not to be confused with the promptings of effacement; we knock down the obstructing prejudices and let the wisdom in us shine. Truth achieved is different from truth imparted. What is thought out by the mind, what is realized by the spirit through service and meditation must agree? We must consort with the great minds of the past, reason about them and institutively apprehend what is of enduring value in them.

Those who have experienced the truth are expected to guide us. The seers owe a duty to their less fortunate brothers to guide them to the attainment of illumination which they have reached.

Faith is necessary for gaining wisdom. Faith is not blind belief. It is the aspiration of the soul to gain wisdom. If faith is constant, it takes us to the realization of wisdom, as wisdom is free from doubts while intellectual knowledge where we depend on sense data and logical inference, doubt and skepticism has their place. Wisdom is not acquired by these means. We have to live it inwardly and grow into its reality. The way to it is through faith and self control.

But the man who is ignorant, who has no faith, who is of doubting nature perishes. For the doubting soul, there is neither this world nor the world beyond, or any happiness. We must have a positive basis for life, an unwavering faith, which stands for the test of life.

The biggest knowledge or *Gyana* is that this world is not permanent and we all have to leave this one day; so sooner we learn to let go is better. The idea of ending recurs in the three great epics of India; *Ramanyana*, Mahabharata and *Bhagavata Gita*. In the *Ramanayana* in the end, *Sita* returns to the earth whence she came from and Ram walks into the river *Sarayu* never to rise up again.

In the *Mahabharata*, in the end *Pandavas* have to renounce their kingdom and walk up the mountains seeking heaven and ultimately facing death. In the *Bhagwat*, *Krishna* leaves the village of cowherds, *Vrindavan*, and makes his way to the city of *Mathura*. He leaves on a chariot whose charioteer's name is *Akrura*, one who is not cruel. The milk maids beg *Krishna* to stay back but *Krishna* moves on to the next phase of his life, abandoning his parents, friends and lovers. That the charioteer is not cruel is a clean communication that one must never begrudge the march of time. Like *Yashoda*, who raised *Krishna* with love and affection only to watch him leave her and go to *Mathura*, we must all ultimately learn to let go.

In a way *Akrura* is *Yama*, the God of death, described in mythology as dispassionate. *Yama* evokes fear in all of us. But *Yama* himself does not seek to frighten; he has no feelings. He is merely doing his duty as the one who separates material reality from spiritual reality. The journey which begins in the womb of mother ends with the arrival of *Yama*. In the mother's womb thanks to *Kama*, the God of love, spiritual reality interacts with and is wrapped in material reality. But a time comes when *Yama* must unwrap the material reality and release spiritual reality.

Vedic wisdom is realization that there is more to life than material reality that is perceived through the senses. It is wisdom that liberates us from the limitations of nature. It enables man to break free from *Prakrati* and realize *Purusha*. *Prakrati* makes us mortal and restless; *Purusha* makes us immortal and serene.

The notion of property is not an objective reality, but a subjective truth, a cultural construction of human beings, not a natural phenomenon. In other words they are creations of *Maya* and components of *Brahmanda*. If man does not exist, there would be no property to possess. Nature does not need man, man needs nature. It is a delusion of man that it is the master of nature, and the owner of nature's wealth and information.

When we self-aggrandize ourselves by being territorial and dominating other human beings, we are reminded that we are still animals, displaying animal instincts of survival and that we have not evolved despite a larger human brain. Wisdom is that which enables man to break free from fear and discover faith. For that we have to surrender to the idea of spiritual reality, to *Purusha*, that which exists beyond *Prakrati*.

In the end I will like to narrate the story of elephant king *Gajendra*.

Elephant King *Gajendra*, who was sporting in a lotus pond with a herd of co-elephants, who adored him; suddenly a crocodile caught hold of his foot and began dragging him underwater. *Gajendra* thrashed about in the water and tried to get rid of the crocodile but the crocodile did not release his grip. The co-elephants tried to rescue him but failed. He was helpless until he picked up a lotus and begged *Vishnu* to come to his aid.

The story draws attention to the human condition. We are all *Gajendra*. Sometimes, we crave for material security even when we get it we become insecure. Insecurity breeds hedonism or may transform into complacency and cynicism as one finds oneself bereft of any purpose. We crave for material growth. It becomes the sole purpose of existence. When we go materially we become arrogant and invulnerable, until circumstance turn against us. In misery we thrash about like *Gajendra* trying to get rid of the crocodile. No one comes to our rescue. We become restless and anxious. Liberation from this state will come only when we surrender to the wisdom of Vishnu.

LORD KRISHNA SAID:

As the blazing fire burns wood to ashes, so does the fire of knowledge (gyana) burn all karmic debt to ashes?

"Ignorance is the root cause of all evils and knowledge eradicates ignorance."

A child puts his hand in fire due to his ignorance. Fire burns the child's hand since that is what fire always does. The child gets the knowledge (gyana) that fire burns flesh. Therefore the child will never put his hand in fire again. This example is applicable to everything we think or do in our day- to-day lives. We learn from the mistakes we make.

---

25. DETACHMENT

I have borne the wicked words of the wicked;
To please fools, when my heart is weeping,
My lips ever laughed.
Stopping my judgment,
I have with folded hands-
Stood before unworthy persons.
Even now, my Desire, why do you make me dance like a
fool?

Philosophers differ, in their views about the universe. Some of them regard it as unreal like a dream, others hold it, as like a body, while still some others believe, in its existence, like water, which always remains in the form of snow, cloud, vapor etc, but never perishes. Thus, they hold different views. But they all agree that perishable matter has no affinity, with the imperishable self. So a striver instead of being entangled in discussions or arguments, whether matter is real or unreal or beyond the real and the unreal etc, should give up affinity, with the universe including this body which is ever undergoing a change, while the soul ever remains the same, without any modifications.

Whatever circumstances we are placed in are the fruits of actions performed in the past; and actions we are performing now, will bear fruits, in future. So a striver should neither be attached to persons and things he possesses, nor have a desire for what he expects to receive in future. He should not have any desire for fruits.

A man should discharge his duty very carefully and promptly, by giving up attachment and desire for fruits, whether it is significant or insignificant. The reason is, that when we are not concerned with its fruits, no question arises, whether the action is trivial or significant and whether it bears meager or rich fruit. An action appears to be superior or inferior, due to desire for fruit.

The term *Kartavya* stands for action which we can perform, which must be performed and which is conducive to perfection. The aim of this human life is to attain perfection, not to enjoy pleasures or suffer pain. Even other beings, such as birds, beasts, creepers, moths, trees and plants etc; come across favorable and unfavorable circumstances in the form of pleasures and pain. But they do not know what actions they should perform. Moreover, they have got no right to attain perfection. The most important thing is relinquishment of attachment to actions as well as to their fruits. .Both Attachment to actions and to its fruits is the main bondage.

So in any circumstances one should not abandon one's duty but should abandon attachment to it and also its fruits. This abandonment leads a man to freedom from worldly bondage. A layman regards abandonment of actions as real abandonment. But real abandonment consists in abandoning attachment, and desire which lead to bondage. If external abandonment is regarded as the real abandonment, every dead person should attain salvation, because he abandons all the worldly possessions as well as his body and he does not even remember them.

A man is more responsible to discharge his prescribed duty than to perform abandonment. If a person abandons his duties, he is considered very much guilty for it. Renunciation of one's duty leads to commotion. Therefore, a person should not abandon his duty whether he is paid more or less for it, whether it provides him more comfort or less comfort. In these days there is disorder in the society because people don't discharge their duty.

Delusion, which is born of sense of duty; where there is delusion there is no discretion: when discretion is suppressed by delusion, the sense of duty, gets blurred.

The pleasure of possession is soon followed by the pain of deprivation, which far outweighs the pleasure of possession. We managed life well, without things which we do not possess. The paucity of things was not as painful as it is, if we miss those things, after possessing them. But these things can be with us for a short time only because these can stay with us so long as our fortune favors us, and they slip away. Thus, we remain the same as we were, without getting these. We had to work hard to get them and now sad, after losing them.

After getting them, we felt somewhat happy only because of our greed. If we do not have this evil of greed, we can never be happy after getting the things. Similarly, we get happiness from member of our family, because of love and delusion. Thus, we see that we derive worldly pleasure out of evil; without evil no worldly pleasure is possible. If there is no greed, there cannot be any pleasure in accumulation of wealth. Greed destroys our discretion, and we cannot think in the right perspective.

It is a rule, that a man cannot perceive his failings as long he perceives defects in others. He feels rather proud of his superiority, that he has no defect while the fact is that everyone generally possesses one defect or the other. If we find fault with others it is also a defect. Being proud of one's own virtues and finding fault with others are the two defects which we do not perceive in us, though we do possess these.

The spiritual journey is a journey towards clarity, but never towards certainty. When you draw conclusions about beginnings and endings, you are a believer. When you accept that you really do not know anything you become a seeker.

No one can remain inactive, even for a moment. Man does not attain freedom from action, by non-performance of action, not does he attain to perfections, by mere renunciation of action. When a man assumes things and actions as his own, he gets attached to them. Moreover, he is also attached to fruits of those actions. But as soon as, his aim is to relinquish the fruit of action, all his actions are directed towards the welfare of the world. The reason is that he knows that he has received everything from the world and so everything belongs to the world. Besides actions and their fruits, appear and disappear, while he ever remains uniform and immutable. Having this sort of discrimination, he ever remains uniform and immutable and he gives up the fruits of actions very easily.

Relinquishment for the fruit of action means to relinquish the desire of the fruit of action. The reason is that the fruit of action cannot be renounced, as the body is the fruit of action, how will it be renounced? Having eaten food, hunger is satisfied, how will this satisfaction be renounced? Having farmed the land how will corn be renounced? Therefore in *Gita* renunciation of the desire for the fruit of action has been mentioned as relinquishment for the fruit of action.

Actions performed during past lives and till now are called 'Accumulated actions". They consist of two portions- fruit and impressions. These are stated in inner sense. The fruit portion forms "*Prarabdha*" and from the impression portion "*Samskaras*", these are fleeting thoughts. Accumulated actions performed in the present life are more responsible for inspiration to action. Rarely accumulated actions of past lives also cause such inspiration. *Prarabdha* has no power to guide our present actions.

Out of accumulated actions, which are inclined to bear fruits are called "*Prarabdha*" destiny. Destiny bears fruits in the form of favorable and unfavorable circumstances.

For example-

1. A man buys some goods and makes a profit or sustains loss, as fruit of his *Prarabdha* but he buys the goods by his own will.
2. A person finds a purse of gold coins and all of a sudden he injures his arm when the branch of a tree falls on him. It is the fruit of his destiny, through the will of destiny.
3. A boy is adopted by a rich man and the boy becomes the owner of the rich man's property; similarly a man's wealth is stolen by thieves. It is the fruit of one's destiny by the will of others.

Destiny results in the form of favorable and unfavorable circumstances, but it does not force a man to perform for bidden action. A man should be satisfied with his wife, son, family, food and wealth, but he should never be satisfied with the study of sacred books, adoration, chanting of lord's name and charity. It means that a man gains wealth and pleasure as is destined and so he should be satisfied with them. But he should never be satisfied with spiritual progress. He should go on laboring for salvation for which this human body has been bestowed upon him.

Ramalala borrowed a hundred rupees from Shyamalala and promised that he would return the amount with interest in a month. But he could not return it. Shyamalala went to Ramalala's house several times but he did not pay the amount. One day shyamalala lost self control and beat Ramalala with his shoes. Ramalala filed a case in the criminal court against Shyamalala. Shyamalala accepted that as he was not retuning his money he was compelled to beat him.

The magistrate smiled and said, "This is a criminal court, you will have to suffer imprisonment or fine for your crime. File a suit in the civil court if you want to get your money. The two courts are different.

Thus the fruits of evil actions lead to unpleasant circumstances. It is a case of criminal court and a man cannot escape it. But as far as the fruit of virtuous actions, in the form of pleasant circumstances are concerned, that is a case for a civil court. The two are different they cannot nullify each other. Thus, sins cannot be counter acted by virtuous actions. But if one performs any good act in order to repent; his sins perish.

Detachment does not mean getting detached from family. As far detachment from children, wife and home, it is not meant that one should have no feeling for them. They are natural objects of affection but when they are not favorable to spiritual progress, one should not be attached to them. The best process for making the home pleasant is *Krishna Consciousness*. If one is in full *Krishna Consciousness* he can make his home very happy because this process of *Krishna Consciousness* is very easy. One need only chant his Mantra – *Hare Rama, Hare Rama, Rama Rama Hare Hare, Hare Krishna Hare Krishna, Krishna Krishna Hare Hare*; accept remnants of food stuffs offered to *Krishna*, have some discussion on books like *Bhagwat Gita* and *Srimad Bhugwat*, and engage oneself in deity worship. These four will make one happy.

One should train his family members in this way. The family members can sit together in the morning and evening and chant together the *Mantra*. If one can mould his family life in this way to develop *Krishna Consciousness* following these four principles then there is no need to change from family life to renounced life. But if it is not congenial, not favorable for spiritual advancement; the family life should be abandoned.

In all cases, one should be detached from happiness and distress of family life because in this world one can never be fully happy or fully miserable. Happiness and distress are non committing factors of material life. One should learn to tolerate. One can never restrict the coming and going of happiness and distress, so one should be detached from the materialistic way of life and be automatically equipoise in both cases.   .

The different manifestations of body and senses among the living entities are due to material nature. There are 84,00,000 different species of life, and these varieties are the creation of the material nature. They arise from the different sensual pleasures of the living entity, who thus desires to live in this body or that. When he is put into different bodies, he enjoys different kind of happiness and distress. His material happiness and distress are due to his body and not to himself as he is. In his original state there is no doubt of enjoyment; therefore that is his real state.

We are all conditioned souls and can be divided into two classes as far as man's search for self realization is concerned. Those who are atheists, agnostics and skeptics are beyond the sense of spiritual understanding. But there are others who are faithful in their understanding of spiritual life, and they are called workers who have renounced fruitful results. In other words only the people who believe in GOD are really capable of spiritual understanding because they understand that beyond this material nature there is a spiritual world and the supreme Lord, who is expanded as *Parmatma*.

Those who work without fruitful results are also perfect in their attitude. They are given a chance to advance to the platform of devotional service in *Krishna Consciousness*. Those who are pure in consciousness and who try to find out the super souls by meditation, and when they discover the super soul within themselves, they become transcendentally situated.

In the modern society there is practically no education in spiritual matters. Some of the people may appear to be atheistic or agnostic or philosophical, but actually there is no knowledge of philosophy for the common man, if he is a good soul, a good listener, then there is a chance for advancement by hearing. This hearing process is very important.

Lord Chaitanya, in the modern world gave great stress to hearing because if the common man simply hears from authoritative sources, he can progress. Therefore, all men should take advantage of hearing from realized soul and gradually become able to understand everything. *Lord Chaitanya* further said that in this age no one needs to change his position, but one should give up the endeavor to understand Absolute Truth by speculative reasoning.

If one is fortunate enough to take shelter of a pure devotee; hear from him about self realization and follow in his footsteps he will be gradually elevated to the position of pure devotee.

Any one who can see three things – the body, the proprietor of the body or individual soul and the friend of the individual soul, combined together by good association – is actually in knowledge. The living entity by accepting his material existence in just so much suffering can become situated in his spiritual existence. If one understands that supreme is situated everywhere, see his presence in every living beings, he does not degrade himself. The mind is generally addicted to self centered processes; but when the mind turns to the super soul; one becomes advanced in spiritual understanding.

In the material conception of life, we find someone a *Demigod*, someone a human being, a dog, a cat, etc. This is material vision, not actual vision. This material differentiation is due to a material conception of life. After the destruction of the material body this spirit soul is one. The spirit soul, due to contact with material nature gets different types of bodies. When one can see this, he attains spiritual vision, thus being freed from differentiations like man, animal, big, low etc; one becomes beautiful in his consciousness in his spiritual identity. How, he then sees the things in an entirely changed view.

So, one should know the distinction between the body, the owner of the body and the super soul. A faithful person should at first have some good association to hear of GOD and thus gradually become enlightened. If one accepts a spiritual master, he can learn to distinguish between matter and spirit and that becomes the stepping stone for further spiritual realization. A spiritual master teaches his students to get free from the material concept of life by various instructions.

One who can see the constitution of the whole material manifestation as this combination of the soul and material elements and also can see the situation of the supreme soul becomes eligible for transfer to the spiritual world. These things are meant for contemplation and for realization and one should have a complete understanding of this with the help of a spiritual teacher.

26. HUMANITY AND HUMAN CONSCIOUSNESS

Many western historians feel that humanity is constantly making progress. Still we see that human consciousness is not so evolved. The progress of history and the progress of human consciousness have two different dimensions. The progress of history is in time and the progress of consciousness is not in time. The progress that we can see of all that is visible, is horizontal, while the progress of consciousness –which we cannot see is vertical.

History can never be in tune with the evolution of the human mind. At the most it can deal with the outward form; it can never get to the spirit. History can never be in contact with the formless; it can only talk about the form. The formless is always transcendental to history and real evolution is always formless. Outward progress is not really evolution. It is simply accumulation.

An event happens somewhere at sometime. So the questions, where and when can be asked about events- it will be relevant- but where and when cannot be asked about spiritual happenings. Their time and space are both irrelevant.

Society will not allow genuine religiousness. It will only allow the false faces of religion. Society creates civilizations not religion. Civilization can have a history but religion has no history at all. It only has certain religious individuals that exist here and there.

Man's success should not be measured by how high he climbs, but how high he bounces back when he hits the bottom. Emotional and physical setbacks often overwhelm us. Stages of life are soaked with such experiences. As a child, we were frustrated by not getting things that we wanted dearly. In youth we may have been bullied and rejected. And so the story goes on in our working and in our lives, as we grow older.

Yet each time, we manage to recover, after a few gaps of silent suffering. During these days we intentionally or unintentionally, disconnect and withdraw ourselves from outward happenings. Silently submitting and somehow connecting with something deeper and mysterious that overtakes us and finally gathering the strength to bounce back. This mysterious power is what drove us to raise above all challenges and carry on with life to the best of our abilities.

This power is fundamental to the universe. Evolution, for example, is inherently driven by an invisible force that is highly creative and intelligent species evolve, adapt and survive because of the force. The entire universe is self evolving because of this.

Mind is an extension of this deeper non-local reality and profoundly influences our action. Originally it is pure, unconditional and resilient. However, the mind gradually loses its resilience to acquire knowledge and conditioning and becomes finite and localized. Consequently we get anchored and habituated to our own comfort zones, secured positions, stability, conformities, familiar situations, relationships and patterns of behavior. We even adapt to our inner negativities and comfortably brood over the past, blame people and situations for our miseries and failures.

One facing new situations, change or a challenge; we perceive them as threats to ourselves. Only a clear supple mind, free from rigid thoughts, beliefs and fears is capable of resilience and is a powerful source of imagination and creativity. To restore resilience of mind; take breaks and retreat into silence with complete faith, and surrender in the life force, and simultaneously maintain an attitude of patience, perseverance, tolerance and optimism.

These traits serve as powerful enablers in developing inner strength, will and clarity that prevent negativity from overpowering and practicing them mindfully helps in maintaining mind-body sync and as we experience inner peace; the mind is able to regain its original purity. Once this is attained the mind inevitably connects with the universal life force and becomes resilient enough to pick new clues and signals and we bounce back. Defeat is in our mind; resilience is in our soul.

It is a matter of belief that some places radiate strong spiritual vibrations. You can feel *Vrindavan* in your heart; *Vrindavan* became one such place around the beginning of 16th century. It was then nothing but a dense forest that began throbbing with deep spiritual vibrations. These were sensed by seekers who started flocking to *Vrindavan*.

Vallabhacharya, a talented philosopher who introduced the pure in non-dualism system came from Andhra Pradesh. *Meera* came from Rajasthan, renouncing all royal riches to immerse in the divine longing for *Krishna*. *Surdas* a blind poet, *Haridas* a renowned Dhrupad singer and many others also moved to *Vrindavan*, feeling a strong presence of *Krishna*.

Then, *Chaitanya* came walking on foot from Orissa, in the year 1516. Until this time, *Vrindavan* has no temples or any other physical evidence of *Krishna's* association with *Vrindavan*. When *Chaitanya* visited the forests near Mathura his heart was intoxicated by the intensity of love. He, as if in a trance, could see *Krishna* performing numerous *Lilas* - acts or pastimes of GOD as he walked in the *Vrindavan* forests. He could identify specific places in *Vrindavan* associated with each of *Lilas*.

Chaitanya identified *Gokul*, a village associated with *Krishna's* childhood pastimes. Here he could see, *Krishna* snatching butler from *Gopis*, village girls. At *Seva Kunj* he could witness the divine dance called *Rasa* where *Krishna* danced with his beloved *Radha* and her eight close friends. *Chaitanya* could see each *Gopi* dancing with the same *Krishna*.

Chaitanya identified three water bodies known as *Shyama*, *Radha* and *Kunda*. Hence he could see *Krishna* performing water sports with his friends. So intense was *chaitanya's* realization, he was dancing with divine joy at all these places.

He identified *Govardhan* hill and saw *Krishna* holding it on his finger tip to save his village folks from drowning in the lashing rains. At *Chitraghat Chaitanya* heard the divine flute sound played by *Krishna* under the tree called *Vamshi Vat*.

He would see naughty *Krishna* sitting on a tree, while *Gopis* were taking bath in the pool. The *Gopis* later realized that *Krishna* had stolen their clothes. *Chaitanya* would hear the request from each of the *Gopis* to *Krishna* for the return of their clothes. *Chaitanya* identified many other spots associated with *Krishna*. *Chaitanya* considered him lucky to feel *Krishna* in full glory. As a pure devotee, he wanted everyone including future generations to get drowned in the same feelings. So he noted the precise location of each of the experiences and got built small temples at each of these places.

Vrindavan today attracts seekers from all over who come here to soak in divine love. They owe gratitude to *Chaitanya* and his team for connecting them to their deeper selves.

Truth is not a concept. It is a tangible reality and has its own decisive action. It is present in every atom of the universe and is continuously evolving in new forms. It represents a new level of consciousness and its continuous descent guarantees our planet a glorious destiny. The truth is the next summit in the evolution of humanity. In a vivid sense, the truth is Transformation.

We can work with this truth. When we do, we become increasingly a reflection of it. We undertake this work through our psychic being the evolving soul and Divine person. This is our progressive and individual truth. The work comprises stages and it all begins when we become conscious of it and invite it into our lives. We must sincerely want it to take over. From that point we learn to live our truth, which involves shunning every falsehood in thought speech and deed.

We have to practice too. At first in a structured way, we open our nature consciously to its influence, devoting regular time to the process. This can be done through body itself. When all is well inside, the body is happy too.

Drop the mind and just observe without judgment from head to toe. Stay present and watch the descending force flow through the body. When the observation is sincere, consciousness does the rest. Consciousness always aligns with force. It is the only way to transformation. But human nature is twisted and there will always be breaks that initially resist the flow. So the patience is necessary and a resolute approach is always rewarded.

When disruption or pain is observed and wherever disease is unearthed, consciousness instantaneously resolves, opening the body to a dynamic, peace, the definitive seal of truth. The well being it brings in indescribable and body vibrates to a new tune. As the inside governs the outside, it is a holistic process that prepares nature for the next stage ahead.

From there onwards, we move into virgin territory. Hence the practice must be broadened in everyday life. Then a spontaneous process of alignment and change will ensure. It needs to become our entire way of living. But the surrender has to be so complete that it is entirely effortless. Our consciousness must be connected, alive and alert 24x7.

The truth is omnipresent and ready always to transfer on. It promises divine life on this earth. To be a servant of truth means to help install it in every facet of human existence. Surely there can be no greater work than this.

◆

27. EXPANSION OF CONSCIOUNSESS

Many people are deeply 'concerned about the overuse of natural resources, increasing global warming and the vastly uneven distribution of wealth. The root causes are greed and competition; attitudes that won't change until there is an expansion of consciousness. *Paramahansa Yogananda* emphasized on high thinking and simple living to correct these attitudes.

A new consciousness of unity is needed. A hallmark of *Kaliyug* was that life seemed to be little more than a brutal struggle for survival. But this old paradigm is slowly breaking down. People are beginning to realize that our life is connected and that survival of the fittest is a misconception. Our role is to become agents of change towards greater global cooperation especially at work, where competition is still highly rewarded.

We have to learn to see GOD through others. The deepest sense of connection comes from learning to see GOD or *Guru* not only in everything, but through everything. If we see GOD in the faces of others, we will naturally feel a deep sense of connectedness with everyone. Even to hold a fraction of that consciousness radically changes the nature of our relationships.

Let the energy flow. Create a magnetic upward flow of energy. An important principle is to create a positive flow of energy up the spine to the spiritual eye. This upward flow of energy through the *Chakras* creates a magnetic field that connects us with others. A downward flow, on the other hand, increases our separation and disunity.

If, we find ourselves slipping into a negative or complaining attitude, we should work first on controlling the flow of energy rather than on trying to convince the mind to be more positive. First feel the energy in the heart and make it positive. A little moment of appreciation works wonders. Then direct the heart's feelings upwards to the spiritual eye. We will find that our thoughts turn positive as soon as the life force begins to flow upward.

This upward direction of energy will also make us magnetic and positive; magnetism will attract positive people. Become channels of Divine friendship. Once you can produce a positive consciously let stream out to those around you; become a wellspring of kindness and support. When we make the welfare of peoples our main priority we generate the positive magnetism which causes the right things to happen and in the best possible way.

The deep sense of connectedness to GOD and other people that we gain in meditation is large which produces an attitude of unity. *Yogananda* said that mediation should be active service and the service should be active meditation.

Bring joy into your work. If we can approach our work with a deep inward consciousness our outer and inner life will begin to meld together into a beautiful harmonious flow. The particular area of our work is not nearly so important as the quality of consciousness with which we work. Make it fun, joyful, cooperative and holy.

In this world of various religions the word secular has achieved a great importance. Secular ethics does not rely on religious principles. There is now a reasonably substantial body of evidence suggesting that even from the most rigorous scientific perspective, unselfishness and concern for others are not only in our own interest but also, in a sense, innate to our biological nature. Such evidence when combined with reflection on our personal experiences and coupled with simple common sense can offer a strong case for the benefit of cultivating basic human values that does not rely on religious principles or faith at all.

This then is the basis of what I call 'Secular ethics'. To some, the very world suggests a firm rejection of, or even hostility towards religion. It may seem to them, in using this word; I am advocating the exclusion of religion from ethical systems or even from all areas of public life. This is not at all what I have in mind; instead, my understanding of the word secular comes from the way it is commonly used in India.

Modern India has a secular constitution and prides itself on being a secular country. In Indian usage, 'Secular' far from implying antagonism towards religion or towards people of faith, actually implies a profound respect for and tolerance towards all religions. It also implies an inclusive and impartial attitude which includes non believers.

This understanding of the term 'Secular' – to imply mutual tolerance and respect for all faiths as well as for those of no faith comes from India's particular historical and cultural background. In the same way I suspect, the western understanding of the term comes from European history. Perhaps, as science began to advance rapidly in Europe, there was a move towards greater rationality and a rejection of what comes to be seen as the superstitions of the past.

For many radical thinkers, the adoption of nationality has entailed a rejection of religious faith. The French revolution which expressed so many of the new ideas of European enlightenment is a good example of this with its strong and religious element.

Of course, there was also an important social dimension to this rejection. Religion come to be regarded as conservative tied to tradition and closely associated with old regimes and all their failings. It seems the legacy of this history that is of more than 200 years. Many of the most influential thinkers and reformers in the west have viewed religion not as an avenue to human liberation but as an obstacle to progress. Hence, secularism and religion are often seen as two opposing and mutually incompatible positions.

When negative attitude towards religion in the west or elsewhere are motivated by a concern for justice, they must be respected. In fact one can argue that those who point out the hypocrisy of religious people who violate the ethical principle they proclaim, who stand up against injustices perpetrated by religious figures and institution are actually strengthening and benefitting the traditions themselves.

However, when assessing such criticisms, it is important to distinguish between criticisms directed at religion and those directed at the institutions of religion, which are two quite separate things. Because close to the heart of all great faith traditions is the aim of promoting humanity most positive qualities and nurturing such values as kindness, compassion, forgiveness, patience and personal integrity.

Most people feel devastated in moments of sorrow because sorrow is painful and if one is a believer one starts to wonder, "Why did not GOD help me"? Sometimes we wonder why GOD does not grant us a life of ease that is a life that is free of burdens. Why do we have to experience a life that is full of health problems, financial, relationship and emotional problems?

We always want GOD to do things that we think are good for us. Whatever we expect in life, we want that to happen; otherwise we become disappointed. When what we want does not happen or unexpected happens, we find it difficult to fathom, why it happened. At that stage, we forget to think that may be this was supposed to happen. So we are caught up in the why and wherefores of what happened. We feel as though we have lost the connection with GOD.

What is important to recognize is; why do we feel that we have lost our connection? If our connection with the Divine is strong and stable, then nothing would make that connection weak. If our faith is great and we recognize that it is under Divine will that our life is being led, and then irrespective of what happens to us, we will recognize that whatever happened was for our good. Then the next time something happens, we will not be as affected by the moments of sorrow and moments of happiness. We will cultivate equipoise that keeps us steady despite highs and lows.

Equipoise comes with stability. For example, when we go to buy a car, we want the most stable car that will not turn over. Stability in a car comes from how strong its connection with the ground is. Similarly our spiritual stability depends upon how strong our connection with the Divine is. If our connection is strong, then nothing will be able to pull us apart and we will remain stable.

That state comes as we mediate and experience the light and sound of GOD. If we sit in silence and focus our attention within, we will find the manifestation of GOD in the form of inner light and sound. Inner journey through meditation will lead us to realization of GOD and feel that all embracing love that envelop us.

Once we truly live like that, then we are able to deal in the best manner possible with any situation that comes before us. Once we realize that is Divine and that is leading us towards our goal we can also accept that just as the boat moving through the ocean and encounters waves, we too may face upheavals. Once we cultivate the strength we are bound to reach our goal. So the strength of our connection is important. If we are weak in our connection, then we have a difficult time in dealing with all these situations whether they are of a happiness or sorrows.

That is why people whose connections are not strong get tormented and have a lot of difficulties in navigating the ups and downs of life. Whereas, those whose connections are stronger and who recognize that strength and who are making efforts to stay in equipoise, are the ones who can pull through difficult times.

———